STEAL AWAY HOME

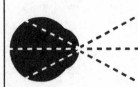

This Large Print Book carries the
Seal of Approval of N.A.V.H.

STEAL AWAY HOME

BILLY COFFEY

THORNDIKE PRESS
A part of Gale, a Cengage Company

Farmington Hills, Mich • San Francisco • New York • Waterville, Maine
Meriden, Conn • Mason, Ohio • Chicago

LIBRARY OF CONGRESS CIP DATA ON FILE.
CATALOGUING IN PUBLICATION FOR THIS BOOK
IS AVAILABLE FROM THE LIBRARY OF CONGRESS

ISBN-13: 978-1-4328-4940-5 (hardcover)

Published in 2018 by arrangement with Thomas Nelson, Inc., a division of HarperCollins Christian Publishing, Inc.

Printed in the United States of America
1 2 3 4 5 6 7 22 21 20 19 18

*For Dad, who taught me
the love of the game.*

AUTHOR'S NOTE

The great thing about writing fiction is that very often you don't need to make anything up at all, or that whatever needs to be made up can be fit neatly within the folds of reality. There was indeed a baseball game played between the Baltimore Orioles and the New York Yankees on June 5, 2001, followed the next night by a strawberry moon. While certain players and personnel of the Baltimore Orioles have been dramatized, the actual play-by-play is a matter of record.

I can well imagine myself sitting down that night seventeen years ago to watch Jason Johnson and Mike Mussina duel it out under the Yankee Stadium lights, just as I'm sure I stood on my porch the next night to watch that moon rise. Maybe that's when Owen Cross stood up and began waving in some corner of my subconscious.

But there are times when I'm certain he's been with me for much longer than that.

7

No writer works from a blank slate. Every character and setting is in some way a reflection of the person who crafts them. That's been true for all the characters in all of my books. Owen most of all.

It breaks your heart. It is designed to break your heart. The game begins in the spring, when everything else begins again, and it blossoms in the summer, filling the afternoons and evenings, and then as soon as the chill rains come, it stops and leaves you to face the fall alone . . . Of course, there are those who learn after the first few times. They grow out of sports. And there are others who were born with the wisdom to know that nothing lasts. These are the truly tough among us, the ones who can live without illusion, or without even the hope of illusion. I am not that grown-up or up-to-date. I am a simpler creature, tied to more primitive patterns and cycles. I need to think something lasts forever, and it might as well be that state of being that is a game; it might as well be that, in a green field, in the sun.

— A. BARTLETT GIAMATTI

What greater thing is there for two human souls, than to feel that they are joined for life . . . to be one with each other in silent unspeakable memories at the moment of the last parting?

— GEORGE ELIOT

PREGAME

1

June 5, 2001

We cross the river when I see in the rearview that the cabbie has something to say to me. His voice carries over the traffic and jackhammering and the bustle of the city: "You ain't got a chance, you know that. Right? My guys, they'll murder ya."

I meet the old man's eyes with my own.

"Always got your number," he says, spinning the last word in that peculiar northeastern way — *numbah.* "Know why that is?"

"Luck?"

He grins.

The cab trundles on. Across the Robert F. Kennedy Bridge and an East River that seems at rest, its skin a brackish and polluted russet. Onward sits a mass of ball fields laid out in clover patterns. Infields more sand than dirt, grass the color of dying wheat. I think, *Nothing can grow here*

11

but concrete.

I tip my head at the thin glaze of grime over the window. "How far's it?"

"Forget about it" — *Fahgetaboutit* — "I'll get you there."

A tangle of brown walls and roofs rises to our right. The cabbie calls it Mott Haven. I see the Harlem River winding like a dirty thread past the maze of cars to our left.

"Where'd you get the call from?"

"Bowie," I tell him.

"Yeah? For good?"

"Only tonight. Cup a coffee, then I'm back."

"Well, enjoy it, mister," he says. He's got me by thirty years at least, but I let it go. "Greatest place to be in the greatest city in the world, that's where we're headed. I coulda made it. You know? Could be you." He shakes his head. At the memory or the traffic, I cannot know. Then he adds, "Knees."

The road dips into what looks like a tunnel, plunging the cab into dim evening. Exhaust trickles through unseen cracks. I wonder how anybody can breathe here. There are no woods. No hills. The only mountains are made of concrete and windows.

"Here, coming up on the right. End of

12

the tunnel."

The cab lurches upward toward sunlight. I press my head against the glass and the residue of a hundred hands. Through a copse of trees rises a curved façade of fading stone like a hand reaching heavenward. The size of it. I have never felt so far from home and so close.

"Yeah." The cabbie laughs a smoker's chuckle and tilts the cap back on his head. Watching me while maneuvering among cars. "You rubes. Crack me up. Haunted. You know? Whole place. Them ghosts rise up. Seen it a thousand times. October rolls 'round, they come. It's our year."

The façade winks from sight amid a jumble of buildings and roads and comes once more as we approach the exit ramp. Two words are writ large along the ring of its top, each letter dark blue and capped and spelling a dream. The green sign above the overpass says *E 161 St Yankee Stadium Macombs Dam Br Next Right.* The cab wheels rightward into the lane. At the curve, the building rises. Here trees and shrubs bloom in the June warmth.

I ask him, "You got any idea where I go?"

" 'Round the side, that's where I'll take you. You ain't the first rook I hauled up here. Won't be the last."

13

At Ruppert Place he throws the gear to park and nods toward a mass of barricades. "Players' lot's over there, and that's their entrance. Should be a guy for you."

I pay him and add a tip. He lays a finger to the bill of his cap. Only the one bag is beside me, a change of clothes and my mitt. I open the door to a heat that steals my breath. The cabbie calls to me from a window he opens halfway.

"Good luck. Coulda been me, but you enjoy it. Just watch those ghosts, you hear? They always watching" — *Dey awlways wahchin.*

"I'll do that. Appreciate the ride."

I shut the door and the cab is gone in a yellow blur, the man back to somewhere in the city or back to LaGuardia, another fare and one more dollar made. The sun is high over the stadium. I sling the bag over my shoulder and realize I didn't pack a toothbrush. Skip, he'd understand. Mom would kill me for it if she were here. Mom'd *moider* me. But as I take in this place of hallowed ghosts and gods, it is neither Skip nor my mother who fills my thoughts. It is a girl I fear has followed me and a man I know is close.

"We made it." I tilt my face to the sun and the blue around it reaching higher and

14

higher. I say, "You and me, we're finally here," but do not know to which one I speak, the girl or the man or both. I settle on both.

2

Where the barricades end I am greeted by a grinning man dressed in khaki pants and a white shirt. A lanyard badge bearing the Orioles logo dangles above a blue tie stained with a dollop of yellow mustard.

He shields his eyes from the sun. "Owen Cross?"

"Yessir."

"Rick Mills, assistant to the traveling secretary. Welcome." He reaches out a hand that is swallowed to the wrist in my own. "Any problems getting here?"

"Nosir."

"Good. Know it's short notice." He winks at me. "Let's get you settled. Clubhouse is this way, then I'll take you to see Mike and get your uniform. Flying back tomorrow?"

"That's what they told me."

"Well, cup of coffee in the Show's still a cup," he says.

I nod. "Sure is."

He leads me down the tunnel and through a door set into the wall that opens into a sprawling carpeted room. Sofas and chairs are set into the center. Lockers ring the sides, each wide enough to fit two people or even three inside. Dangling from wooden hangers affixed to the corners are jerseys bearing the names of players spoken of in the bush leagues with the hushed tones used for royalty. I spot Bobby Kitchen's jersey hanging near where two wide-screen televisions are set into the wall. The sight of that jersey sends a shiver from my toes to my head. It births an image of home and a childhood now long past, me and Travis Clements and Jeffrey Davis riding our bikes down to the 7–11 and sorting through the Topps and Donruss baseball cards we'd bought, me squealing when I came across one of Country Kitchen himself.

Though a little before noon on the day of a night game, already a few Orioles players are there. They mill about, joking and shuffling a deck of cards before shaking my hand.

"Here," Rick says, finger pointing to the last locker in the row. "Put you here since it's just for tonight. You can leave your stuff. Mike wants to see you first off."

I drop my bag onto the metal chair and follow him through the clubhouse to a narrow hallway where a door stands. *Manager* is stamped on the frosted glass. Rick knuckles the frame and enters, motioning me forward. The man behind a battered metal desk stands to welcome me. Mike Singleton has been the Orioles' manager five years now, a journeyman outfielder in the seventies whose claim to fame is a '79 World Series ring and the fact that he collected home runs off four Hall of Fame pitchers during his career.

"Thanks for making the trip up," he says.

"Thanks for the call."

He sits but doesn't tell me to join him. "Wish I didn't have to. Hate calling up guys for one game, least of all in June. Hate it more against the Yankees. But our backup catcher's on bereavement down in Tallahassee with a sick daddy until tomorrow, and, well." He studies me. "How old are you, son?"

"Twenty-nine," I say. *Thirty next month,* I don't.

Mike shakes his head.

"Rick'll get you suited up. We got Johnson throwing tonight. Pitchers' meeting's in an hour. Doubt you'll see any action tonight, Carter —"

"Cross," I tell him.

Mike waves that off as though my name doesn't matter. "You're insurance, nothing more. Brooksie's our catcher, and God willin' he'll keep in one piece until Lopez gets back tomorrow. You just do what needs done. Meet the guys, enjoy yourself. Get a taste of the Show."

"Yessir."

Steal Aw ay Home

"Skip or Mike'll do."

"Yessir."

Rick leads me out and farther down the hall, past the video rooms and where the trainers are already at work on the players who need them. The equipment room is on the end. "Scooter," he says. "Been with us forever."

I am greeted by an elderly man with a face of white stubble who asks my sizes. Scooter repeats my last name back to me slow, letter by letter, as if Cross could be spelled a dozen ways.

"You come back, I'll have you ready. Take this for now."

He hands me a hat. The fit is good.

"Welcome to the Show," he says. "You a preference for a number?"

"Nineteen, if you got it."

Scooter says "Nineteen" the way he spelled my name to me. "Nawp, ain't anybody using it. That your uni down in Bowie?"

"Nosir." I swallow hard. "Was my daddy's."

3

I get settled and greet a few of the players before sitting in on the pitchers' meeting. Jason Johnson is there. He is quiet and does not acknowledge me, too focused on the game. Brook Fordyce, our catcher, runs through the strengths and weaknesses of the Yankee hitters. Brooksie lets me sit near the front as he takes over the meeting. It is a mass of numbers and formulas and computer charts mixed with what can only be called superstition — according to the pitching coach, tonight's moon is near full.

"Pitch'm off the plate," he says to Brooksie and Johnson. "Keep'm off balance, but make sure to pitch'm low. Full moon makes the balls fly."

A new uniform and a fresh pair of spikes are waiting at my locker when I'm done. Number 19 across the back, *Cross* in a slow arc above. I change and follow a group of guys down the tunnel toward the dugout. They make fun of my accent, call me Hillbilly. I am informed of the best restaurants close to the hotel and where I can find the best women after the game. It does not matter I'm a seven-year busher. None care I'm

19

here for a cup of coffee. They hold their own memories of sorry hotels and buses stinking with sweat and grime, truck stop food and showers that would leave you howling each time someone flushed a toilet. For this night, I am one of them.

The way is brightened by a wedge of blue sky framed by the tunnel's end and a section of the right field stands. Sounds reach out like angels calling me home — laughter and shouting, ball meeting leather. I find a spot at the end of the bench as the players separate each unto their own kind, outfielders and infielders and pitchers last. Breathing deep the smell of dirt and grass, the aged wood and steel of a place that until this day existed in my dreams alone.

I stand and walk toward the dugout steps. The new spikes clack against concrete littered with tobacco spit and empty husks of sunflower seeds. Where the field meets the dugout I stop and rest my hand upon the railing. Below me is a straight line of groomed dirt to one side and the dugout to the other. I wonder how many steps I have taken to arrive at this place. Years of fear and doubt and trying flood me, the faces of those I've lost along the way, but as I move from dirt to grass so thick and soft my spikes sink to the ankles, I know I belong here.

I have always belonged here.

Most of the veterans along with Mike and the hitting coach are still around when my turn comes for batting practice. They gather with reporters or lean their arms against the netting. I grab a bat and enter the cage with that quiet murmur surrounding me. Taking my stance in the box, setting the bat to hover over my left shoulder.

I think, *The Babe stood in this spot. Gehrig. The dirt behind this plate belonged to Yogi and Dickey and Howard and Munson.* But where I should look for the pitch, my eyes instead wander to the third deck of stands in the far right. I see my father's words scrawled on a long-ago note left next to his living room chair and a baseball for me to sign. My eyes pick up the pitch too late. I muscle the swing and catch the ball at the end of the barrel, sending it dribbling along the infield grass before it veers foul in a slow curve. Talk behind me falls to quiet. Heat builds at my back. I cannot bear to turn my head.

The BP pitcher reaches for another ball from a crate of dozens. I tap the plate and remember it's seventeen inches like Dad said, seventeen whether at the high school field in Camden or at Yankee Stadium, and at the next toss I feel that bubble of eternity building and hear the bat connecting with an echoing crack, the ball arcing high and long out toward right, landing deep in the third deck with an echo against a seat I barely see. Another there, another, chased by early fans wearing the battered gloves of their youth. Now a voice behind me tinged with humor, one I pray is Country Kitchen's but that may belong to a manager believing me too old and spent to be here:

"Dang, son, what they feeding you down in Double-A?"

I finish my swings and step out to nods and quiet cursing. Fans gather along the first row of seats above the dugout. A boy leans over the edge with his father close and holds out a pen and a ball peppered with scrawled names. He says to me, "Sign my ball, mister?"

"Sure? Ain't worth as much as some a these other guys'."

But the boy says I'm a player and today I am. I take the ball and the pen he hands me.

"What's your name?" he asks.

"Owen Cross. How 'bout you?"

His daddy says, "Named him after his granddaddy's favorite player."

"Oh yeah? Let me guess: Babe."

The boy chuckles.

"No? Yogi? Thurman? No, wait — Lefty."

I find a spot where the seams of the kid's baseball come near together and scrawl *Owen* and part of *Cross* as the dad says, "Mickey."

The pen freezes in my hand. The boy grins, flaring something in me, anger or sadness I cannot tell, they feel so much the same. Buzzing in my head.

"Your name's Mickey?"

The father looks away. He says, "There's Ripken," and louder, "Hey, Cal, Cal, sign a ball for my boy." He reaches to take the ball from my hand and sees it only half signed, tells me to hurry. I can't. I can't sign the ball because of the boy's name, hearing it said. "Hey, c'mon, man, it's Cal Ripken."

I hand the ball back and watch the two of them scurry down the line of seats to the far end of the dugout. The boy looks at the ball and me and I hear him say, "He didn't sign it all the way, Daddy," and hear the father say it doesn't matter, that guy's a nobody but it's Cal Ripken over here, and all I can do is duck inside the dugout and find my place at the end of the bench, murmuring the boy's name over and over again.

4

I was twelve when Paul Cross moved Momma and me from Stanley. That was June of '84, after Dad lost his job at the mill where he'd spent twenty years of his life after blowing his elbow in the fifth inning of a doubleheader against Virginia Tech. I was old enough to know we were dire but too young to comprehend its depths. Dad looked for work everywhere. He would have taken anything. That's how he ended up being the janitor at a high school sixty miles away in Camden and how we ended up in a tiny ranch house at what felt like the edge of the known world near the Shenandoah National Park.

He spent much of those first weeks learning the ropes down at the school, coming home every evening wearing a wearied grin and a county uniform of blue pants and a gray shirt that stunk of cut grass and floor wax. We'd go into the backyard and have a catch while Mom fixed supper, him the pitcher and me the catcher, working on my movement and pitch calling as I crouched behind a trash can lid set down as home plate. We ate mostly in the quiet tones that come with a family growing accustomed to a new life. Each of us recalling the day's events, Dad's at the school and Mom's at the job she found shelving books at the library, me telling of the friends I'd met, Travis and Jeffrey and the boys who gathered every morning at the ball field in town. In the evening Dad would retire to the spare bedroom down the hall where his old trophies and baseballs were kept, relics of a life Paul Cross felt was stolen from him.

I am able now to understand the weight he must have borne, the burden of so many golden yesterdays from which such a sour present was birthed. He was a hard man, my father, and from that hardness came a love for Momma and me that we mostly shriveled under. And he was proud in his brokenness. I believe that was why he turned us to religion after our move — Dad's way of seeking out what meaning could be had from what his life had become. Two weeks later Reverend Alan Sebolt baptized the three of us along the muddy banks of the South River. Jesus laid hold of Paul Cross with a vengeance I can only compare to my daddy's love of baseball. He spent a week in our shed making a woodburnt sign that said *As for me and my house, we will serve the Lord;* he hung it above the front door and wielded the Bible as one would a truncheon. As for me, I could only suppose my dunking some form of punishment. I thrashed about in the current as the preacher's hands clamped down, wanting every sin washed away. Some creature, fish or devil, took a nibble at my knee.

Weekdays were mine alone, and I spent them in the only way I knew: playing ball. I had arrived in Camden too late to join school and Little League, but there were always pickup games in the mornings before going our separate ways in the afternoons. It didn't take me long to insert myself. Even at twelve, I could hit. And I was the only kid around willing to squat behind the plate against the fastballs Travis Clements fired at frightened batters like little Jeffrey Davis. They were my first friends in Camden, though not the most important. Travis and Jeffrey would remain so more or less until I ran away to college in the late summer of 1990 carrying my own burdens.

I sit on the bench of the visitors' dugout at Yankee Stadium watching Country Kitchen taking BP and Ripken signing autographs, watching the stands begin to fill, but even here I know those first weeks I spent in Camden were the happiest of my life. It was nothing but play and sunshine, old bicycles with crooked handlebars and sketchy brakes, Slurpees from the 7–11 and long drinks from garden hoses. All our lives stood before us, magic as unrecognized as water to a fish because the magic was everything.

Then she came, and everything changed.

5

It rained that morning in early July, not so much to make a gully washer of things but enough to call off our pickup game. The clouds broke in the afternoon, beckoning me to go exploring. Our house sat at the end of Maple Street where the backyard met a stand of white pines. Wilderness lay beyond: a meadow of mustard and wildflowers untended but for the groundhogs and rabbits living there and then the rolling foothills building toward the Blue Ridge. Between the two stood a grassy hill topped by a single towering oak like a candle on a cake. The kids called that hill cursed — not only the scrubs but Travis and Jeffrey too, good players whose words carried greater credence. Their story held it was not a hill at all but a burial mound protecting the bones of an ancient Indian chief. None stepped foot on those slopes, not even on a dare, but that hill had called to me since I first caught a wedge of its crest from my bedroom window. I can say it no other way.

I found no arrowheads, only that tree, but

27

the view of the pine trees and far mountains to one side and Camden's edges to the other was enough to hold me. I sat where the bit of rain caught in the leaves wouldn't drip down and tried not to think of a skeleton hand rising up from the earth to lay hold of the heathen white boy. The wind tossed sounds I could not decipher. The world smelled as though it had gotten washed and hung to dry. Thunder rolled along ridges clothed in thin sheets of fog. Squirrels chirruped. A sparrow called from what could have been a mile away. Then another noise, small but rising, blending with the songs of robins and cardinals.

Up the hill's western slope she came, nothing more than a growing dot clad in a muddied pair of cutoff jeans and a plain white T-shirt. A length of black rope was slung across her shoulders. An Atlanta Braves cap, soiled with the dirt and sweat of adventure, sat cockeyed over hair so blond it looked dipped in gold. The girl appeared my age or close and no stranger to the wild places beyond Camden, as evidenced by the confidence of her stride. Near the crest of the hill she lifted her face and flashed a look of surprise. Her expression faded to a smile I could not bask in long. My eyes caught the thing draped across her shoulders. Its head lay motionless against the girl's neck but its tail quivered, brushing the side of her stomach.

She said, "I don't know you."

My head turned one way. The other.

"Well, what you doin' here? Ain't nobody told you this hill's cursed? I'm only playin'. Don't mind what folk say, it's just a plain old hill. You live 'round here?" The girl smiled through a set of yellowed teeth and placed her foot inside a broken bar of shade. "Well then, you must be new, 'cause I ain't never seen you afore. Not here and not in town neither. And you sure ain't from the Pines."

It moved, what she had wrapped about her.

"This here's my spot. I come up here all the time. You can too if you want, it ain't no private property. But you better keep away from me."

I said the only thing I could: "You got a snake on you."

She laughed. "I know that, stupid. It's a blacksnake is all. I killed it. Wanna see?"

"That thing's movin'."

"They fidget a little after sometimes, because they don't know yet."

"What don't they know?"

"That they dead."

She plopped down beside me and shrugged the snake away. It landed on the ground near my feet and twisted like a toy about out of batteries, pink mouth sliding open like a yawn. Fear kept me from running. Fear and pride.

"You from the city." A statement, not a question. "I ain't never knowed nobody from the city. But you best be goin' on now."

"Why?"

" 'Cause I'm a Dullahan. My daddy's Earl and my momma's Constance. We live down in Shantytown." She pointed to the sea of trees between the hill and the mountains.

I waved out toward the town side. "I live over there." Not looking, not with that snake laying at me.

"That's why you better go. Don't nobody from Camden talk to a Shantie. It's unheard."

"But we are talking," I said.

The way she stared at me, so full and complete, scared me even more than the snake between us.

"Because you got to know you'll get in trouble. Or me. Earl finds out I'm up here talking with a town boy, he'll skin me. Earl Dullahan's fierce."

"I don't want you getting in no trouble," I said. "I'll go on."

30

"No, you have a turn. It's pretty, ain't it?"

I said it was awful pretty, but I wasn't talking about no hill.

She turned with a wave and a "Seeya," skipping over the ruts and ridges with a sureness I could not fathom. I looked down as the snake quit its flopping and I called out, saying she'd forgotten it.

"You can keep it," she said, "so long as you don't tell nobody you seen me. Okay?"

"What's your name?"

"Michaela," she called.

"I'm Owen."

"Good to meet you, Owen."

I watched the pines below claim her and then sat upon that hill until suppertime to see if Michaela would return. Next morning I walked up there again and laid a handful of dandelions, tied into a bunch by their stems, beneath the oak. That afternoon the flowers were gone. In their place was a small chunk of quartz set in the middle of a finger-drawn circle.

The next days brought the same and the same. We came to the hilltop all that summer, sometimes finding each other and other times only a rock or a tangle of dandelions the other had left behind. Then, right about the end of July, Michaela and I agreed we'd meet daily after the sandlot games were done and before my folks got home. Sometimes I'd get there first. Most times she'd be waiting, and those would be the best days of all because she would smile at my coming. She'd say I shouldn't be there and then scoot over so I could sit beside her.

She was Micky to me by the dog days of August, when you are fooled into thinking summer will last forever. Then came the first edges of autumn and rumors of school and a sadness creeping between us.

"We can't talk to each other at school," she told me, this less than a week before summer's end. "Dullahans is soiled. 'Sides, you're from town and I'm a Shantie. Can't nobody know we're friends, else we won't be friends at all."

I struggled with that logic but found no hole in it. Micky was right about the Dullahan name. It was spoken in town only with either a sneer toward her daddy, Earl, or a sad shake of the head with regards to her momma, Constance, a good woman gone tired by a life spent chained to the wrong last name. Dad spoke of the Shanties as a crop ripe for spiritual harvest. Momma would go silent whenever those of the Pines were mentioned, staring into her plate of supper or cup of coffee.

"We can still meet here," I said. "After school. Momma's never home until six. My dad too. That's like two hours almost."

Her hand slipped into mine, birthing a shiver no friend should give. She said, "Okay. After school, then. And if one of us can't come, the other'll wait. Like an hour. To make sure. We'll leave a marker for the other to find so we'll each know we been here. I'll leave a rock, you some dandelions. Or grass if it's the wintertime. Only knot it so's I know it's you, okay?"

It was more than okay. Micky and I may not have met every day, but it was most, and as one year turned to two and three, our time together became a constant in my life second only to baseball. I guarded those stolen hours between the end of school and suppertime as treasure. Fool that I was, I believed that secret could be kept forever. But two young children running off every evening, even for a little while, are bound to raise suspicion.

It was Constance who spied us together first. She followed her daughter one afternoon not long after my first year of school in Camden began, watching us from a spot just inside the Pines. The next morning she sought out my momma. Turned out the two were already familiar with one another, the library being one of the few places in Camden where the poor could get something free. I don't know if Micky ever realized how close our friendship came to ending that day; she never knew of our mothers' conversation, and Mom made me promise I would never tell. According to her, "Constance only wanted me to know where all you were going, Owen. She begged me not to put an end to it, so I won't. You just don't get in any trouble with that girl, and don't you ever tell your daddy."

"You ain't mad?"

"There's no sense folk not having a thing to do with other folk just because of what they are or aren't. I'd've listened to a thing like that, you'd've never been born. And besides, Constance thinks you're about the only thing holding that poor girl to this world."

And maybe I was, if only for a while. Micky had found out about her momma's bad heart only months before. Constance was sick, Earl no more than a mean drunk, and I the only friend Micky had. She kept to herself in school as one more poor kid among many, wearing the same cutoffs and white tee every day except for when the snows blew down from the mountains, at which point Constance would take her to

34

the Goodwill for a threadbare coat. And Micky was right — Camden kids and Shanties may have been thrust into the same school, but they did not mingle, not ever, nor did their mommas and daddies in town. Least of all did any in Camden have a thing to do with a Dullahan, who were to a person considered plain white trash.

But what my momma never knew, what maybe no one but Micky ever did, was how much that plain white trash out of Shantytown kept me in the world too.

6

After batting practice everyone retreats to the clubhouse for a last little bit of ease. Players mingle and gripe about their slots in the order or how they are not in the order at all, how the Yanks are throwing Mussina tonight and he always gives us a rough time. The card game at the center table is intense. Someone turns up one of the televisions to help drown the noise of the crowd above.

From the chair in front of my locker I spot Country sitting off to himself. He wears a smirk as he watches the goings-on, too tired or old to join in the games of youngsters. I want to go over there. Say I grew up watching him, even copied his stance all my junior year of high school until Dad asked why I'd started holding the bat so high off my shoulder, I'd never catch a low fastball. Instead, I only watch him, kept in place not by the awe of being so close to a genuine hero but by memory alone, and dig into the back pocket of my jersey pants. From there comes a small bit of quartz I hold aloft to let the facets play among the room's lights. I have carried this rock for a dozen years whether to Youngstown or Bluefield or Bowie. Now New York. In many ways it is the one thing that remains of her. I may have come from Maryland in such haste that I forgot my toothbrush, but I would never leave behind Micky's first gift to me.

I don't know when our hours together grew to something more than friendship. The summer before we began high school. Maybe earlier. Maybe at our first meeting when I was twelve. It was the slow-building kind of love you can't help but yield to. The kind that, looking back, seems all but inevitable. Our mothers' blessing helped things along — Mom sneaking us into the house for summertime lunch when she was off and Dad was working. Constance scraping up enough to take Micky and me to the matinee in Mattingly after I'd spent the morning with Travis and Jeffrey.

Yet it was the hill that drew us together as

much as anything. It's funny how a place can feel like home, like that's where you belong. There was only that old oak above and the soft ground beneath, a whisper of wind laced with the scent of pines and wildflowers on some faraway peak, but it was all we needed. There our trials were left away such that nothing else existed, nothing mattered, and that was a lie Micky and I would do just about anything to believe. On our hill I was overcome by a sense of time and place stripped to their barest elements. It was a thing I could manage only in bits and pieces on a ball field. Leaning back into my stance and feeling the barrel of the bat lowering, counting the stitches as the ball left the pitcher's hand to judge their spin and direction. But it was always the fleeting sort of peace when I was at the plate. Never the lasting kind, not even now.

"I tell you something?" she asked me once, this during the long summer before we started at Camden High. "I think God sent you. I never did believe in God. Ain't no church in Shantytown" — looking down over the slope of our hill toward that sea of pines — "Daddy says God won't go there. But I think God comes here, and I think He brung you with'im."

"Only reason I first come up was to find

an arrowhead."

"You can think that. But I think He knew I needed somebody. Don't matter up here I'm from the Pines and you're from town, Owen. This is our spot." She moved a piece of blond hair behind her ear and took my hand, pointing with the other out where the Blue Ridge rose tall and regal. "How long you think it took to make something like that? Billion years, I bet. Bet it took a million more for all them pines and wildflowers to grow on every ridge and holler just so we can smell this sweet wind. Probably it was a thousand years to make this hill for that wind to climb up, a couple centuries to make this oak so the wind can sing through."

I said, "I ain't never thought of that."

"Well, I have. And you know what I think? I think all that creating was did for us alone. Just for you and me to have this little while. And I think maybe you better kiss me now, Owen Cross, or else I'll burst."

And so I did, right there and then so as not to disappoint a God who'd spent so much time doing all that making for us. It was a tangle of lips and teeth that felt awkward but so utterly fine that Micky and I kissed again after and every time we came to the hill from then on out, and I don't know if that's what you call love but it's close. To us we were held together by a bond unbreakable, and the forbiddenness of what we had only grew our passion more. We kept ourselves secret all through high school until that terrible summer of 1990. There was no choice otherwise. My father would never allow a girl to come between him and the future promised through his son. The scandal of a townie boy like me, golden and destined for greatness, mixing with the plain white trash of a Dullahan girl would be too much for either of our families to endure.

What held us was the small promise of a few hours on the hill and the bigger one of the years to come. By my senior year I had signed a full baseball scholarship to Youngstown State, Ohio, which may as well have been darkest Africa to a people whose business rarely took them away from the valley. The *Camden Record* carried a nice article. Mom saved it along with the picture (me, Dad, Coach Stevens, and Youngstown's head coach, a muscled ex–minor leaguer named Frank Solis). From there it would be a quick road to the minors and the major leagues. And Micky would be coming with me. I was going to take her away from everything.

Until that summer I had only been to Shantytown once, when Constance Dullahan's heart finally gave out. Micky was the one who found her sprawled out in the front yard. The day's mail had blown from Constance's hand like so much chaff. That was the first time my trips to the hill almost got me in trouble. We had only a few hours together before Dad got home, but I couldn't leave Micky there in such mourning. She clung to me and wouldn't let go. Daddy near skinned me when I got home, saying he was near to calling Sheriff Townsend. Momma was the one calmed him down. She told him getting out in the fresh air never hurt anybody, and she said the same for the next three nights so I could comfort the girl she knew I loved.

News came out of the Pines of Constance's death and funeral. Mom made Dad's favorite supper of pork chops and grits. She fawned over the exploits of his day and nodded in agreement when Dad said it isn't education kids need these days but the Lord, then took that opening to give her speech.

"They're laying Constance Dullahan to rest tomorrow. Poor woman loved her Flannery O'Connor, though I expect she understood little of it."

Dad humphed.

"Think I may go down there. For the service."

"To Shantytown?"

"Be the Christian thing, Paul. Don't you think?"

"Ain't no wife a mine stepping into the Pines by herself, Greta. And I cain't go with. Got to get the field ready for the game."

"I'll take Owen then."

I wore the only tie I owned, a red one with blue stripes Mom said would suffice so long as I kept my shirt tucked. The knot in my throat felt to tighten that whole way, poking at me like a fear. Not far along Route 340, Mom turned right onto a narrow strip of road hidden by a tangle of briars to one side and a thick stand of pines to the other. A fog of gravel dust engulfed the car. The only marker in that place of dead fields and withered trees was a bullet-riddled sign that read *25 MPH*. Above us sat a wide sky empty of even the crows and carrion birds.

All I had ever known of Shantytown had been told by Micky, and only from the vantage point of our hill. Names mostly, people and roads, though none with any detail that painted living there as anything different from the rest of Camden. The stories told by my parents and kids from school declared it a bleak place of poverty and addiction — anything from moonshine to heroin could be had in Shantytown — where the only power greater than want was ignorance.

From our oak the place looked little more than a labyrinth of mud lanes hidden by pines as tall as buildings and thicker than a wall. Yet as Mom drove on, checking the directions Reverend Sebolt had drawn for her on a piece of library stationery, there was neither distance nor obstacle to keep me from beholding what so many in Camden chose to ignore. Past my vision rolled shacks and single-wides pitched in the final battles of a losing war against time and gravity. Dogs near feral pulled against thick chains wrapped around porch posts, screaming mad barks. Diapered children hid behind leafless trees. One boy no older than three answered Momma's wave with a raised middle finger. An elderly woman stood in the knee-high weeds of her tiny front yard, cursing us while making shooing motions with her hands. Faces numb and dead of hope peered out from blackened windows opened to the hot breeze. Hulks of rotting cars. Piles of trash — old appliances, crumbling furniture, an overturned sofa. Creeping vines covered everything, as though the land sought to heal itself of some deep wound or merely cover its own shame.

I said to Momma, "This is how Micky lives. This is how they all live here."

She turned at a cut in the narrow lane, studying the paper in her hand. Earl Dullahan's truck sat just inside. Two shovels were propped next to the lowered tailgate. A small group of mourners were gathered in ragged Sunday clothes, though I paid them no mind. All I could consider was the slight rise of land through the windshield and the small clapboard cottage atop it no bigger than our woodshed. Never before had I seen Micky's house. In all our years she had never described that place, nor given an account as to the hardness of her life. That she was poor needed no saying. Most in Camden were. But the hovel in front of me was of a poor I had grown up not knowing existed, and not merely because the windows were streaked with filth and the siding had begun to peel and the roof shingles curled like black scabs. The house looked wrong somehow, on some deeper level. Like sadness had distorted it as despair can a person. It spoke of a life beyond mere want, worse than disease. Shantytown was like a bruise on an apple that reached all the way to the core. I wondered then if that was why we had all come that day. If such hopelessness had been Constance's end.

"Lord," Momma said. "This breaks my heart so."

We got out of the car and made our way to the house as the Harper twins, Barry and Gary, stepped out from the open door and onto the porch. Their frayed jeans and plain T-shirts were dampened with sweat. One of them (I couldn't tell which — not even Jeffrey's daddy could tell them apart even though both boys worked at his grocery) waved at Mom with a dirty hand.

"Those boys bury the folk here," she said. "Out in the Shantie cemetery."

Earl Dullahan stuck his bearded face through the wide window from what I assumed was the living room, woozy-looking and drunk. I did not see Micky. Mom led me up the steps as the knot in me tightened. Stars flickered at the corners of my eyes as I entered the house. The lump in my throat pushed upward, wanting out. There was no place for it. All the paltry living room could hold was a small television and a worn green sofa standing on its end against one wall. The rest of that narrow space was taken up by the pinewood coffin set in the middle of the floor.

It's the smell I remember, a cloying scent of cheap air freshener that could not mask the mold and rottenness beneath. The Harpers kept on the porch, gawping through the big open window like it was something they were watching on cable. Reverend Sebolt stood at the casket's head. Earl swayed next to him. He swiped at his beard and stared at the box like he was trying to figure out how it had gotten there. And though my mind raced and my heart broke and it felt as though I would scream at any moment, that was all I could consider as well — how that front door was much too slim to maneuver a coffin through.

Reverend Sebolt clasped his Bible. He possessed the solemn countenance of a weary traveler through a world of dangers and snares. He asked in a low voice, "We ready, Earl?"

The man nodded slow, then turned to shout over his shoulder: "Get out here, girl. Folks is waitin'."

I heard a knob turn. The door behind them creaked open. She walked out in silence, head down. I would have wept were I not so frightened. Micky seemed no more. Or rather the Micky I had known since that first day up on the hill, the smiling girl who

45

glowed by some great shining star within, was no more. The blond hair and deep-set eyes, the curve of her chin, these were the same. All else of Micky Dullahan looked a stranger to me. She came forward in a pair of black jeans and a faded gray tee (the nearest clothes for mourning I suspect she owned) and settled between Earl and the preacher. Not once did she lift her head. Her eyes remained instead on the box. I felt as alive as the body we had come to restore back to the earth.

Reverend Sebolt began: "We are gathered to mark the passing of Constance Marie Dullahan, wife to Earl, mother to Michaela . . ." as a heaviness settled over the room. He talked on, glossing over all but the rudimentary facts of one woman's life, whatever Micky and Earl had shared with him earlier. The hard life Constance endured. The toil and trial. The Dullahans were not churched, which offered Alan Sebolt no true path to speak of rest and glory found. He stuttered and paused and broke to prayer when the words ran out.

At his amen the reverend paused to ask if anyone would like to speak. Micky's head lifted. On her face were a million words she could not tell. She looked not to the box nor to the others but to me alone, moving her chin in a silent no.

Earl was the only one who tried, offering what were perhaps the truest words he ever spoke: "She was a good woman. I did not deserve her."

Reverend Sebolt nodded as to the truth of that statement. To the Harpers he said, "Boys."

One twin shuffled inside as Earl and the reverend lifted the casket's front end. The three of them placed the bottom edge at the windowsill. The Harper boy then moved outside to his brother and they maneuvered the body through and onto the porch. Micky followed last. Her hand brushed my arm as she passed, a gentle touch of fingers running from elbow to wrist that stole my breath and melted every bit of that lump.

The Harpers slid the box into the truck's bed with a sweet gentleness and added the two shovels with which they would bury her. Micky walked toward the lane with the preacher. I could not hear what the reverend said. Whatever it was, she answered with a shake of her head.

"Owen," Mom said. "Come on now. We'll leave them to bury their own."

I stood and watched as Earl got into the truck. The engine wheezed to life as Barry and Gary took up the rest of the seat. Micky

47

climbed into the bed alone to take one last ride with her momma. She sat atop the hump made by the wheel housing and laid a hand to the coffin, steadying it as the truck lurched forward and off to the graveyard with a passel of Shanties trailing behind.

At the turn onto the road, Micky looked back. There was no hidden wave. No smile. Hers was instead the same dead face that had greeted us from behind darkened windows and withering trees, the look of the lost. It was as if in that brief glance I could see all of Michaela Dullahan's tomorrows laid out in one long unbroken line, years as hard and empty as any who were cursed by being born into that bruise upon the world. Ridiculed because she was poor, ignored because she was the wrong color poor. Called lazy and backward and trash. Micky kept her hand to the pine box, and I knew hers was a despair not only at her mother being taken away but at the taking of something even greater. Like a part of her, the best part, was about to be laid in the ground as well, never to shine again.

From our first kiss on the hill I knew I would love that girl forever. But it was on that day at the start of summer in 1990 when I vowed to save her someday too.

8

Twenty minutes to game time. The raucous clubhouse quiets to a professional calm as the card games end and the music is turned off. Players one by one gather their gloves and bats to make their way up the tunnel. Someone calls, "Hillbilly, you coming or what?"

I place the chunk of quartz back in my pocket and follow. At the tunnel I hear the growing crowd and the organ music, the clacking of spikes. There is a part of me that questions how it can be that on this, the greatest day of my life, I would be thinking of a girl long passed. There is the greater part of me that doesn't question it at all. I find my spot at the end of the bench and look out upon a field of gods, but I know now the cabbie was right. There are ghosts here, truly.

And they rise up.

TOP 1

1

We gather in a line outside the dugout railing, hats over hearts as a local high school band plays the national anthem through tubas and flutes and saxophones. A sky of reds and deep blues unfurls above the stadium. Rising over center field is a blossoming moon nearly full. Goose bumps break out along my arms and the back of my neck and channel beads of sweat down between my shoulders. I think of how our high school band played the anthem before that championship game back in '90. Those about to take the field or wait their turn at bat fidget between rolling notes. They rock on their legs or cant their heads heavenward, thinking of all that long road to this place before stating a plea for one more good game. A shout rises at the last notes. Applause and cheers and smiles from teenaged children as their gleaming instruments are carried off. A cry from the umpire: "Play ball."

No one in our dugout sits. Some of us place towels upon the hard concrete wall that ends at chest level to the field and rest our elbows there to peer through the railing or sit atop the long padded backrest of the bench. Others walk from one end of the dugout to the other as the Yanks take the field, keeping loose.

I lean forward when I spot 35 for the Yanks stepping out of the dugout. Mike Mussina takes the mound and rubs down the game ball between his hands. He's a crafty one, a veteran with four pitches and half a dozen arm angles. On our side of the field, Brady Anderson and Mike Bordick are at the on-deck circle. Both inch closer to gauge Mussina's stuff as he begins his warm-ups. Peppered between chatter of "Start us off, Brady" and "Show me somethin', Mikey" is talk of the moon. Many prophesy a big game in the same way my father once spoke of the Lord's holy judgment. At the end of the dugout, Mike Singleton stands with the bench coach going over the lineup.

Mussina makes quick work of the first two batters, getting Anderson on a deep fly to center and Bordick on a routine grounder

51

to Jeter at short. But I can tell he's struggling. His fastball is flat tonight, the curveball — his crutch — not biting. Worse is he's shaking off Joe Oliver behind the plate. The two meet midway between the plate and mound as Chris Richard, our right fielder, readies to step in. Three pitches and one changeup later, Richard sears a line drive to deep left and holds with a stand-up double. Mussina's frustrated at the inning going long. I spot him looking over his shoulder, not at the runner on second but at the moon beyond, missing all but a sliver.

Oliver jogs out toward the mound once more but doesn't stay long. Mussina doesn't want to talk and I chuckle to myself, thinking of Travis Clements back home. Travis with his hundred-dollar arm and nickel head. I hear Daddy's voice in my head — *Ain't a sorrier soul in all the world than a pitcher, Owen, which is why the catcher's got to take care of him* — Paul Cross saying that even though he was a pitcher himself. Jeff Conine walks to the plate but it's Travis I see, that game I remember, and how we almost lost it all because of a pitcher's pride.

2

It was a May afternoon on the cusp of summer in 1990, a few short days until our senior prom and a little over twenty-four hours since Constance Dullahan was laid to rest, but all the town could talk of was the state championship game between us and nearby Mattingly. Classes let out early. Businesses locked their doors and placed *At the game* signs in the windows. Jeffrey's dad shut down the grocery for the afternoon and Travis's daddy the car lot, which apparently hadn't happened in Camden since Hurricane David back in '79. As evidence of the rivalry between our two schools, Sheriff Clancy Townsend summoned most of Camden's police department to attendance. It's a wonder Mayor Henry didn't call up Governor Wilder and ask that the National Guard be sent down from Stanley too.

Our field was a large one — 325 feet to the poles, 390 to dead center. Two rows of bleachers sat behind the fence at home plate, separated by a concession stand and score box. By the time batting practice began, both sets of bleachers were filled. The Mattingly folks arrived in waves that settled in along the third-base line and spilled all the way to deep left. Mom came. Dad too, taking his accustomed place at the fence to the left of our dugout where the grass had been worn to dust. *Paul Cross's Spot — No Trespassing* may as well have been written there for all the games he'd seen from that location.

He waved me over after I'd finished warming up Travis. Fingers stuck through the metal diamonds in the fence, like a kid begging to play. He leaned in as though trying to squeeze himself through the gaps, pressing those blue pants and that gray shirt into the fence. I smelled floor wax and urinal cakes.

He nodded toward Travis. "How's he look?"

"Fastball's good. Curve ain't, but it never is."

Barry and Gary Harper walked past, sporting their empty grins. The Harper boys never missed a game. Nothing made them happier than wrestling kids twenty years younger and two hundred pounds lighter for foul balls. There came our mayor and a crowd of others, a gaggle of Shanties arriving en masse with Earl Dullahan leading them, a whiskey bottle peeking up from behind the pocket over his vanished butt. Micky wasn't with him, nor had she been to school that day.

Our denizens of the Pines forsook the bleachers. They sequestered themselves along the foul line in right instead and stood there unblinking, their smell of sweat and dirt drifting to us on the breeze. Not a single member of Shantytown played for Camden. None could afford the twenty dollars for uniforms and warm-up jackets, though I always got the feeling money didn't matter. Plenty of kids in town couldn't pay, and Coach Stevens always found the money.

"This is your game, Owen. You call your pitches and bend that idiot's will to your'n, and then you take your swings. Watched that kid warming up for Mattingly. Name's Hewitt. Got signed to a minor league deal. He's good, so you pay attention. People's watchin'." He cocked his head leftward. "First row, aside your momma."

I leaned around him and gathered in the man sitting next to Mom. "That Frank Solis?"

Dad nodded. "Come all the way from Ohio."

"For what?"

"For you. State championship's a big game, even if it ain't his state." He stuck a finger through the fence. "You're his player, though. So you show him something. Might make the difference between starting your freshman year and riding the pine."

3

Conine's up, and he's a pro. He doesn't bite when Mussina tries to paint the corners, and instead works the count his own way in a duel of mind rather than muscle. When his pitch comes, he's ready. The bench erupts when a fastball that's gotten too much of the plate is sent to left on a line. Richard scores, Conine stands at first. He points in acknowledgment when his teammates yell, and I hear the first smattering of boos (*Bronx cheers* — Dad speaking to me again) roll like a wave onto the field. Mussina keeps his cool but he's rattled, giving up a run with two down in the first. I know because he looks like Travis out there, and here comes Oliver again to settle him down.

4

The pep band played the anthem. I stood at home plate with my catcher's mask covering my heart and my eyes pointed at the flag past center field, trying to concentrate on the game. Only once did I avert my gaze long enough to glance out toward the parking lot in front of the school, hoping I'd see Micky. Reverend Sebolt delivered a prayer that came out shades more confident than the one he'd delivered in the Dullahans' living room.

Travis took the mound in the top of the first and promptly walked the first two batters. I settled him down long enough to end the inning with a strikeout and a double play, bringing a roar from the gathered.

Junior Hewitt strolled from Mattingly's dugout with all the care of a preacher out for a Sunday walk along the river. I'd never seen a boy so big. He looked like he belonged on the offensive line of some college football team instead of a high school pitching mound.

Jeffrey led off and struck out on three pitches. He passed me on the way back to the dugout, the color gone out of his face. "You'll hear it," he said, "but you won't see nothin'. Swear to God."

Travis hit second and fared little better, though he did manage to see five pitches rather than three before the ump punched him out. He walked slump-shouldered back to the bench and put on his jacket to keep his arm warm.

The crowd cheered as I stepped into the box, Mom and Solis too, though Dad offered nothing. I dug my back foot into the dirt when Mattingly's catcher started in: "You the big dog, huh? College boy."

I gave him silence.

"That's our big dog out there. Think he's

scared a you? Let's see."

The first pitch confirmed everything Jeffrey told me. Junior Hewitt coiled his giant's body and threw out not a baseball but a blur, a white dot the size of a pea that I barely saw but heard fine as a sizzle, ending with a shotgun blast when it smacked the mitt.

Strike one.

Mattingly's contingent cheered and mocked. I stepped from the box and back in, tapping the end of my bat at the inside corner of home plate. Finding my balance. Relaxing. Hewitt nodded at the sign. I raised the bat off my shoulder and leaned backward, ready, ready. My eyes locked in on an imaginary square that my mind had drawn two feet to the left of the mound where Hewitt's hand released the pitch, that square representing everything and nothing, and I saw Micky there, her face staring out from that spot and her blond hair spilling down along its edges, those eyes staring at me just as they had at that pinewood box, helpless and de —

The pitch was upon me before I could move. It crashed into my right kidney with all the force of a truck, releasing a bark as much pain as surprise, sending me to the ground. Mom screamed. Dad cussed and shook the fence. The crowd near came unhinged with all the yelling, half of them demanding Hewitt be tossed from the game and the other half planning a parade in the boy's honor once Mattingly claimed the state title.

Above me loomed the catcher's shadow. A voice like God's spoke: "Hurts, don't it?"

I picked myself up and tried jogging without looking like I was stumbling toward my own death rather than first base. Cussing Junior Hewitt and his minor league arm, cussing myself. I'd let my focus wander from what was important, only I didn't know which thing that was, the game or Michaela Dullahan.

Anger replaced agony. I stole second and third on the next two pitches, chasing a bit of Junior Hewitt's stupid grin, then rattled him enough that he sent a curveball into the dirt on pitch number four. It skittered under the catcher's glove and rolled toward the backstop. I broke for home. Hewitt's tag came too late. I'd pee blood the rest of that night but knew it was worth the pain. We were up 1–0.

There the score remained for the next five innings. Travis kept up his end, delivering every pitch I called without hesitation and keeping the Mattingly hitters off balance enough that they never really threatened. Hewitt matched him. Micky was still there. I felt the brush of her fingers each time I flashed Travis a sign. Glimpsed her in the crowd before every at-bat, mistaking a stranger's face for her own. Hers was the sole voice rising from the crowd chanting my name. Camden managed three hits through the sixth inning, none of them mine.

Dad motioned me over after my third at-bat resulted in a weak ground ball down the third baseline. Coach Solis stood with him. They asked if I was good — if I was hurt — and then Frank said, "That's college pitching out there, Owen. That's what you'll be facing."

The look in Dad's eyes was almost a plea.

We played only seven innings in high school ball. By the top of the last our lead still held, and you could see the dawning realization of loss on Mattingly's faces. They had a final chance at bat but were already beaten. Three outs to the only state title Camden had ever won. The crowd stood jittery and yelling, ready to fight should the situation warrant it. Even Shantytown cheered Travis's warm-ups.

The umpire called for a batter. Travis grooved one last fastball that I would then throw down to second base, which would then be tossed to the shortstop and finally to Jeffrey at third. A throw I'd made at the start of each inning I'd ever played, repeated so much as to be mechanical. And yet as I yelled "Comin' " down to second and stood to release the ball, I saw her. Standing alone past the right field fence with that same corn-silk hair, now teased and hardened with a can of Aqua Net hair spray. She had changed out of her mourning clothes and into a pair of cutoff shorts and a black Def Leppard T-shirt. Aside from the cigarette raised and lowered to her mouth, Micky never moved.

All of this registered in the time it took for me to release the ball, which sailed over second base and rolled meekly into center field.

Hoots from Mattingly's dugout, calls of "Candy arm" and "College boy." I took my eyes from Micky long enough to fully appreciate my awful throw and to see Youngstown's coach — the man who would hold my future for the next four years — dip his head. Dad looked as though gripped by the pains of labor.

Micky watched.

The first batter grounded out to Jeffrey at third, the next hit a lazy fly to center. Two outs, the Camden crowd frothing and wild, stomping their feet on the bleachers. Coach Stevens leaned in close to the fence, ignoring whatever it was my father shouted at him. Coach always did agonize over the last outs of a close game. The Witching Hour is what he called it, when anything bad that could happen most often did. It was a sentiment once more proven right that day, because that's when Travis's pride got the better of him and everything went to hell.

Mattingly's left fielder, a scrawny nine-hole hitter who hadn't touched Travis's heater all day, stepped in as their final hope. I put down a single finger for a fastball. Travis shook me off. I laid down a finger again. Wiggled it, saying, *This is the pitch.*

He shook me off.

I slapped a fist into my mitt and looked at Coach Stevens, whose chin had settled at his chest in one final prayer to the baseball gods. Dad merely shook his head in shock. I looked out toward Micky, then Travis, and put down two fingers for the curveball I knew he wanted. Travis nodded. Before anyone could blink, Mattingly had the tying run on first after a clean single up the middle.

As proof that pitchers possess the emptiest minds of any known form of life, Travis shook me off again with the next batter. And again. I let him serve another curveball that resulted in Mattingly having the tying run at third, the go-ahead on second, and three-quarters of the crowd descending into a weeping and gnashing of teeth.

I called time and walked to the mound, taking my mask off so Travis could understand me plain. "You think maybe it's time you start throwing what I tell you? Or you want these two runs to score so we can all go home?"

Travis scuffed the mound with a cleat. A low murmur of doubt washed over the crowd.

"Curve feels good," he said. "Daddy says I need to be throwing that more often."

"You serious right now?" I asked him. "Biggest game a your life, and you're standing out here thinking of what your daddy wants you to throw?"

"They already seen my heat. Need to show'm the slow stuff."

"They seen your heat," I said. "They can't hit it."

Jeffrey jogged in from third, popping his gum like he was above it all. "Hey, what y'all doin' later? I need a ride to pick up my tux for prom. And my cap and gown.

Sheesh, I forgot all about that. Y'all get yours?"

I tell you this: should you ever have need of empty conversation and have no pitcher close by, go find yourself a third baseman.

Travis said, "Got my tux," and needled me with his elbow. "Got yours yet?"

To him, Jeffrey said, "What you doin' after the dance?"

"Goin' to the party. And it ain't what I'm doin'," he said, "it's who. As in Jen Hamrick."

Jeffrey chuckled. I punched Travis in the chest with my mitt. "Get your head in the game 'fore you blow it."

"You got your tux, Owen?" Jeffrey asked. "I got to get mine. Stephanie keeps on me. Why ain't you taking nobody?"

Travis smirked, said, "Owen's gone take his mitt."

The ump came forward, barking at us to get on with things.

"I'm throwing curve," Travis said.

"I'm the catcher," I told him. "It's my call."

"Think it all you want, I don't care." Travis leaned down and spat into the dirt. "Why'n't you go on back to the plate, Owen, tell your daddy come clean that up."

I showed Travis my back and walked off.

Not looking at Micky or the crowd or either coach, new or old. Certainly not my father, who would have given up his ghost right then and there if he'd known what I was about to do. Mattingly's next hitter was their best, a kid named Barnett. I put on my mask as I reached the plate and spoke a single word:

"Deuce."

He looked at me, shook his head a little, and stepped in. I didn't even give Travis a sign. Travis, idiot that he was, nodded. The only thing that moved faster than his arm was his head as it spun to watch the ball arcing out toward the alley in left center, where it smacked the top of the fence. The Barnett kid ended up with a triple. Mattingly led 2–1.

It took a mere three pitches to strike out the next batter, all of them fastballs.

Travis never shook me off again.

By the bottom of the seventh it was mostly silence, the crowd hollering for so long that everyone had worn themselves out. Momentum had shifted from one team to the other so many times that no one quite knew what would happen next and so stood or sat in nervous twitching. We batted 9–1–2, which meant someone would have to get on base for me to have a last chance against Hewitt.

Our nine-batter struck out, bringing Junior Hewitt's total that day to fourteen — a state title game record. Jeffrey then managed to set aside his need for a tuxedo and walk on six pitches. Travis stepped up to the plate. I came out on deck and loosened up with my bat, watching Micky.

Travis hit a weak pop fly that the first baseman caught just outside the foul line.

Two outs.

I strolled to the plate easy-like and flicked at the air with the barrel of my bat, an old thirty-three-inch Easton Black Magic with a picture of Ted Williams taped near the handle. The crowd wasn't so much cheering now as shouting. Hundreds of voices calling out my name, calling, "O-wen." Mom yelling for me to wait on my pitch and Coach Stevens standing still, too afraid to hope. Dad standing at the fence with a quiet grin. Frank Solis looking out from beneath his Youngstown State cap. I saw him mouth four words: *Come on now, son.*

My last look was out toward right. Micky leaned into the fence.

Stepping into the box that final time was like entering a three-sided room of silence, the only opening pointed straight to where Junior Hewitt stood. I breathed deep the smells of earth and sweat. Felt the breeze at

66

the side of my face, carrying out.

And I knew then, beyond all doubt. That game was over.

Perhaps it had simply taken that long for me to shake the sadness of all I had seen in Shantytown. Maybe I simply wanted to impress my girl. But I don't think so. I think what locked me into that moment was Micky's mere presence. I found peace in knowing she was okay, at least for now. And for now was good enough.

Jeffrey took his lead off first base and gained an extra step, though that step meant nothing. I knew what was coming. Everyone believed Junior Hewitt's best pitch was his fastball, but it was in fact his curve. His curveball had movement, had bite, and while his fastball could carry in the mid-90s at least, it came at you as straight as a clothesline. And when it flew out of that tiny square I had drawn in my mind, Micky's face had no need of being there. I saw that ball alone.

There is a moment as a hitter when all the leavings of the world fall away. You are drawn into a bubble of absolute stillness and perfect simplicity that exists beyond all time and space, where pressure and fear cannot reach you and conscious thought is rendered meaningless. I felt no pain of the hit I'd taken at the start of the game. I heard no sound. To hit is to forget yourself entirely, it is a great letting go, and that is why it is an art. It is poetry set to action and music strummed by the soul, but it is also more, for those endeavors are fated to forever fall short of perfection. Yet a swing can be just that. It can be perfection, and perhaps the only perfect thing you will ever do. I always thought that if I could somehow live in that bubble stretched out to the half beat of a heart, I could live forever. If that was heaven, I would do anything to get there.

I never felt the ball meet the barrel. My bat met Junior Hewitt's fastball so clean and square that it felt like I'd swung through air. My eyes lifted up and out in my follow-through, leaving me to stand for an instant to watch it go. The ball shot high and far toward right, where Micky stood watching. It soared like a seed carried on wind.

The ground shook beneath me. I kept my head low and rounded the bases quick as I could. But I heard each cheer and every scream, every yell of my name. Sheriff Townsend moved his men into position to make sure no fights broke out in the parking lot. The team mobbed me as I touched home plate. In between high fives and slaps to the butt, I glanced back toward right, wanting to see her and needing to know she'd seen me. But that spot was bare except for the sight of Barry and Gary Harper racing a gaggle of elementary school kids to where they believed the ball had landed.

5

David Segui's our five-hitter. Big guy, good stick, handles himself pretty well with the glove around first base. He needs to let Mussina pitch here. Wait for that one mistake he can send out to an alley somewhere. Another run is what we need. Put the Yanks down two before they even get a chance to hit. Make them feel the pressure. Conine's got his lead off first. Mussina checks him. You think there's not much action in a ball game until the late innings. That's not true. There are battles, sure, but the little skirmishes through the early innings often carry as much tension. Our bench knows this is one. Segui comes up empty, though. He manages a grounder that Jeter snags and tosses to second for the force play. The inning's done. I glance over at Jason Johnson two places down from me. He stands and shrugs away the jacket that has kept his arm warm and looks out toward the moon — hoping is my guess, wanting that near

full globe to be working only one way this
night.

Bottom 1

1

Coach Solis took us out to eat after the game. I couldn't refuse the invitation even though I knew Micky would be waiting on our hill. Mom sensed hesitation on my part and pulled me aside to say it wouldn't be long, this man had driven all the way from Ohio and deserved a little of our time.

I fidgeted in my seat. My side hurt from where the Hewitt boy had hit me. Changing in the locker room after the game, I had inched up my shirt to find a purple-and-green bruise the size of a grapefruit sprouting beneath my jersey. Black spider webs reached from my side outward, skimming my stomach and back like some dark hand laid hold of me. In the center of the blotch rested the gentle curve of a baseball's seams as two dappled red lines sank into the skin.

Dad dwelt more on my poor performance prior to the seventh inning than anything else. To his credit, Coach Solis refused to view my game as anything but exemplary.

"I got big plans for you," he said. "You and me, Owen, we're gonna have some fun."

But it wasn't the next year at college that filled my head, it was getting home to Micky. Dad said nothing when I told him and Mom I was going to take a walk around the woods to stretch out and catch my breath. Mom winked while he wasn't looking and said to be back before too late. I pushed open the back door and made for the other side of our pines and the meadow. By the time I reached the slope of our hill, I could barely walk for the pain at my kidney. I climbed slow and favored my right side as much as I could. Pulled forward neither by duty nor by expectation, but by a simple desire to be with the girl I saw waiting beneath an oak so tall and wide it had no business being in this world or any other.

"There he comes," I heard. "Camden's crown prince. All hail."

Micky grinned out those last two words as much as she could, flashing an unbearable sense of pain and loss beneath them so the *All hail* stretched to sound more like *Aww, hell*. Her slight smile disappeared when she saw me limping.

Her hand at my arm, the scent of cheap

perfume mixed with pollen and forming dew. "What's a matter with you? Is it where you got hit? Barry and Gary told me."

"Ain't bad. Just help me down here is all."

She eased me to the oak's trunk and inched up the bottom of my shirt. Micky's quiet cursing was all I heard. Enough moonlight reached through the branches that I could see the two red welts laid in curving rows across a great purple sun.

"Have mercy, Owen, you been branded."

I don't know why that made me smile, but it did. It was the way Micky stared at the bruise like the wound hurt her as much as me, or how her fingers settled at my hip bone. Her eyes glistened. It was a wonder she possessed tears at all after burying her momma, yet it looked as though more would spill at the prodding of a single breath.

"You need to get a doctor," she said. "Your folks seen this?"

"It ain't bad. I've had worse." Which was true. Broken fingers and busted knees and bruises left by foul tips to my shoulders and arms. Catchers grow old before their time. I held my faint smile, wanting it to show, because I knew Micky was upset over more than some bruise. She had kept from our hill the night before, laying only a pile of river stones as a marker along with a note that said Shantie folk were coming to offer scraps of supper to her and Earl.

Micky needed me. The Rapture wouldn't be enough to bring me down from that hill.

Her protests ended there. She sat against me and her mouth said, "You're an idiot," but her eyes, those two watering sapphire globes, offered thanks alone. For a while we only stared down upon that vast sea of trees and the waves of mountains cresting behind. Mosquitoes whined in my ears. Micky nudged me as a star shot across the crown of the sky's bell, streaking white and orange and red. I knew her wish and mourned the star's refusal to grant it. The dead rose only in movies.

She said, "I knew you'd hit that ball. They scored them runs and I could hear everybody moaning. But I said, 'Not yet. Only one guy gets on next inning, Owen's coming up. We'll all go home smiling.' " Her gaze lingered on my face. "I ain't never seen a thing like that in all my life. That ball kept so high and far I almost spent a wish on it."

"Wouldn't've had to do that if Travis had thrown what I wanted."

"I seen him shake you off." Micky shrugged like that was backstory and so inconsequential. "He's an idiot."

"I'm just glad you came. I seen your daddy there but not you. Got worried."

"You know I wouldn't miss that game."

"Couldn't do anything," I said. "Played like some freshman. I needed to know you were okay. Soon as I did, it's like everything came together. Guess you won that game as much as me. It wasn't hard. I knew what was coming. I was laying fastball."

"You was what?"

"Knew he'd throw a fastball. That's the Hewitt kid's crutch — his heater. Every pitcher's got a crutch. One pitch he'll always fall back on when he needs to wiggle out of a jam. He mixed up his pitches good all game, but when he got in trouble he always went fastball. You knew I'd hit it out. So did I."

Micky blinked — no tears, though they gathered — and tilted her head. Often I would catch Mom looking at me in such a way, like in awe, which I either shrank beneath or brushed aside. But that same expression from Micky made me want to freeze that moment forever and store it away for all those times I felt small and alone.

"Sometimes I forget how smart you are," she said.

"Missed seein' you at school."

She flinched a little and drew her hand

75

down to pluck a blade of grass, which she tore into small strips and left to the breeze. "I was trying to right the house all day," she said. "Earl went off to wherever and left me with all Mom's stuff. Whole house smells like her. Only thing got me through's knowing you'd be up here tonight, that we could sit and talk and look down on everything. I think that's why I always liked this place. Nothing looks big from here."

A tear dripped. Micky wiped it before it fell. She'd never cried in front of me, refusing to be anything but the strong woman she pretended to be, the Shantie who could be stepped on by life yet still stand. I was not fooled. There were cracks in Micky's steely armor.

"She was the best woman I ever knew, Owen. She kept in marriage because a me and said a million times a child needs her daddy. I told her once I never did have no daddy to need, all I had's an Earl, and she'd say nothing to that because she knew it's true. But she did always love him. Especially at the beginning. Earl was handsome once, and he was always a fine talker. Then it all got too hard is all. Toward the end I guess she loved Earl still, but only that part a him Momma thought could yet be saved. Some shred of light she could claim."

"She was always kind to me. Little things like smiling when I saw her about in town. Wanted to say something like that at your house."

A hoot owl called from somewhere along the dark bruise that was Shantytown. Not far, a mockingbird answered from loneliness.

"You think there's a heaven?" she asked.

"Sure."

"Sometimes I think there is. I walk around down there in the Pines and see what goes on, all them people suffering through this life, and I think there's got to be a heaven if only to balance things. I want to believe it's so. That Momma's up there right now looking down on me. Loving me. She never did hate me for what I was to her."

"What you were?"

Micky nodded. "Ruination. Momma never told me she got pregnant before Earl put a ring on her finger. He speaks of it like it was a proud thing to do. Like he'd been the one out of every man in Camden to claim the prettiest rose there was, only then to tear that flower petal by petal. I was the one kept Momma from living what life she was meant. But she never showed it. Not one time. Momma was good to me."

"You ain't no ruination. Don't you say that."

"It's true. All Momma ever wanted was for me to be good. She died hoping."

"I think you're good," and at those words I realized I remained the only person left who believed as much, me and my momma. Micky was a Shantie, after all. Nothing good ever came from those pines.

Her hand graced my arm. "I'm glad you're here, Owen. If nothing else than because I love you, and the count of the ones I love in this world has now been halved."

"Summer'll be here soon, then it'll be time to go. Coach Solis was at the game. He's gonna take care of me at college. Means I'll take care a you. All we got to do is hang on, and I'll get you out of that place down there. I swear it."

She laid her head to my shoulder and we remained that way, talking some but taking in all that silence, looking down on all the small things. Micky never cried. And just as those tears had welled upon seeing the bruise on my side, I wanted to think I had a help in keeping them away that night as well.

2

Brook Fordyce has bounced around the majors since the midnineties, playing for five teams in both leagues. His bat doesn't have much pop but he's solid behind the plate, and he's shown me nothing but kindness. There are veterans who won't turn their heads to somebody up from the minors. Others are downright nasty. This speaks little to their personality and more to the reality of the game itself. There is always some younger kid behind you, some hotshot player waiting to take your spot the moment you hit a slump or do a long stint on the disabled list.

Johnson starts off well on the mound, getting the leadoff Yankee hitter on a lazy fly to left. But now over the intercom come the deep tones of Bob Sheppard, the man they say possesses the voice of God Himself, and Jeter is up. I lean forward as the crowd sets to buzz. He is a tall man, thin but muscular, built to play shortstop. A gamer, as my father would say. Brook and Johnson pitch him well, getting Jeter to hit a sharp grounder to second, but that's a hustler moving down first, head down and legs pumping, forcing Hairston at second to throw the ball wide and the crowd to utter a roar I feel in my bones. The bench grumbles. Johnson looks off to the pale moon.

David Justice is next. Johnson is rattled and lets loose a breaking ball in the dirt that

Fordyce can't handle, sending Jeter to second as the tying run.

"Go out there," I whisper. "Get him easy before they even this thing up."

Fordyce is thinking the same. He takes a walk to the mound and lays a hand to Johnson's back, his mask on so the Yanks on the bench cannot read his lips. A pat on the butt and he's gone. Whatever words he says are enough. Williams and Martinez both fly out, ending the inning and preserving our slim lead. The dugout joins my clapping. I stand and bump fists with the Oriole players as they come in. Fordyce meets Johnson in the dugout, going over what went wrong and how to adjust. Brook calls me over to listen. It's an escape, that inning. We all know it. And it's a long way to go.

3

Mom and Dad were in bed when I got home from the hill. On the table next to Dad's lamp were a baseball and two notes. The first had been scribbled by my father on a sheet of paper with *Augusta County Schools* stamped along the top. It reads: *440' measured. Harpers found it. Sign and take to Pr. Taylor in morning. Third deck Yankee Stadium.* An arrow was drawn from the bottom of the page to the ball.

The second sheet of paper was folded like a card and standing upright like two sides of a triangle. *Owen* was written on the front. I looked down the darkened hallway and conjured a ghost of Mom coming along once Dad had gone to bed, shaking off his second skin of janitor's clothes for a few hours before putting them on once more. Her glancing down the hallway toward the bedroom before laying down her own bit of thoughts.

Owen, I just want you to know how proud I am and always will be to have had a hand in raising such a fine son. Love, Mom

I crumpled the notes and pushed them into the trash can beneath the table, then picked up the baseball I had smacked a distance few ever managed, so great that it would have landed in the upper reaches of Yankee Stadium. Turned it in my hands. Held the seams crosswise as Junior Hewitt would have thrown it. I signed and dated it with Dad's pen and dropped it off at Principal Taylor's office the next morning, three days before prom and the beginning of everything's end. Mister Taylor vowed that ball would remain in a hallowed spot in front of the Camden High School's trophy case alongside mementos from football and basketball teams long forgotten, and first-place plaques the school's Future Farmers of America had garnered in parliamentary procedure competitions. I suppose that ball is there even now.

The memory of crumpling those two pieces of paper and tossing them into the trash has followed me like a curse. The crinkle of the pages in my hand; the edge of Dad's letter nicking the side of my forefinger, drawing blood; the faint smell of Mom's perfume. None of it mattered to me then, none of it felt real. I slipped down the hallway and fell to bed, forgetting how far that ball had traveled and how proud my mother would be regardless. I could have gone oh-for-five that afternoon and sacrificed a puppy between innings, she still would have left me a note that said *Love, Mom.*

It meant little to me then. It means near everything now that she's gone.

Top 2

Our batboy is a kid named Ethan. So far he's kept close to the rack and refused to stray from his duties. The players joke with him, flick the bill of his hard hat and lay their hands to his shoulder, squeezing the bone. His grin is a tired one, like smiling is something that until late he has rarely done. Mora and Gibbons grab their bats and head out toward the on-deck circle to start the second. I leave my spot on the bench long enough to pull myself up on the top step of the dugout. Keeping my back and legs loose, but also staring out into that great mass of bodies and faces.

They are kids mostly, children as I once was, wearing their Yankee caps and shirts, streaks of ketchup on their faces and the grime of the seats on their elbows. Most hold a glove close by for a wayward foul ball or benevolent act by a player who has caught the last out of the inning. I see fathers and mothers. Brothers, sisters. Grandparents stooped over spiraled scorebooks with ballpoint pens shaking in their hands. I see a few alone but content, the smiles on their faces like Ethan's — maybe recalling loved ones with them on nights like these long past, or maybe experiencing the magic of how a simple game can stanch the pains of loneliness.

That is all baseball resembles to most — a simple game. A thing to pass time on a warm spring afternoon or a hot summer's night. It has always been true enough to me. A game is all it has ever been.

Yet it has remained for me the only thing I ever truly mined the depths of, like a puddle of cloudy water you think will reach only your ankles until you step into it and are swallowed whole. I have never known anything but this game. My mother once said my name came from her not an hour after my birth. She cradled me at her breast and looked into my still-shut eyes and said, "We're going to name him Owen." And in her account my father brushed a sweat-slick forelock of her hair away and then settled his eyes to my hands, taking one in his thumb and marveling at how my fingers reached clear around the knuckle and squeezed. His pronouncement would seal my future more than even a name: "We gone make him a catcher."

I look at those hands now as Mora steps to the plate and sends a lazy pop fly that lands in the first baseman's glove. These hands. By the time I'd won Camden its championship, I could hold four baseballs in my splayed fingers. Often on our hill, Micky would press her palm to mine and laugh at the result.

She would say to me, "God really did make you a catcher, didn't He?" and I would answer, "No, Dad did."

He had been made a pitcher by his own father's will at the age of ten, when on a quiet April evening of catch after his chores were done my father threw an errant pitch that knocked a hole clean through the Cross family's chicken house. My daddy played league ball growing up, then on to high school. To my knowledge, Paul Cross remains the only pitcher in Stanley history to throw four no-hitters in a single season. The Hewitt kid paled in comparison.

Dad managed a scholarship to Georgia Tech but lasted only his freshman year before his arm went, and with it every dream he had ever possessed. Schooling itself meant nothing to him. He came home a failure and found work at the mill, met

Momma some years later. He was a broken man by then. My mother's parents wanted no part of him. But Momma saw something in this man she loved, a goodness that had been beaten down and she believed worthy of coaxing back, even if Paul Cross was nothing more than a tired mill worker with a bum arm.

His greatest fear was that his life would come to nothing, which was why he felt such renewed purpose when I came into the world. My father gave me many things in his life. Most of all, he gave me baseball. In that diamond pattern of dirt and chalk I found a sense of beauty and truth and the answer to every question sprouting in my heart. We played constantly in our small backyard on Stanley's outskirts; it was no mere work or practice but love made through effort, sweat gathering beneath the small brim of a Cubs cap I found under the Christmas tree and grass stains Momma could never get out of my jeans.

A single by Jay Gibbons trickles through the middle of the infield. Ethan grabs the bat from the grass in foul territory and stumbles over his feet halfway to the dugout, drawing jeers from the fans. His head is low when he reaches the dugout. Mike claps him on the back, tells him good job. Fordyce is the next batter and strikes out looking. Two down. Mussina looks to have settled down on the mound before Hairston makes up for his earlier error and singles to center, allowing Gibbons to reach third. Shouts from our dugout. I sit back down at the end of the bench and tell myself to keep my head in the game. Can't let my thoughts wander.

Anderson's up, our DH. He's built like a tank and you can tell he's always been the best at what he does. Every field and sandlot in his youth, Brady was the man. Looking down the bench and out onto that emerald field glowing in the dim evening, all those Yanks on the other side, I know we were each once that — the cleanup hitter, the stopper on the mound, the kid you pitch around in high school.

I was eight when Dad took me down to the Ruritan club and signed me up for my first year of Little League. Tryouts were held the following Saturday. I stood in the box a lefty ("Better able to handle the curve," Dad said) and watched in abject horror as the first pitch given me by a volunteer coach lobbed in so slow that I let it by, believing the throw a mistake. I stepped out and looked at Dad, who chuckled and nodded. The next four pitches sailed over the fence, and I knew then there was not a single boy on that field who could match me. Not one kid in Stanley or anywhere else. I could hit farther and throw harder and run faster than any of them. When you come across something you're good at, something that sets you apart, the conviction of that being the thing you're going to do forever isn't far behind. I was born to play ball, yes. But I was born to play it because that's how Paul Cross raised me. Because that was how he'd been raised himself.

Hairston steals second and I don't know why. I hear a grumble from the other end of the dugout and see Mike Singleton shaking his head. Anderson's got a big stick, likes to drive the ball out to the gaps. But with first base now open Mussina has the option of pitching carefully. Anderson walks. The crowd groans as the bases load. We may have the makings of a little two-out rally here, but Hairston's stolen base may cost us in the end.

Think, Dad would always tell me. *You got to think out there, Owen. That's your job.*

Mike Bordick is our shortstop. He takes a fastball from Mussina and sends it on a line to center, scoring Gibbons and Hairston and sending Anderson to third. The boos descend sharper, fueling our dugout's yells and clapping, though I notice much of the celebration is for Ethan's charge out to the plate to retrieve Bordick's bat, giving a clear path for Gibbons and Hairston to touch the plate.

A guy next to me, Stills, a utility player just over in a trade by the Dodgers, nudges my arm. He says, "Ethan's a good kid. Daddy's in jail and his momma's drying out in some rehab. Kind of broken, I guess. We all adopted him."

Richard steps into the box as the pitching coach for the Yanks comes out to calm Mussina down. Their meeting at the mound doesn't bear much fruit. Richard cracks a deep ball into the left-center gap that scores Anderson and Bordick and gets the Yankee bullpen stirring. A wild pitch to Conine sends Richard to third, but Conine can't capitalize. He strikes out, ending the inning, but we're up now five-zip and our dugout is feeling good. Johnson nearly sprints out to take the mound for the bottom of the second.

I leave my spot and wander up the dugout to where Mike and the bench coach stand, lingering over the bats. Ethan eyes me. To him I say, "Good job out there, little man," and hold out my fist.

He bumps it with his own and thanks me
with a quiet grin.

Bottom 2

1

Dad used to say that in any game and any life, momentum makes all the difference. He knew this from experience, so close as he came to foundering after both his injury and his layoff at the mill. We're the ones with momentum now. Our guys have an extra hop in their step as they take their grounders and long throws. Johnson zips the ball even on his warm-ups. Mike rocks back and forth on his heels by the dugout steps, sensing a rare win at Yankee Stadium. We're feeling good.

With nothing to do at the bottom of each inning, Ethan takes a quick look to make sure the bats are in order before sliding down the dugout. He takes a seat not far from me. O'Neill is up, a tough out to be sure, but Johnson catches him off balance and gets the leadoff hitter for the Yanks to ground out to third.

"First out's always the hardest one." It's Ethan says it. "You get that first one right off, it'll be a good inning most times."

"I'd say you're right."

"You the busher they call Hillbilly?"

"Yep."

"Where you up from?"

"Bowie. Double-A."

"Lopez's daddy's sick. They say he's in the hospital. You got a daddy?"

"Not no more."

"Me neither."

He takes up another few inches of the bench. I move my mitt out of his way. It is a bond of understanding between us, both our fathers gone. Like two veterans comparing wounds from some dark war.

"Johnson," Ethan says, "he'll be all right so long as his shoulder don't fly open. It's always trouble if he does that. Plus that moon out there." He won't look, superstitious I suppose, and instead shakes his head in the wizened way of one who has seen too much in this short season. "I don't think this one's over. It ain't over 'til it's over. That's what they say."

"Could be you're right."

Ethan stretches forward as Brosius steps to the plate, says the Yankees' third baseman is one of his favorite players. When he settles back on the bench, he is almost atop me. I see the happiness of his eyes and the pain at rest beneath. Kind of broken. I know that look well. Seen it in all those Shanties back home. Seen it in the kids most of all.

2

In no other place are the discriminations of the world laid so bare as the nearest high school cafeteria. There the line separating those who belong and those who do not is made clearest, with those two groups divided even further: what your last name happens to be; the color of your skin; your degree of ugliness or beauty; your address. By these we are judged by a common jury of peers driven by the deep human need to classify every person, ourselves most of all. Which I suppose gives at least partial reason why Todd Foster decided he was going to sit at the wrong table that next afternoon, three days before prom.

The Camden High cafeteria was a wide room set along the school's west side. Illumination relied more upon the bank of windows facing the parking lot than the rows of fluorescent lights Dad climbed a ladder each month to repair or replace. Cinder-block walls painted dull gray gave hint to the food we ate, dished by old women wearing hairnets and scowls. Rows of tables laid end to end covered most of the cracked linoleum floor. Three narrow paths ran the room's length. The chairs were red plastic disks bolted to the table bottoms.

Ours was the table nearest the food line and the trash cans, a spot coveted not only for the ease of movement but the commanding view it offered — the popular table. Travis claimed the chair at the head the same as Dad did his La-Z-Boy in our living room, like it was the throne from which to gaze upon his kingdom. The seat to Travis's left was a revolving one of the prettiest girls in school. In the days leading to prom it was Jen Hamrick there — the who rather than the what Travis was doing. Jeffrey sat on the other side with Stephanie Sebolt, the preacher's daughter. The final spot was mine.

I was never ignorant of the reason I was afforded such a prime spot to dine on little smokies and fish sandwiches. My friends hailed from rich homes, or homes as rich as any in Camden could be. Bubba Clements, Travis's daddy, owned the biggest car dealership in Camden, leaving Travis with looks and athletic ability and money all. Jeffrey's father owned the IGA — the only grocery in town. Jen's momma ran the flower shop, and her daddy was responsible for the tile or laminate or carpet in just about every house and business in twenty miles. Some were of a mind the Hamricks were richer even than Bubba. And while the Sebolts were not overly wealthy, Stephanie at least strolled the hallways with knowledge that her father was the Lord's mouthpiece to us all, or at least those who believed in a Lord worth listening to.

But the Cross family was ever doomed to occupy that thin space between Emerald Hills, the fancy subdivision where Travis and Jeffrey and Jen lived, and Micky's home in Shantytown. I never possessed much in the way of looks. My clothes came from sale racks at J. C. Penney. Mom made little more than minimum wage at the library. Dad pushed a mop in front of every single one of my peers. Were it not for baseball, I would have been cast off with the rednecks who claimed the table closest to the FFA room or the stoners who held court by the pay phone near the doors. I may well have even been banished to the loser table where Micky and the rest of Shantytown's kids kept to safety in numbers. I'd won a spot at the popular table for one simple reason: I had been born with the unique ability to square a rounded ball against an equally rounded bat.

Lunch was the only time Micky and I crossed paths at school: twenty minutes of trying to steal looks around all those tangled bodies, to smile and dream of each other before darting away. On that particular day her eyes lingered. Looking back, I am left to wonder if she had some premonition of what was about to happen.

Jeffrey was regaling us with a re-creation of his gutsy seventh-inning walk the day before. Travis leaned across his tray to kiss his current flame. I looked toward the double trash cans not twenty feet away where Dad kept duty, looking like a prisoner, a man convicted. He plunged a hand down into the slop and pulled out a fork some student had tossed away, a man robbed of pride and future both standing at semi-attention over bags of trash he would pull and knot and carry to the Dumpster out back.

Todd cut through my stare as he passed, a slim body of little more than gristle and bone wearing stone-washed jeans and a bright T-shirt. Blue that day rather than purple or green or (Todd's favorite) neon pink. Two smooth hands with neither callous nor blemish gripped the sides of his tray. His fingernails were long and carried a constant shimmer many swore was clear nail polish. But it was Todd's hair that stood out more than his attire, an auburn mane brushed to wings and sprayed stiff. The running joke was that of all Camden's girls, Todd's hair was prettiest.

Travis moved his mouth along Jen's neck. Stephanie Sebolt bent in close to say she wished they'd get a room already when Todd stopped, forming the apex of a triangle with our table and the Shanties' the remaining points.

His chin dipped as though weighing options never considered until that moment. He pivoted (it was a graceful movement, a girl's pirouette) and made straight for us.

Todd Foster sat.

He looked a frightened thing that barely took up the space beside Stephanie, staring down at his tray and the fork wrapped inside a thin paper napkin. Not a word fell from his lips. Jen sat so shocked that all she could do was stare. Silence fell. Jeffrey's mouth went agape. A bit of half-chewed chicken fell out, dappled with ketchup and saliva.

The only one within sight unaware of our guest was Travis, too busy working his tongue from Jen's neck to her ear. She pushed him away, provoking a "Hey, what's . . ." that evaporated at the sight of

Todd. Every dark emotion Travis kept hidden sprang out all at once, and with such fury it left his eyes narrowed and his cheeks a bright crimson. He managed, "What you doing, Foster?" in a voice so deep it didn't sound like Travis's at all.

Todd kept quiet. He freed the fork from his napkin with two trembling hands.

"Hey, man," Jeffrey said. "Seriously. You can't be sitting here. That's your table over there." He pointed at the long row that made up the cafeteria's center, where Micky sat staring.

The other Shanties joined, bony and acne-stricken elbows nudging into the sides of those beside them, forming a long line of expressions that were half admiration and half a guilty thankfulness. The Losers may be poor, may have spent their entire years of schooling bullied and mocked, but at least what was about to happen to Todd Foster was not happening to them.

Micky mouthed to me from halfway across the room: *Do something.*

"Seriously, man," I said. "You should really go."

Todd looked up at me, no one else. And in a soft falsetto voice laced with the smallest bit of Virginia drawl, he said, "I can sit where I want."

Noise at the cafeteria's other side continued unabated. Trays clanging and voices raised in the chatter of a hundred conversations. Our side, though, had taken on the hushed stillness of a crowd anticipating a fight.

Travis was more than obliged to give them one. He said, "Pick your stuff up and get out of here, Foster. I'm not kidding. Last warning."

Todd didn't move. I don't know that he could have even if he'd wanted to at that point, as scared as he looked.

"That's it," Travis said. "This fairy's taking a ride."

Principal Taylor's head turned at the collective gasp that arose. As Travis went to stand, Micky also got up. She walked toward the front and around the tables, putting herself between my father and us.

She said, "Todd, why'n't you come sit with me today."

"You heard her," Travis said. "Get on over there with Michaela."

Again Todd: "I can sit here if I want."

Travis sprang. The force of his movement was so sudden and pure it forced Todd to his feet. He was walking at a brisk pace toward Micky with tray in hand, russet hair flapping, when Travis kicked out his shoe and sent him flying. The cafeteria burst into laughter, bringing Principal Taylor our way. He had almost reached us when Micky reached down to Travis's tray and grabbed a handful of gray meat and browned peaches, shoving it all into Travis's face. Jen let out a scream.

Laughter turned to a chorus of *Oooh* as Principal Taylor jerked Micky by the collar of her shirt and herded her toward the steps leading to the hallway and his office. Todd ran, banging open the door to the parking lot with such force that a corner of the glass shattered into a hundred tiny webs, and I laughed, oh how I laughed, because laughing was all I could do. It didn't matter I'd spent four years at the popular table just because I could play a game better than anyone else. Didn't even matter the popular table was really no different from the dozens of other wobbly and stained tables that had sat in that lunchroom for years. It was enough to know I had a place to sit. That I fit in.

Travis swore vengeance. The bell rang. Dad came forward with a mop bucket and a roll of towels. I used a napkin to wipe up what I could of what had spilled on our table, then stacked the six trays that remained.

"I'll get that," Dad said. "You get on to class."

"Let me help."

"No" — not even looking at me — "told you I got it," he said, and nothing more.

3

The only Dullahan I saw at school the rest of that day was Earl, wobbling his way into the school after the last bell, demanding someone tell him where the office was and that whore of a daughter he was cursed with, she done gone and disrupted his afternoon.

4

"Was an awful thing," Dad said at supper. "A hateful thing, and my only comfort is you weren't there to bear witness to it, Greta."

Mom looked across the kitchen table to me. Said nothing. Only stared in that way of eyes that had gone soft and lips slackened, as though what she'd heard couldn't be.

"Watching you with that stupid grin splayed on your face. Know what I thought, Owen?"

He waited for my answer, motionless with a bowl of mashed potatoes in one hand and a serving spoon in the other. "Know what I thought?" he asked again. "I thought, *I ain't never been so sorry to call that boy mine.*"

I knew better than to reply with anything other than "Yessir," which at least got the bowl passed to Mom.

She took it and sighed and spooned her own portion. "Kids these days, so mean and nasty. Isn't a thing they won't do or say or try. And Stephanie Sebolt drawn up in it, of all people. Wonder what the reverend will have to say toward that." The bowl crossed the table to me. Mom held on to it as she voiced what I hoped would be the final thought on the matter. "That poor child. Todd Foster, you say?"

Dad went from being unable to look at me to being unable to take his eyes away from mine, and I couldn't figure why. It wasn't me who'd stood up and threatened Todd Foster with a beating unless he crawled back to his own table. Wasn't me chased Todd out.

"Wasn't me," I said. "I told Todd he should go before all that started. I didn't say it mean."

"Didn't say it mean. You still told him to go."

He stared. I was seventeen, as tall as Dad and twenty pounds heavier, a grown man who by summer's end would be going off to college, then the minors, then the Bigs. But whenever he looked at me that way I always shrank to a boy no older than six, looking up at a man who possessed unquestioned authority. Mom may have been the rock of our family, but Paul Cross stood as its moral center.

Dad shook his head and stabbed his half a chicken like he meant to kill the bird all over again. Wiping his hands on the napkin settled over his lap, careful not to stain those blue pants. My father had been a proud man once, a pitcher with a golden arm. Now he would be a high school janitor until the day he died. His destiny lay in a dustpan. I had grown to look down upon him as much as up.

He asked me, "Think you better'n him? That boy ain't worthy of the space you occupy or the air you breathe, Owen?"

"He's only a boy, Owen," Mom said, as though that fact was one that none of us had considered. "I pity him."

Dad's stare turned to her. "You what?"

Mom blinked. She quit chewing her food, started again. Between movements, she said, "Pity him."

Dad stood and balled his napkin. "I can't be here right now," he said, and turned to leave.

I heard the front door open and shut, the sound of his shoes on the sidewalk. Mom rolled her eyes and shook her head in a noncommittal way, as though saying, *Well, there he goes again,* looking over her shoulder out the window above the sink to catch Dad's direction. Maybe go after him.

That was Mom — the family apologist. She was a pretty woman until the cancer ate her away. Hair fashioned so that it draped over the sides of her face like a picture frame, parted on the left and curled inward to the point of her chin. Brown rather than the coal black Dad's genes had bestowed upon me, though so light it looked more copper when a high sun lit upon it. Eyes sparkling blue. A mouth quick to part with either a kind word or a smile. I miss her.

"Don't mind your father," she said, and began collecting plates. I gathered my own and took it to the sink, happy to know the food I'd left would cause no concern. Mom pulled the cobbler from the oven and set it on the counter to cool. The kitchen smelled of blueberry bushes and peach trees. From the other side of the screened back door came the noise of a cardinal's call and the sound of a spraying hose, Dad watering the flowers.

"I didn't do anything to Todd," I said. "All I did was sit there."

"Inaction is still action, what your grandma used to say."

I scraped the plates. Mom started the dishwasher. She asked me, "Was really Michaela did that? Shoved that food in Travis's face?"

"Every bit of it."

"She got a fire in her, doesn't she?"

I had to agree. "Didn't think she'd ever do something like that, though. Take up for a Shantie."

"A Shantie's what she is. Like your daddy's what he is. He's a hard man to know, Owen, but he loves his family and does his best to provide us a good life. And you a good future."

"That don't give him license."

"No." She offered a smile that reminded me of a bright ribbon tied to a broken gift. "But you have to remember your dad had promise before he got hurt. Those years in the mill took most the rest. The little left over . . ." A shrug, a tilt of her head. "He tells me sometimes, you know. The things he hears from kids down at that school. How sometimes they'll make a mess just to watch your daddy clean it up. The way the teachers talk down to him, even though Paul

Cross is about the smartest man I ever knew." And then this last little bit, slipped as a slender blade into my heart: "Talks, too, of the times you go about ignoring him if your friends are close by."

"I don't do that," I said, though I couldn't look at her.

"I hope that's the case. The years haven't been easy, Owen. Your father and me had our struggles, many of them mighty. But we carved a life out of this place, and it's a good bit better than the life given to some. And it's all been for you. Maybe what happened today with Todd cut a little close to the bone. Could be the rejection that boy got was the same your dad feels every day, only turned outward. Maybe he got mad at you because to him, you were casting out someone besides a boy who didn't belong. Was a man who didn't belong neither, and never would."

Half of Dad came into view, one arm and part of a leg. The hose's nozzle swung in a slow arc from the grass to the far rosebushes set against a shed the size of Micky's house. The shoulder of that arm looked slumped and tired. Mud streaked the cuff of his pants.

"That ain't how I meant it. I didn't even laugh."

She stood on her toes and placed her hands to my cheeks. Looked at me in that way mothers do, parsing my words. It was as if she knew one of the two things I'd just said was a lie but couldn't figure which one, whether I was in fact ashamed of my own father or whether I had in fact laughed at Todd Foster's embarrassment. But then the question in her gaze was gone, replaced by a measure of grace.

"I know that," she said. "You're a good boy, Owen. I'm happy for you. You're about to go off and start a new life. But I confess I don't quite know how to act sometimes. A mother and wife is all I've ever known to be, so now it feels like half of me is gone. Like there's a hole now. There'll be one in your daddy too, and I think that bothers him more than he'll ever say. He's proud a you. What you've become."

"Sometimes I ain't so sure what I've become, least of all to him."

The fan twirled a strand of her hair. We stood in silence for but a little while with nothing but the whirring blades and the outside sounds between us, a passing car and the far barking of a dog, the hose at work to loosen the dirt beneath our flowers.

Until finally Mom said, "Why, you are his proof, of course. That's why he wants nothing more than your love and respect turned back to him. By you he aims to show the world his life has not been a waste." She held my face as though it were a mirror reflecting back the best parts of herself. "You are your father's path to redemption, Owen, however unfinished it may lie."

5

Brosius strikes out swinging, bringing a groan from Todd (*No, Ethan,* I say in my mind, *kid's name is Ethan*) that he barely covers. I never saw the pitch Fordyce called, don't even see Brosius walking back to the dugout with his helmet already in his hands. It's Micky I'm thinking of, and how I found out later that I hadn't been the only one held to account for what happened with Todd Foster. How she came to the hill that evening with an Earl-sized welt on the side of her face, red and swollen.

She'd tried in her own limited way to cover it with whatever makeup she had on hand, which looked little more than some lipstick and a bit of rouge. I took one look and vowed to lay Earl Dullahan upon the ground. Only thing kept me from it was Micky saying going down into the Pines wouldn't matter since Earl was passed out drunk. She possessed a ready answer to counter every point — "Earl won't ever change" and "He hit Momma some too" and "You doing something will only serve your anger, not my safety."

All spoken from half a heart through those unlit eyes. I don't know what scared me more: that Micky had been beat on or that she hadn't looked to have felt any of it. Some wiser part of me spoke out then with a sureness that shook me, whispering, *She's on a precipice, Owen, that girl's on the ledge of something and she's going to jump, she's going to jump soon* —

"— your daddy," she said.

"What?"

"I said I always thought similar of your daddy. Way he's pushed you so with baseball. Your momma's right. You are his redemption, and that will be your burden. Wish Earl'd pushed me similar. He never did. Less you count the time he made me go tumbling down the root cellar when I was a kid."

"He ever lay a hand to you wasn't balled to a fist?"

"Earl was never one for affection. I think that's one reason my momma died. I thought about that. How maybe her heart didn't swell up as much as it grew brittle from not being handled."

"You loved her."

"Weren't the same."

We faced east as we were sometimes wont, looking out over the bit of town the hill's height provided. Side by side, our shoulders touching, and Micky's bare leg next to mine.

She asked, "You get your tux yet?"

"I'll get it Saturday. Your dress?"

"Found it at the Goodwill. I tried it on for Earl. He looked at me like I was a Democrat. He always did want a boy."

"Probably for the best you ain't. I'd hate to be up here every day with the prettiest boy in town."

"You're so stupid," she said. And in a soft tone meant as a comfort, she added, "It'll be okay, Owen. Prom. We'll have fun the best way we can. I just wish we could be going together."

"Won't be the same. Won't be as it should be. Everybody's asking why I ain't taking nobody."

"What you tell them?"

"That there ain't nobody I want to take. Which is a lie."

"Lying's what we do." She sat there, looking to where the ridges fell into the distance. "I didn't want to get Todd hurt. Travis woulda lit into him. He wouldn't have stopped until Todd was half dead, seeing it as some challenge to his manhood or something. And Todd would've sat right there and let it happen, if only to prove his own point. I had to do something."

"What point?"

"That Todd can do what he wants. That just because a where he was born and what he is, it don't mean he's something less. But Travis is just like everybody else in this place. Just like his daddy and Jeffrey's daddy, like them girls who was with you. Even the preacher's one. They all the same. All people's ever gonna see of Todd Foster is he's a queer from Shantytown. Which is why I always thought I needed him."

"Todd Foster's about the last boy in town you've need of."

"You're wrong there. People's just lost, Owen. Shantie folk 'specially. It's like we don't even understand what living is no more."

A star streaked across the sky and disappeared over the mountain in a long tail of silent fire. Micky didn't nudge me. I wished anyway. "I think about all anyone can do is get from one end of it to the other the best way they know."

Her hand found my leg with a touch so soft it felt like the brush of feathers. The bruised part of Micky's face turned to mine.

She kissed me.

"Yes," she said. "That's the very thing. Whole town knows what Todd Foster is. He was like that long before you got here. I remember this one time in kindergarten we had show-and-tell. I brought a snake I caught down at the river by the house. Travis brung a football Bubba give him. Todd, he brought a doll. Like a baby doll. He was always doing stuff like that."

She faced town again and those few strips of avenues we could see, darkened husks of housetops and the world gone to slumber. Though we shared the space beneath the oak with our bodies so close and the feel of our breath mixing with the air, Micky had never looked so alone.

"It's a horrible thing I'll say, Owen, but I got to because it's true. So you'll understand. People in this town'll always call me trash. I'm the drunkard's daughter, girl of the woman whose heart gave out because those pines took it. But I figure so long as Todd Foster's in Camden, I can look at him and hold my head some higher. I can pass Todd on some street and think, *Least I ain't as bad off around here as him.* That's why I need him. So long as I'm here, I need Todd Foster to be well and outlive me by a day."

6

The crowd's groan shakes me. I blink to see the Yankee catcher turn and walk back to the dugout and Fordyce rolling the ball back out toward the mound. Johnson has struck out another. End of the inning, that's the way to do it. Score some runs on one end and shut them down on the other, that-a baby. That's the way to pitch a game.

Ethan stirs beside me, says, "Gotta get back to work."

"You go show me something."

"I will."

He grins again and doffs his cap as he walks down toward the bat rack, showing me a shock of Todd's auburn hair. The air hums around me, claps and atta-boys and let's-get-'ems, but it's only buzzing in my head, a hazy wall of electricity between my now and my then. A cricket sings out . . .

7

. . . from a tangle of brush somewhere down the slope, turning Micky's head. Calling out into all that silent dark for the promise of summer and company, though the night would bring neither. I wondered how many in the world were like that. Calling out in our darkness for some relief that told us we were not alone. Grabbing hold of anything

113

near to convince us of that, no matter its cost.

"All we got to do's hold out the summer," I said. "Then we're off to Youngstown. You'll never have to see this place again. I promise you that. Rest of it, all that stuff you think about you and Todd, it's all lies."

And Micky grinned a little, no more than a thinning of her painted lips. "Why, Owen Cross, don't you know all we got's the lies we tell ourselves? Like your daddy thinking his life may come to something so long as yours does, or my daddy thinking his girl is but a misshapen boy. But there comes a time when those lies become known for what they are, and all we've left is to buckle under them. Five whole years we been coming up here," she said. "You realize that? Don't seem more than a week sometimes, and now it's almost over. 'Nother month we'll walk across the stage for graduation."

"And be gone," I said again.

"It's times I'm afraid to believe that. Don't many ever get a chance to leave Camden and never come back. Nobody from the Pines. Most us? All we do is stay right here because there's no choice, live and work inside our own coffins. But not you," she said. "You are destined."

I snorted a little, wanting it to be so but

afraid of it just the same.

"Don't you laugh. I always believed it no less than that the sun will rise. You've a gift like I never saw in anybody. The way you play ball? It's like . . . well, I don't know what it's like. A poem, I guess. Like everybody else out there is just flailing about while you glide along without a care. Your daddy says you were born for the game. I never thought that was right. I always thought it the other way — the game was made for you. I can't imagine what it's like being able to do a thing so well. To be you. It would be about the greatest thing there is."

I said, "Might let you sit here all night telling me that if I believed a word of it."

"It's true or I wouldn't waste the breath to say it. You're too humble is all. Or maybe it's you're too scared to know. But I ain't. You're gonna make a name for yourself. You realize how precious of a thing that is? That you're special? That your heart's built such that it can love something so completely?" She looked off then, down toward where the grasses swayed as the night critters moved through them and then farther, past Shantytown to where the mountains rose like masses of departed souls. "That's all I ever wanted, I think. To lay my mark however I can."

"You can do that."

Micky shook her head. "I'm a Dullahan. That's all I'll ever be. Just an echo of all the Dullahans come before with the same blood running through me and the same bent nature. You can't change an echo. Don't matter what anybody thinks or feels, we never can be more'n we are. Even if you do take me away from here."

"I am taking you away from here," I said.

"You promise me?"

I took her hand . . .

8

. . . "Promise," I say across the years.

"What'd you say?" Ethan asks.

"Nothing. Go get 'em."

TOP 3

1

It is a crowded place, a baseball dugout. Could be you're stuck inside that cinder-block hotbox we had in Camden or the one in Bowie (my spot there reserved next to the bat rack where Skip stands, rather than all the way at the other end alone). Can even be Yankee Stadium, it don't matter. You hear everything. And while you may be led to believe much of the talk is centered around the game, that isn't so often the case. For as many guys as there are talking of Mussina's stuff (which doesn't look so good to any of us tonight) or how the wind is moving the fly balls or how the ump isn't giving the batters the outside corner, there are more simply looking to vent and gripe.

Somebody's getting a divorce.

Somebody's being audited.

One guy is in the middle of a contract negotiation and the guys upstairs are playing hardball.

There are players who are hurt and ones who don't care anymore, those traded here months ago and still can't sell their houses back where they used to play, and hearing them makes me feel this is a sorry bunch of people who think they have problems but don't, at least compared to most of the people sitting in those stands. And lest I forget, I count myself right along with those living the major league dream. Doesn't matter I'm a twenty-nine-year-old catcher still stuck in Double-A, I'm still getting paid to play. I'm still a ballplayer, and between Johnson's warm-ups out there on the mound I hear the cabbie's voice fresh in my mind:

I coulda made it. You know? Could be you.

You get a bunch of guys all bunched in together, there's bound to be accidents. Get hit with a rocket of brown tobacco spit or walk right through someone's wad of bubble gum. Get sunflower seeds thrown on you. Catch a whiff of stink off someone just in from the long run way out in left. It's as much of the game as anything else and something I've always enjoyed as I could. Makes you family, being in such close quarters. That's what all the good teams are, family.

So I don't mind a bit when Gabe Caldwell comes walking by and jukes out of Ripken's way, cleating my foot. Caldwell's a good kid. I saw him come through Double-A a few years back (cup of coffee for him, he wasn't in Bowie more than a few months) and from there he climbed the ladder straight through Triple-A to the majors. Baltimore has been his home this entire season. Already he's had more than twenty at-bats and seen some action out in left.

No, I don't mind. Don't even flinch when one of his spikes sinks through my shoe and clips the edge of my big toe. But then Caldwell's hand shoots out as his legs jump back. His eyes bulge as he says to me, "Sorry, sir."

Sir. Like I'm some kind of senior citizen, Caldwell's daddy. I wave him off with a "Don't worry none" and he nods his head quick-like before moving off down the dugout to where the starters are talking about Mussina's stuff. Head bobbing like all the world's a song playing for him alone.

Twenty years old, already in the majors. Already seeing some playing time with the big team. Kid was still in grade school when I left Camden for Ohio, and Lord, I suddenly feel ancient.

Youngstown State University occupies one hundred and forty acres just north of the town proper, a stone's throw from the Pennsylvania border. That's where I ran in mid-August of 1990. My aim was double in nature and had nothing to do with schooling: to become the Penguins' starting catcher by spring, and to put away everything that had happened back home. I managed only the one.

Dad insisted on driving me up. Mom came along. The ride was six hours of small talk with a good measure of silence thrown in. Dad looked like he had aged years since the start of the summer. Much of the light was gone from him by then, though its passing had softened a few of those hard edges Mom and I had spent years scraping against. He kept his blue pants but had added a white shirt and red tie for the occasion.

Mom spent much of that ride watching the miles pass through her window. Whole seasons crossed over her reflection through the glass: a wintry look of despair that yielded to a springtime softening of the creases around her mouth; a weariness that spoke of long July days; an autumn bursting in rosy cheeks and bright eyes. I looked away rather than suffer the punishment of seeing her in such a way. Too much had happened in too short a time. Nothing of the world looked as it once had.

The ensuing months are lost to me now, tangled and frayed at the edges. My scholarship came with a housing allowance healthy enough that I kept my own apartment near campus. I settled in and made friends where I was able, which was no easy task given the culture shock of university life. A walk across campus was like taking a shortcut through strange places I could only imagine seeing. I shared space with people from China and India and Africa, from lands so far-flung I struggled to pronounce them in ways that would not offend. Protests everywhere — abortion and the death penalty and equal pay and rights, the war just begun to kick Saddam Hussein out of Kuwait. It felt good to be small and forgotten.

There were calls from home. Coach Stevens and Travis and Jeffrey, Mom each night after supper. Her questions were the sort any kid fresh from home would expect — if I was eating and studying, and whatever Dad shouted at her from the recliner across the living room. My questions back were equally vague and designed so they offered the lowest odds of treading anywhere close to the subject of Michaela Dullahan.

Baseball was what saved me. Conditioning began in my first week of school, followed by untold hours of working on my swing with Coach Solis and the rest of the staff. Going over pitchers and spray charts, learning the conference. I hounded them, picked their brains, made myself a better player. The game became my education, the prism through which I viewed not only the world but my place in it. My crutch. It's not only pitchers who have those. We all do, every single one of us.

By the time the season began, I was a starting freshman positioning the infield and calling pitches for juniors and seniors. Proving myself not to them but to my father, and not to my father but to myself. I hit seventh those first few weeks of the season. Mom and Dad made the trip up for an opening day that felt more like winter than spring. I went two-for-four with a double that glanced off the fence in right center. By the month's end I was hitting .377 with two homers and batting fifth.

But the past is a living thing, and I could not outrun what chased me. There were days I never thought of Camden at all, or of Micky. Weeks I floated from class to class and one corner of campus to the other thinking it would all be okay — that it was over.

Those lies I told myself about things being over and okay caught up with me eventually.

Lies always do.

3

It's the five-six-seven hitters up for us in the top of the third. Every light in the stadium burns to beat back an encroaching dark. It's dreamlike out there between those solid white lines. Green grass and dirt near the color of coal. A few more runs, that's what I'm thinking. We break this game wide open and who knows, maybe Mike will call me up. Put me in as a pinch hitter or maybe even let me spell Fordyce behind the plate for the last couple of innings. Give me my shot. Throw a bone to the old man at the end of the bench. He bends my way, looking through the bodies of the players walking back and forth through the narrow way between the bench and railing.

One shot is all I need. One chance to prove this is where I belong. Could be the past will go away then, finally and for good.

4

We were at a home game against Valparaiso
in early April of '91 when I spotted him
along the first base side, peeling an apple
with his Buck knife. He watched me the
entire nine innings. I struck out twice that
afternoon and took the collar, going oh-for-
four. It was my first bad game as a college
player.

The baseball field was away from campus,
which meant we took buses before and after
games. I lingered in the dugout as long as I
could and ducked out in a crowd of teammates, hoping to get away unseen. Cap
pulled low, shoulders hunched. Wanting to
look small. I never looked up until I was in
my seat and had a tinted window between
me and the world. An hour later I was coming up the walk to my apartment and saw
him leaning against the iron railing, grinning like I was a prodigal returned.

In a place as diverse as any, no one appeared so out of place as Sheriff Clancy
Townsend. His eyes were narrowed beneath
a scruff of pale hair and thick brows that
always looked furrowed, like he was looking
for something gone lost. A red flannel shirt
helped ward off the spring chill.

He shook my hand and pulled me in for a

124

bear hug. "Let's eat," he said. "I'm starving."

There was an Arby's at the corner of the next block. The sheriff ordered enough food to see him through supper and the ride back to Virginia both. We sat in a booth near the back of the restaurant. He tore into his sandwich and chased it with two slurps of soda, winking at me.

"Greta give me your address," he said. "Said it'd be nice for you to see somebody from back home, 'specially since her and your daddy can't get up here all the time. Still took me near all afternoon to find it. Found somebody told me you had a game and I thought that sounded just fine. Ain't seen you play since the championship last year." Clancy shook his head. "Didn't think I'd ever find that dad-gummed baseball park. Go on an' eat. Don't let me keep you."

I did. Nibbled at my roast beef and a few curly fries, wanting to show Clancy I wasn't worried. Every bite I swallowed tried to push itself back up.

"Ast your momma not to let you know I's on the way. Wanted it to be a surprise."

"Guess it is. How's Louise?"

"Right as the mail." And after some thought, "Better. Getting there, leastways." Clancy chewed, marveling at how it was he could be so far from home and yet be eating food that tasted the same in the land of rust as it did a block from the sheriff's office in the heart of Appalachia. "Speaks to a certain equality of things, don't it?" He swallowed and shook his head a little. "We ain't found him yet, Owen," he said.

"Don't guess so. Thing like that, I'd've heard."

"Mayor Henry's all in a twaddle. Says it don't matter it was Shantie folk, they should be as much a part a Camden as anybody other. Sad thing, ain't it? Takes something like what happened to get some sense in folks' heads. I tell Mayor keep his head, wait awhile. Men like Earl Dullahan don't stay hid long. Ain't their nature. Sooner or later he'll get an itch to take more'n he's got already, or he'll run through what he's got and have to come up out whatever hole he's in. I don't expect it to be close to Camden. Earl's ignorant, but he ain't dumb. Somebody'll let me know when he does. I got word out to about every law enforcement agency there is."

"You believe that?"

Clancy said, "I do."

"Could of just called with news of Earl, Sheriff. Though what all you told me couldn't even be named news at all. And I

126

don't see how you'd think I'd be interested in it either way. I'm gone from Camden now."

"Ain't nobody ever gone from Camden. Truth is I had to get away. Even if it's only for a mornin' and evenin'. It's a wound running through town. I reckon you care as much for Earl Dullahan's welfare as much as anybody else does, my own self included. But he ain't the only one I'm lookin' for. You gone eat them fries?"

I pushed the cardboard container toward him. Clancy took a handful and bit down. His eyes bored into me.

"Can't find Michaela neither. It's like she up and vanished from this world with nary a trace. And that's the thing matters. Only thing far as I'm concerned, because it all began and ended with that girl. I been talking to Shanties and townies both. Don't nobody know. Then I remembered." He cut his eyes in a way that reminded me this was the sheriff beside me, not some friend from back home. "We had us a deal."

I stared at my hands. "Thought I knew where he was. I'll swear it. But I got there, Earl's gone."

"Remembered you tellin' me that too, once it was over. Like I said, comin' here's mostly an excuse to get away a while. Most in town are of a mind once Earl turns up, Michaela'll come right along with him."

"I don't think you're gonna find her, Sheriff."

"Why's that?"

I spoke the lie I'd told myself over and over since leaving Camden. Mixed with a kernel of truth, as all good lies are. "She run off is all."

"Wish I's as sure as you. They both gone, ain't no argument there. But Earl up an' snuck off before Michaela did. You ever think on that? He left day before that barn burned, but I talked to Shanties who seen Michaela the next morning. Why'd they do something like that if they was planning on running off together?"

"I don't know."

"Because they didn't. That's my idea. I think that girl went and got herself killed. Once that place burned and folk found out all that money's gone?" He shook his head. "People's apt to turn to violence. Shantytown folk 'specially. Ain't a long road to hurtin' folk when you been hurt yourself."

Clancy rubbed the salt from his hands and the ketchup from his mouth. He leaned back in the seat and fished a pack of smokes from his shirt pocket. Staring at me. His every movement seemed designed to be as

128

slow as possible so he could judge my reaction — the cigarette going into his mouth, the flick of his lighter, how he drew in deep and let the fumes out slow.

I said, "Them people loved her for what she did."

"Don't got to tell me that. Some believed, some didn't. Ones who believed held Michaela Dullahan up to be some kinda savior. Ones didn't . . . well."

"What you gonna do, then?"

"Keep asking questions. Do my job. So I guess to make this whole trip up here to the cold North worth it, you got anything you want off your chest? Some folk in town talking about how you and that girl were around each other some when it all started. That day in front of the grocery. Simpson's field."

"Simpson's field?"

"You'd be surprised what might help." There was no grandfatherly way about him. Across the table there sat a man of the law, and nothing less. "Sometimes putting a finger to the start of a thing can lead a body to its end. I ain't gone sit here and bust your chops on what happened at that party after the prom. It's too much water under that bridge. But you saved her that night. Michaela."

"That a bad thing?"

"I'd never say it. But she said she seen something. Said you did too."

"I got nothing for you, Sheriff. Wish I did. And I'm sorry you had to come all the way up here. Truth is I don't know what happened to her. I don't know where she is. And the only thing I saw that night was my own death comin' for me."

I spoke those words with all the calm and surety a liar could, then broke only at the end.

"I will say this," I told him. "Never once have I thought saving her was the wrong thing. But there's times since I wished she'd of saved me right back."

5

Mussina settles in to get Segui on a strikeout and Mora and Gibbons on two lazy fly balls that calm the restless crowd. It's three batters, no more, and yet a tremor unheard but felt works its way down our dugout. What momentum had carried us through the top inning is wavering now.

"We up five," I hear someone say, "let's go shut'm down," and that's true. But this is still the Bronx and it's still the Yanks and forty thousand strong behind them, and a five-run lead in the bottom of the third is nothing.

130

It's nothing, and I know that's what Mike Singleton is thinking over there by the dugout steps. Gonna need all hands on this one. Gotta keep those starters in.

It's nothing but I know that's what Alice singing is thinking over there by the dugout step. Clemens used all kinds of the once, three ring those statues in

BOTTOM 3

1

Johnson goes out to throw his tosses knowing he'll face the nine-hole batter and the top two in the order. The stands buzz. They're good fans here, and to a person they seem to sense this is the time to crawl back into this game. Three runs, two, even a threat, is all their Yanks will need. A game is never over in this stadium. Few leads are safe. Those ghosts rise up, and perhaps in expectation of that very thing, over the loudspeaker comes a piano's play and the first keys of a song I have not heard in ten long years, a voice soft and smooth speaking of oceans apart and drifting away. I chuckle to myself, not believing it, Richard Marx singing to me again. And then that smile fades, fades . . .

We could not go to prom together. Dad didn't want me going at all, deeming the event an invitation to fornication. He only relented when Mom set her foot down. Never once did he bother asking whether I was taking a girl. It would have been a rare opportunity for me to be honest with him and say I wasn't. Earl Dullahan would never abide his daughter dating a boy, likely for fear Micky would end up chained forever to a drunkard of a husband as did her momma. My mother alone saw the 1990 Camden High School for what it was supposed to be — one final night for us all to be the kids we were before having to transition into whatever adults we would become. She could not bring herself to speak what was surely in her heart — it didn't matter what folk thought. Shantie, townie, the Pines or Camden, those were mere words used as walls we all built around one another. I believe all she wanted for her son was a single night spent without the judging eyes of a people who wouldn't matter to me a bit when I went off to college.

But Micky would not budge from her assertion that prom night should be no different for us than any other. How would it look, a boy still lauded for hitting the homer that won Camden its first state championship, walking into the high school cafeteria with a Shantie girl on his arm?

"It'd be even worse than us going separate," she said. "They'd make you feel so awful."

So it was settled. But as I drove to town that Saturday morning on the nineteenth of May to pick up my tux, I found myself slipping a quarter into one of the pay phones at the 7–11. No special occasion, no dire need beyond merely wanting to hear Micky's voice and to pretend we were together in more than our own eyes. It was a risk calling the Dullahan house, yet I found the threat to our secrecy well worth the price of hearing the day had found her bright and well. If Micky answered, I would keep her only a short while. If Earl, I would simply cut the line. It seemed a plan without flaw until an electronic voice informed me the number had been disconnected. I had forgotten Earl's inclination to drink the money that should've paid his bills.

3

I arrived at school that night to find the cafeteria windows open to the cool air, rendering the slender wedge of night beyond them in the pale whites and yellows of evening. People arrived from every direction. Clumps of them, four and six and eight, all dressed in what amounted to the finest clothing they had ever put on. Music thumped from speakers placed near the locked side door, Poison singing of every rose having its thorn.

Travis and Jeffrey met me on the walk with their dates. Even in high heels, Jen Hamrick stood nearly a foot shorter than our star pitcher.

"Where's your mitt?" Travis asked.

"Shove it. Weren't for me, you'd've gone down as the guy cost us the state championship."

Stephanie Sebolt pulled at the neck of her dress, unaccustomed to such an amount of skin left open to the air. Jeffrey fidgeted in his tux and pronounced wonderment at the lengths to which he would go in order to get his girlfriend alone at a party.

Jen turned to me. "Come on, you can walk in with us."

"Think I'll stay out here a little while. Get some air."

Travis wouldn't allow it. "Ain't gone let you stand out here like some retard. Come on."

I looked out toward the lot and realized I had no idea how Micky would get there unless she'd manage to take Earl's truck. Travis dragged me on. We made our way inside to where the music faded and swelled again. Light flooded the hall to our left, bright and hot. We moved off toward the cafeteria like five souls reaching far into that long tunnel leading to the afterlife.

The cafeteria lights had been extinguished in favor of hundreds of stringed bulbs hung in swooping arcs from the ceiling and wound about the three support columns near the kitchen. The sort of lights that looked borrowed from untold proms before. They dangled above us by a series of hooks and carefully placed strips of tape, enjoying some use before being boxed once more until time to ring a pine or spruce next Christmas. Balloons of maroon and white, Camden High's official colors, were fastened to the sides of a leaning archway near the doors. Beside the arch sat a weary-looking photographer leafing through a copy of *Rip* magazine.

Flowers everywhere. Large arrangements stood at attention in the corners and on a center table where the punch bowl lay in full view of chaperoning teachers. Smaller vases were placed next to flickering candles atop the lunch tables, each of which had been draped in white cloth to hide the stains beneath and pushed to the cafeteria's side, leaving a wide space to dance beneath a glowing disco ball.

Glitter covered the floor in patches. Napkins were stamped *Camden High School Prom 1990 — A Night in Paris.* And at the far end of the room stood our prom committee's crowning achievement: a seven-foot likeness of the Eiffel Tower shaped by pounds of papier–mâché, all the Paris any of us could want.

Stephanie took Jeffrey's arm. "Isn't it wonderful? It looks so pretty in the dark."

I managed, "In the dark," nothing more. I only saw spotlights that shifted color on a pile of confetti Dad would have to sweep and one fragile-looking statue. The place smelled of the previous day's pizza and body odor.

We moved through the crowd gathered at the doors to find an empty table. All those smiling faces, those hearts filled with fancy and sureness, and yet I knew everything of that night was a lie we could all tell ourselves. That was the only magic our senior prom offered. Our clothes were borrowed, worn to hide the hollow bones beneath. The decorations and flickering lights were merely a sham to banish to the shadows what was worn and stained, kept from sight so we could think of them as nonexistent. They were there to make the ugly look beautiful, if only on the surface and only for a while.

It was plastic, our prom, in the same way that most of our lives were doomed to become. The final week of school for us meant freedom, though with conditions. Few of us could hope for true deliverance from the weight of living in a place with attitudes unchanged since before the Civil War. For most, college was a dream not worth chasing. What my friends embraced was more a commutation of the life sentence handed down when you were born here, which meant graduation on Sunday afternoon followed by a Monday that marked the beginning of your adult life in whatever work you'd arranged, if any — a death from one world through a violent birth into another.

That was why I could only sit in numbed quiet while the room roiled in cheer around me. I pitied these people and feared them the same, because I realized that were it not for baseball I would share their fate. Marking my days according to what meaning had been lost inside them rather than gained. Never had I loved my father so much for pushing me. Never was I more thankful for the gifts given me. Never had I wanted away from Camden more.

The DJ moved through songs voted on by the senior class, "Every Rose Has Its Thorn" begetting "Sweet Child o' Mine" begetting Chicago's "Look Away," each rolling to the next without introduction. We moved to the center of the crowded room and took our place among classmates the years had made so familiar as to be kin. Travis held Jen close as Stephanie ensured there was enough room between her and Jeffrey for the Holy Spirit to mingle. I drifted away to a table alone. Waited.

It wasn't long. My friends had joined me from the dance floor when a shadow danced near the hallway steps. Micky entered without notice except for our own. Her dress was a pale satin that reached to her thighs, yellowed with age. No sequins, no ruffles, merely a bit of lace along the sleeves that ended short of her wrists. She had made her own corsage of flowers that looked like those that grew on the lower slopes of our hill in the dry summer months when all else had gone to browns and grays. Her hair, loose off her shoulders, was brushed to a shine but unsprayed. Makeup covered the bruise Earl had given her.

Jen said, "God, wonder where she found that dress."

"Goodwill," I whispered.

Travis snorted.

Stephanie punched me in the arm. "That's so mean."

Micky's eyes roamed about the room in open awe but never settled upon my own. She offered a shy wave to a group of Shanties clustered in the dark and made her way to them. Twice she stumbled over her shoes, so unaccustomed was she to walking in heels. In the warmer months when she came to the hill, Micky preferred nothing covering her feet at all.

There we both remained for most of that whole night, watching one another and everyone else, not dancing once even as a few Shantie boys asked Micky, and I turned down Jen and Stephanie both. Toward the end of the dance, the DJ paused to announce Camden High's king and queen for 1990. A cheer rose when Stephanie's name was called. It was a roar at Travis's. Then came the song, good old Richard Marx singing in that moldy backwoods cafeteria then as he sings from the rafters of Yankee Stadium now, "Right Here Waiting."

Jen and Jeffrey joined them at the end of the first chorus, followed by the rest. I looked across the dim room to where Micky sat. In so many ways, that prom felt like an ending to our last bit of adolescence, the final days of which we would all look back upon as a freedom truer than any we believed waited, and in that freedom I found I no longer cared what would be said of me or her.

I cut through the center of all those tangled bodies, aiming for Micky's table. There came a softness to her eyes when they met my own.

"Dance with me," I said. "I don't care if anyone sees. All of that is over now. And besides, everybody'll get so drunk tonight none of them will remember a thing by church in the morning."

I held out my hand. Micky took it without a word and kicked off her shoes as though she'd been waiting for my invitation all night. We kept to the dim light near her table and let darkness shield us from the prying eyes of others. My hand holding hers, our free arms around one another. There was no unease in the way our bodies pressed and turned; the two of us moved as one.

Micky asked, "Isn't it amazing? All those lights and candles. That statue thing. It's all about the most beautiful thing I ever seen. Never even dreamed I'd be in a place so fancy. I feel like a princess in a fairy tale."

The words were spoken in veneration almost, which broke my heart and convicted me the same.

I said, "It's pretty. You're prettier."

"And you're sweet. Our first dance." Her hand let go of mine. It joined the arm wrapped around my middle and pulled me into an embrace that spoke more than passion and love and friendship. "I can hear your heart beating."

There we moved as a single thread stretched through all time, the two of us as near in body as we could ever be again. Letting the world slip away from us silent and unseen. Even when the music ended, we danced. And in my deepest longing I sometimes believe that were it not for the bright cafeteria lights turning on and a raucous Jeffrey Davis leaping atop the nearest table to shout, "Let's party," Micky and I would be dancing still.

4

It looks like Alfonso Soriano is holding a telephone pole, so big is the bat in his hands. But he can wield it with a blur you wouldn't believe, especially for a nine-hitter, and Johnson gets him to fly out to right. I barely see it, though. Can hardly hear the crowd roar when the ball goes out there and then moan when it settles into Richard's glove. I'm still dancing with Micky at the prom, feeling her next to me, letting my thoughts travel on to after, where I don't want to go. Because the sheriff was right that day he came all the way up to Youngstown so many years ago. There at Brutal Simpson's field — that's where it started. Right on those railroad tracks.

She wouldn't let me drive her back out to the edge of Shantytown where the party waited. Micky said whoever didn't see us dance at the prom would surely see us arriving together, so she took Earl's old truck instead. We didn't even walk out together. Micky left for the house and said she would change there and leave the truck. Wasn't but a little ways through the woods from there to Brutal's, she said, if you knew the way.

Leaving alone didn't stop me from pulling out of the school parking lot knowing the world had never felt so fine. Air cool enough to keep you awake but so warm you had to keep the windows down. The wind licking at the warm spot at my neck where my bow tie had sat. The feel of cotton and denim and my fingers on the wheel, guiding the truck around the sharp turns of the back roads that wound toward Shantytown. Easing into those curves and catching the crickets in half a chirp as I rolled by. Earth and trees filling my nose, making me feel alive.

I followed Jeffrey's truck and tried to keep close. I knew the Simpson farm to be nearby, but in Shantytown nearby was just enough information to get you lost.

Brutal Simpson was one of many farmers whose fields and pastures lay at the borderlands between Camden and Shantytown. Like most of those farmers, he looked as old as the dirt he plowed. The two hundred or so acres that made up Sunny View Farm scattered out in all directions to encompass timber and pasture and what looked to be miles of cropland. But in those days Brutal kept mostly to the fifty or so acres close to his house and let hired help (Shanties, mostly) tend what remained. Included among this modern form of sharecropping was the wide swath of pastureland set at the southernmost border of Sunny View, which ended at a lonely place along the railroad. All of which is to say that bit of lonely earth was just about a perfect spot for the sort of party people throw when they realize they're about to grow up in a hurry.

A bonfire fed by scraps of wood, dried cow chips, and what looked like a dozen large pallets raged at the field's edge. There girls danced with glass bottles in one hand and abandon in the other as though calling on ancient spirits. Boys looked on with hunger. Clumps of bodies made up of little more than flickering shadows huddled beyond the flames, where the air felt cooler. Tubs of ice. Cheap beer and cheaper wine — all anyone could afford after giving a cut to an older brother or sister willing to purchase it at the IGA or the 7–11. Music blaring from boom boxes leaning against primer-painted hoods, guitars thundering, voices wailing in anger and angst.

The fire's heat came at me like a wall. Far at the field's edge, the railroad tracks glimmered like two silver threads stretching onward in the moonlight. A new Camaro sporting dealer tags, a convertible top, and cherry-red paint so glowing it looked like hell's hearse sat by itself. In front were Travis and Jen. He lay in her lap, one leg cocked in a lazy upside-down V. Stacked beside them was a small pyramid of empty beer cans.

I reached for a beer from one of the tubs and shook off the ice before popping the tab, drinking deep until I loosened. Someone yelled for the music to be turned higher. There came a yelp from the darkened circle of vehicles, and I saw Stephanie scampering from Jeffrey's truck, face red from anger or embarrassment, a wave of laughter rolling over the field as she announced, *"I am not like that."* She clamored toward the bonfire while buttoning her shirt (and missing one, leaving herself lopsided) as Jeffrey followed. Panic sprouted over his face.

"Seen you strike out plenty of times," I said. "Never that bad, though."

A contingent of Shantie kids had broken off to the edges between the fire and the tracks. They drank and judged us in their own way. Atop a shabby blanket strewn across the dirt sat Micky. In her hand rested an unopened beer. I had never known her to drink, knowing what drink had cost her family. She stared at the label as it glinted in orange firelight as though pondering the dark powers held within that thin sheet of aluminum, then set it down beside her and stared at me. I raised my beer to her in an ill toast of social lines that separated poor from poorer.

On the party went, the fervor increased by an abundance of alcohol and the lateness of the hour, each of us to a person invincible in our own private ways, seventeen forever. It was near to one in the morning when the amber light appeared in the distance. A whistle calling across flat-topped fields and answered by a chorus of drunken whoops and a voice — Travis's, Jeffrey's, or someone else's, I have never known — calling out, "Chicken. Let's chicken the train."

"Chicken the train," said another, mocking the bird's call.

Travis stood. Said, "I'll do it," against Jen's laugh. He walked off wobble-legged away from the fire and on through the field, followed by others, Jeffrey and Stephanie and Jen, drawing the same crowd that had followed them since kindergarten. Shanties as well, drawing up from the dust and dirt they had sat upon all night. Every one of us following so we might behold for perhaps a last time the stupid courage Travis Clements wore as a tin badge. Micky rose and motioned me to go with my friends.

The train bore on with its triangle of lamps. The whistle sounded a siren's call, and Travis the doomed sailor stumbled toward his own death. A slight grade of rocky land rose up from the field to where the tracks lay. I heard the rails sing as we neared. Travis climbed to the center and spread his arms wide, laughing, Jen's meek "What you doing?" coming as Travis's arms opened wider as though to embrace the engine barreling on.

He shouted over the noise, "Ain't none y'all got the guts, do ya?"

Jeffrey yelled, "Dude, get down from there."

I could not move. None of us could. Then the shadow of a figure moving up the grade —

5

I jerk with the bat's crack and see Knoblauch sprinting down the first base line, Hairston fielding the grounder and throwing to first. Two down, Johnson commanding the game on the mound. Jeter up to the plate and the crowd stirring, the voice of God saying over the speakers, "Der-ek Jeeter," and some now standing, wanting to see something, hoping to see —

6

— the train bearing down now and a whistle sounding not as a call but a warning, three short pulls followed by a long wail that pierced the darkness. Micky stumbled over the ties. She brushed Travis aside and stood afore him.

I shouted, *"Micky,"* not caring that no one else knew her by that name, not the town kids who considered her as little more than Earl's daughter or the Shanties who called her Michaela. The whistle rang out again as she opened her arms. Travis leapt from the grade as the sound of rolling steel blew and I ran, pushing him away in my ascent as he himself descended. Scrambling on all fours, I reached the first rail. The steel shook in my hand. I pulled myself up into a tempest of angry roars and wheels turning. Wind gathered in a hot swirl. Dust and cinders shot into my face. Micky's arms had lowered. She gaped not toward the long line of cars bearing down but to the rock and wood at her feet, streaked with oil. To her fingers. Her hands.

I grabbed Micky's wrist. What spell had captured her broke at my touch. Her head spun, her eyes showing panic at seeing me there. She yelled, "Owen, no!" as the massive brakes bit down with the sound of the world tearing itself in half, a howl as frightening as it was mournful. The noise drew me. I gathered in that approaching light and found myself frozen by fear. Every muscle and impulse to run froze. My body betrayed me. It was as if my mind had fled, leaving my bones as lifeless as the ties and rocks beneath me.

The train could not stop. It shrieked and buckled and smoked but rolled on, the triangle of lights in front of the engine growing to three suns that meant to swallow us both. I braced myself as I could, sucking in a final breath I believed would never be expelled. And as that great wind swirled about inside a darkness I have not known since, all I knew was cut away in a single stroke.

It was as if Micky and I had somehow found ourselves back on our hill, or as if I stood in the box with my weight shifted to my back foot and my stride already taken, bat angling toward some racing fastball. The world compressed to a dot no larger than the bubble of eternity formed around us — all the eternity I had ever sought. No sound of the train's brakes reached me. That long black snake slowed to a speed imperceptible, leaving only glaring lights. The gale surrounding us was silenced to little more than a soft rustling of silk. In this bubble, only silence reigned. In that space came the flutter of my breath spent outward, only not mere breath. It was a mist that came through my lips, golden and silver-tipped, rising upward just beyond my eyes and hanging suspended before bursting to tiny suns I could not count before spiraling in directions I could not fathom.

Micky went rigid with wonder. Her hand thrummed in my own. Our eyes met, and in them we each beheld entire worlds. Her lips parted to breaths that came in the soft noise of joy wedded to bliss, leaving her own golden suns to rupture and race. When that breath crossed my path, I felt every ripple and hidden atom. They caressed me like a mother's touch, the tickle of a dandelion held at your chin. What felt like warm water flooded down my arm into Micky's. Tingling, almost probing me, the way a fish will nibble at your toes when you dangle them just over a pond's surface. That arm rose as Micky lifted the hand I held. It came into sight bathed in the train's honey-yellow lights — all the outside world the bubble allowed to penetrate. Our fingers were laced, and with a terrible awe I realized those were not our fingers at all, not our hands, but two joined objects so filled of wonder and horror that I felt my mind strain and bend and finally snap.

Our skin was gone, stripped away, the bones and muscles left as thin translucent strips that held together not merely blood and vessel but a universe of tiny pointed lights laid in the shape of ringlets. They ran up and down the length of our hands, billowing into and out of our fingers before disappearing from sight past our wrists, coming back, undulating in a dance I could only process as cosmic, while what remained of all rational thought could only speak three letters —

DNA.

I am looking at my own DNA.

Molecules swam. The very blood within me trilled and chanted. Micky's face had taken on the sheen of one peering into the very face of God. Our hands lowered. Clear but shimmering eddies of gravity rippled outward into a night that had come alive in a way that exceeded life itself. A moth floated motionless at my periphery, wings spread, and I saw upon them every intricate design and heard the slow rocking of its tiny heart. Every rock glowed. The wooden ties beneath us were no longer wood but everything wood could be, everything wood was meant to be. All beat and danced and played in a symphony guided by a great Source that felt at once everywhere and separate. The air itself lay charged, dense with quarks and leptons, with gluons, bosons, and neutrinos, and it mattered not I had never heard of such words nor possessed any capacity to understand their meaning because I knew their meaning then. In that moment I knew everything, and my smallness most of all.

And then the bubble around us felt to expand and contract as though from a great shaking. Far away came the rustle of a great storm building. The train's lights settled into a growing intensity. The pop of a brake. A release of steam — the world being un-paused, rushing back. I wanted to scream for Micky to

(Jump)

but the word would not form inside my rapture. I felt her hand tighten and looked to find the true beauty of it gone. Only her perfect skin remained, chipped nails colored red for prom night. All of the peace I had felt now fell away. Every bit of understanding. What remained of my heaven was knowing that here, at my end, I would at least leave this life with the only one I had ever loved.

Time rejoined us. All the clamor and swirl of hot wind and screeching brakes and blaring whistle came at once, leaving no time to even speak. Then came the force from behind us, toward the side where nearly a hundred kids stood screaming next to a bonfire. A giant hand took hold of me like death and shoved. I slammed into Micky's side. We went sprawling over the rail and down the slope. Rocks tore at our clothes and skin. Stars moved from above us to below as we tumbled down the opposite side of the slope as the train wailed past.

The world returned with the sound of my name and Micky's face hovering above my own. Upon her was a stillness of fear gone to shock. Acrid smoke that smelled of smelting iron engulfed us. The train had skidded to a stop well beyond. I turned my head to see a measure of railcars behind us. Faint screaming on the other side of the grade — the train had cut us off from the field.

Her mouth moved but made no sound except for a whimpered shriek that held multitudes. I took Micky's hand. We ran toward the back of the train. Afterimages burned into my eyes, resembling little more than flashes and streaks. Even then, some part of me had begun to forget.

No, I tell myself now, shaking my head as Jeter lets the first pitch go for a ball. I never forgot what I saw as that train bore down. What I felt. It was more that as I pulled Micky toward the last railcar and then around to our side of the track, I had begun to tuck it all away. Pushed it down and down into a drawer labeled *Do Not Open* in that far inward place where the walls are black and the floors are covered with the ashes of fairy tales told when you were young, into that drawer where go all the things that do not affirm all you believe.

I heard the faint call of a man and spotted

a shadow climbing from the side of the train's engine. Then another. Our classmates ran in every direction but toward us. Trucks and cars tore away. Headlights bounced over the field's dips and ridges.

Micky's hand had gone cold and clammy. Twice she stumbled. I led her around my truck and opened the door to get her inside. In the far distance I saw a light on Brutal Simpson's porch and a man standing there. Micky sat crumpled in the seat, empty eyes staring out the windshield as I gunned through the field, so numbed that she accepted a torrent of my screaming with neither word nor sound.

"What were you doing . . . thinking?"

She would not hear me. Could not.

Miles away, a siren set to wailing.

She said nothing of substance beyond simple directions to guide me: "Left" and "Right" and "Keep straight" and, some minutes later, a simple "There." I doused the headlights and pulled into the lane well away from the little shack, wary of waking Earl. The windows were propped open. Pale curtains fluttered in the night breeze like wandering souls.

She said, "Take the road all the way to the fork. Bear right, then make every left you see. You'll come out along Route 20. It'll be a drive, but you won't be seen." Much of Micky's makeup was gone, leaving her skin looking like the blemished skin of a peach. But there was no hurt on her face, no pain.

I studied the house. Waiting for Earl to stumble out onto the porch wearing a pair of soiled old skivvies and one sock and swinging a shotgun, but that never happened. And truth be told, I knew Earl wouldn't. He'd sit watching in the darkness if he woke at all. The man was a drunk and a scoundrel but a coward most of all.

Micky opened the truck door and shut it and spoke through the open window. "You saved me, Owen." A robot's voice, mechanical and dead of feeling. Or maybe there was so much feeling that nothing but a false voice could be managed. She stepped away but kept a hand to the door. "You saved me," she said again.

She walked away barefooted in a pair of cutoff jeans but with a royal's gait. My hand reached for the gearshift. I wiggled my fingers and touched each with my thumb. Only a hand. Just a hand was all. I could not back my way down the lane without the reverse lights shining and so pushed the gear into first, intending to make a quiet circle around the front yard. When I'd turned away from the house I kicked the lights on again and stopped dead when they swung onto Micky's form. She stood blocking my way.

"What did you see?" she asked.

It was hard to tell how much of my expression lay visible behind the headlights. Not much certainly, little more than a blackened blob over the steering wheel, though her eyes were square to mine.

"At the train, Owen. What did you see?"

My hand gripped the wheel. Just a hand. Four fingers and a thumb, three of which lay slanted from where they'd been broken and jammed over the years by foul tips and headfirst slides. Catchers age, oh they age.

"Nothing."

"What happened to us?"

"Nothing," I said again.

My foot eased off the brake. The truck inched forward. Micky stepped aside and let me pass. I could never speak anything but the truth to that girl. To do otherwise simply wasn't in me, and Micky would know it if I tried. Like she knew then. I lied. Oh, how I lied, because the truth was already an unbearable thing wedged in that place far down in me. I lied many times in the days and months and years after. A lie is what my life became. But never once did I lie with such conviction as I did that night in Micky's driveway. Nosir, not once.

7

Jeter swings and misses for the third strike, bringing Johnson's total to three. He near leaps off the mound, runs rather than walks to the dugout. Momentum has swung back our way. The players crowd into the dugout bumping fists. Gloves slap onto the bench. Ethan readies the bats we'll need. Far to the end near Mike, I see Country Kitchen eyeing me.

There are games within the game. Baseball is not nine innings but three innings played three times. As in life, a night of baseball contains within itself a beginning, a middle, and an end. As the top of the fourth readies to commence, I know my beginning here this night is now done. The middle innings stretch out before us as once did that old field on the outskirts of Shantytown, empty and dark and filled with unknowns.

And then comes the end, as must come the end of everything. I look out over the diamond and try not to give thought to the sense building inside me. The beginning has begun and the middle is now and then comes the end, and what of the end? What happens at the last out when the bases are cleared and the crowd is silenced and there is nothing but some tomorrow that may never come?

I shudder as the teams trade sides on the field, what Momma used to say was a rabbit running over my grave.

TOP 4

To my father there lay an order to the universe far beyond the ability of human-kind to know, and an Orderer both fear-some and mysterious. Such was the sum of his religion. The world as it lay before him was a simple place, all straight edges, nary a curve to be seen. You worked and you got by and could call your life well spent if you managed both.

I believe he and Momma both adopted themselves into the Lord's family as an act of thanksgiving. They saw it as God's hand, us getting away from a waiting poverty in Stanley to a somewhat comfortable life in Camden. I always felt Momma had been drawn to faith — the searching out of that great Mystery — which goes long in explain-ing the choices she made that summer. For Dad, faith was what waited at the other end of a long and hard life. He could otherwise make no sense of his hardships. For him must be some waiting reward or explanation. A hope that the grainy picture of his days would someday be made clear and he would find his rest.

He clung to church more for that than for the milk and meat Reverend Sebolt preached each Sunday. Religion became his religion, more even than baseball, and so long as he obeyed the rules and ensured his wife and son followed, so long as Paul Cross manned the door at Sunday service and we poured out our hearts at Wednesday-night prayer meetings and once a month took our wafer and grape juice and imagined them the Body and the Blood, we would keep strong. His family would live on always.

I myself have always struggled with things divine. I cannot abide what I cannot see, and when seen I cannot accept them. That is why I put what happened in front of that train as far from my mind as I could — that event so holy but that seemed to me then so threatening. And yet I call myself a superstitious man no less than any other upon this field or in these stands. Baseball makes us so. No other game is so entwined with the mystical and the groundless. I know players who refuse to wash their jock in the middle of a hot streak, players who will trip themselves rather than step on a foul line or must eat the same meal before every game. Any pitcher throwing a no-hitter after the fifth is shunned. I will not sit with him on the bench, will refuse to visit the mound. Bats are considered living things. Sex is either the key to a streak or the curse of one; for as many guys who swear by lying with a woman before a game, others are monklike in their abstinence. Chicken bones are good luck, the sight of a cat inside a stadium bad. Rally caps hold magic. Full moons make the ball fly. Ghosts rise.

I see them displayed now, batters making the sign of the cross before they step into the box. How they point heavenward after a hard base hit that finds a hole, a gap. The rituals of the on-deck circle done to a precise formula governed by the mind alone — pine tar upon the handle and the weighted donut over the barrel and the swings, never wavering. The same circuitous route Mussina makes around the mound after each out. How Johnson sits in the same spot on the bench and will not move from it unless he comes in from a bad inning, that spot now poisoned. The way Ethan will hold some bats by the barrel and others by the handle alone as he retrieves them, according to the wishes of his players.

Upon a baseball field I am more a believer in God than anywhere else in this world. I am no nearer heaven than when I play. My crouch behind the plate is my penitent bow.

Yet what magic we call forth for the top of this inning falls to deaf ears beyond the arc of lights that reach high to the full dark. There is greater power here than the workings of mere men. Fordyce and Hairston and Anderson each go down with strikeouts, two swinging and one frozen by Mussina's knuckle-curve.

Though no one speaks of it as the players clutch their gloves and run out onto that hallowed field, I believe we all are thinking the same. Those ghosts, they lurk. It is said that in the dark mountains of Appalachian Virginia the past is never dead, never even past. The same is true for baseball, where curses are living things to be borne and where players and times long dead are spoken of as though they still breathe. In fact they may, and that is why the game is eternal.

Bottom 4

1

I woke that morning after prom in a panic because I couldn't feel my right hand. The shade was drawn tight against a dull sun struggling to leak through the bank of clouds that had moved over the mountains. Fear kept me in place. All I could imagine was turning down the covers to find the skin of my hand stripped away, whirligigs of color and chromosome in tight formation, singing their songs. It was only when I rolled over I realized my hand was pinned beneath the pillow — numbed, nothing more. I wiggled my fingers, sending the feeling of needles pricking at my palm. Like nothing had ever happened.

Yes. Just like that.

Mom knocked twice to rouse me for church. I found her at the stove, swirling eggs in a cast iron pan, and Dad at the kitchen table in his tan suit. Their smiles were laden, their words few.

Dad had the Sunday's *Record* spread out before him; no headline screamed of a nearly derailed train and a group of wayward children, no story accused. The only mention of prom was one Mom attempted to make in passing, asking if I had a good time.

"Sure," I said. "It was great."

2

There were fully a dozen churches in Camden but only one Baptist; Reverend Sebolt would never allow otherwise. I broke off from Mom and Dad when we arrived and found Travis, Jeffrey, and Stephanie gathered beneath a maple near the picnic pavilion. Their faces smiled at my parents and the others who passed, but their movements were sharp and awkward and their eyes could not seem to hold steady for more than a few seconds.

I waited until it was just us there and asked, "Anybody have trouble last night?"

Travis shook his head. It was a lumbering effort that bore witness to the hangover he suffered.

Stephanie said, "My folks were in bed."

"You do that for, Travis?" Jeffrey asked. "Get up there with that train?"

Travis shrugged as though trying to remember. "I wanna know's why that Shantie whore got up there. I was gone move out the way. She just stood there. And you," he said, boring his eyes into me. "The hell you doing going up there and trying to grab her? You two's the ones stopped that train."

"We wouldn't have been up there if you weren't," I said.

Jeffrey looked at me. " 'We'?"

"That girl an' me."

A pale-brown cruiser limped into the lot. Two blue lights on the roof. One was cracked on the side. The car stopped near the doors, and Clancy eased himself out before going around the other side to retrieve his wife. Travis said, "Don't nobody look."

But the sheriff was looking. Even as he took hold of Louise's elbow and guided her to the steps he looked, and then only looked away when he spotted the Sebolts and Jeffrey's parents and my own greeting them from the open door to the foyer. The group lingered there for some time. Dad's eyes looked across the expanse of cars and met my own. Reverend Sebolt sought out his Stephanie.

"Dammit," Jeffrey whispered. "We're busted."

"No you ain't," Travis said.

"Clancy gets in there and finds Bubba," I said, "you'll be busted too, Travis."

"Daddy don't care."

Stephanie said, "Well, mine does."

"Wasn't us," said Travis. "No matter what they say, no matter what anybody else tells them, wasn't none a us on those tracks last night. Don't nobody say nothing. You neither, Owen. 'Less you want word to get out to that college coach a yours."

Clancy nodded, turned our way. He went on inside with Louise aside him, and then followed Jeffrey's parents and my mother. Dad and the reverend remained.

"Come on," Stephanie said. "Won't look any better for us if we all keep out here."

We went around the front. Jeffrey suggested making our way in through the side door, which cut through the Sunday school rooms, but Travis said no, it would look guilty. At the foyer we entered. Dad handed us each a bulletin and said to me, "We'll have us a talk later."

Golden bars of sunlight streamed through stained glass windows adorned with stories I barely knew in spite of all my churching. The pews were polished to a shine. Banners of every color were tacked to the walls, a name of God festooned to each with ribboned paper.

I sat near the front next to Mom. She looked at me. "What happened last night, Owen?"

Though unreligious, I could not bring myself to lie in church and so answered nothing. Organ music faded and stopped, creating a bubble of silence filled in short order by coughs and whispers. Somewhere in the back a baby cried.

Reverend Sebolt cast a wary eye to his daughter. He kissed his wife, Abigail, on the cheek before striding up the two carpeted steps leading to the podium. The order of service went as unchanged as anything else in Camden: a welcome and then prayer, followed by an open call for announcements. A few in the congregation stood to remind all of Bible school coming up and the Wednesday meeting, as well as the canned food drive for the Shantytown poor. Clancy sitting at attention. He turned once, withering me with his stare.

"Like to mention one other thing," the reverend said. "Heard through our sheriff was some trouble out at Brutal Simpson's last night. Those who have not been blessed and sometimes cursed with young folk may not know it was prom at the high school. Seems afterward many of them decided to trespass and have themselves a little party.

Also seems at least two got it in their heads to play a round a chicken with the midnight train out of Mattingly."

Mom took my hand. Squeezed it. Every head in that place went to me or Travis or Jeffrey or Stephanie.

"No real damage done according to Clancy, who gave me permission to speak on it in church so long as I offered words of spiritual caution at the end. Which I will. Seems all them kids run off after the train stopped, so Clancy don't know who they all was. Left behind a mess a tire tracks and beer and liquor. Shanties, that'd make the most sense. Though I can't seem to figure why they'd take a bunch a cars and trucks up there, seeing as how they could all just walk to Brutal's."

Someone gasped.

"But I will mention it nonetheless," said the preacher, "if only to hold up these as a warning to all our fine young kids here ready to graduate and get out in the world. This is as good a day as any to take stock of which direction you'll go."

The reverend paused. I wished for an aneurysm.

We prayed then. Baptists love a great many things, but praying over the lost and fallen away above all. Reverend Sebolt

169

altered his sermon from the promise of the future to the folly of youth. Us kids took it like champs. Whatever guilt was meant for us to swallow didn't take.

What did you see? At the train, Owen. What did you see?

I stared at my hand. A hand is all it was.

The value in spending most of your Sunday morning having to sit still and listen to the most boring person you have ever known go on about your own badness was always lost to me. That Sunday, however, was the first time I ever felt thankful for Stephanie's daddy. His slow monotone was all the numbing agent any of us could have asked to quash the nasty looks thrown at us. I watched an outbreak of yawns begin in the back and build to near epidemic proportions by the time it reached Mom. Bulletins fluttered in front of red faces. Pews creaked against shifting weight. By sermon's end only Abigail Sebolt remained at attention, and I felt for the first time that all of what happened in Simpson's field was destined to become a mere afterthought. Was sure of it, in fact, until I heard the front door open.

I turned a little but couldn't see for Dad blocking the way. Then he stiffened, and I knew. Jeffrey did as well, for from across the aisle beside me I heard him mumble, "Oh my God," in a way bereft of the Holy Spirit. I turned all the way as Michaela Dullahan entered the church.

Reverend Sebolt's mouth caught in the middle of the Lord's name, turning "Jesus" into something akin to "Jay . . . ziz" as Micky lingered behind the back pew. Dad gathered himself enough to step forward and point to an empty spot at the end. He could not bring himself to touch her, knowing who and what she was.

"Mom," I whispered.

She looked. I could not tell what was on her face.

The organ sputtered to life as the first chords of "Softly and Tenderly" leaked through the pipes and the reverend cast his end-of-service net into the deep waters of souls afore him. "Should any of you have need of salvation, should your heart long for the peace and grace of our Lord Jesus Christ, should your spirit yearn for quenching waters that never dry or still, then come . . . come."

Hymnals were raised. I turned once more. At the first verse I watched Micky place one dirty tennis shoe into the aisle. Then the other. Two long legs wrapped in faded denim. Micky's smile wavered to a grimace. Dad backed himself into the foyer. Micky bit down on her bottom lip.

She stepped forward. Faces twisted aghast and curious as she reached the end of each pew, hesitating before lurching onward. Her neck corded to thin strips of straining muscle. The organ played on even as all but a few of the outermost worshipers went silent.

Halfway down the aisle she stopped, overcome by a rush of emotion so primal that I believed the human heart incapable of producing it. It came as a muffled explosion of grief and joy, discord and peace, lost and found. The gush brought Micky to her knees directly beside my mother and me. I reached toward her in something of shock and looked to Mom for help. In her I saw concern and pity and the first flickers of love.

Micky crawled. She made the last steps to Reverend Sebolt's feet on her hands and knees with blond hair tacked to her tears and the neck of her Metallica T-shirt slung low to the ground, *Kill 'Em All* printed there like red roads leading toward a promised land.

Reverend Sebolt bent to lift her. I heard him say above the music, "Now ain't no need for all *that.*" He held Micky close. Stephanie's mother joined them, and the three formed a tight circle like a huddle on a pitcher's mound. Whispering, their jaws moving. At the song's end they turned Micky to face a congregation so stricken that any notion of Simpson's field had long vanished.

"Today we welcome a sinner saved," the preacher said. "This here's Michaela Dullahan, and I hope you'll welcome her. The angels rejoice, my friends, for she was once lost and yet now is found."

Amens rose up. Hands clapped. The crowd descended upon Micky in a manner familiar to that which she had seemed to fear all along, only with love rather than scolding. They surrounded that girl, friend. My mother stood first to greet her. She bid me come along but I could not. I remained apart even as Micky searched me out. And while there flowed in that holy place happiness and joy abounding, I felt touched by neither and knew not why.

3

"Never thought I'd see it," Dad said over dinner that afternoon. "A common Dullahan inside our church. And coming forward, no less."

Mom winked at me. "I thought it was beautiful. Most heartfelt thing I seen in church for a long while."

"Best not let the reverend hear it. I love your innocent heart, Greta, but it is a gullible thing. I expect it was all for spectacle. Probably the girl's way a heading off whatever trouble's coming from what all happened on Brutal's farm." He took a bite of his fried chicken. "Which we should speak on, Owen. Where'd you go after that dance?"

"Didn't go nowhere." Looking at Mom. "Stayed after to help clean up and then I come home. Some a the others were goin'."

"Who? Travis? Jeffrey?"

I shrugged.

"You tell me the truth, boy."

"Ain't none a my business what they do," I said. And at the next words, my mother rose to excuse herself: "Ain't none what no Dullahan does neither."

"Well, maybe you should think on it then. Maybe you should think hard. Because we come too far, Owen, and we too close to the end. There's far more ahead than behind. You got to remember that."

" 'We'?" I asked.

He looked at me.

"*We* come too far?"

"That's right," Dad said. He pointed his fork at me and said it again. "That's right."

4

I have to get up off this bench, stretch a little. It's Justice, Williams, and Martinez up for the Yanks, but we're out in the field and there's nothing for me to do, no chance I'll get called to pinch hit or run. Shoot, Mike will hardly know I'm gone at all, he's so busy watching Johnson out there on the mound. Only Ethan sees me duck down into the tunnel. I think I spot Country looking over at me from his spot, bat tucked against his left knee.

Down the tunnel to where the crowd noise softens to a murmur and then to nothing. Only the buzzing of the lights here, wedged inside their wire cages.

I find Scooter in the clubhouse. He nods and moves off toward his little room of uniforms and caps and leaves me to silence. I don't know what to do. Can't sit at my locker, can't make a quick call home because nobody is left. Dad is gone and Mom and Micky as well. Micky gone now for years and yet still here. I can feel her lurking. Watching me. I have felt this way before.

5

Late that afternoon she stood waiting beneath the oak's canopy with her hands to her hips like it was past high time I arrived, smirking in a way that did not mean mischief but more a twisted kind of joy. It occurred to me for the first time that I no longer knew what sort of Michaela Dullahan I would find on our hill. In the days since the funeral I had kept company with the poor girl needing rescued and the grieving one who pined for her dead momma, the philosophical one who had thought long on the value of even the Todd Fosters of Camden. But as my steps slowed and the smile on my face greeted her, I knew this current version was different though not foreign. This was a Micky I had known from long before. A ghost from a time when we did not yet know all we did not have.

"There she is," I said. "Camden's crown princess. All hail."

She stepped forward with arms outstretched to swallow me in the way she had reached for the light of that oncoming train. Her chin turned inward to fit the crook of my neck. We turned there as though in dance. My nose filled with the clean scents of cotton and soap.

"I been waiting near forever. Almost come looking for you. We should talk, Owen."

"Yeah. I believe we should."

Micky broke her hold of me and took my hand. We sat facing town rather than the mountains. Somewhere close a mockingbird called from its loneliness. Wind sighed through the oak's upper branches.

She said, "I picked some flowers by the river after I got back from the church. Took them to the cemetery. It's still a mess down there from where they put Momma in. It's all tramped up. Reverend Sebolt must've tole Barry and Gary there's a baseball somewhere down in that ground for all the digging they did. I thought Earl'd pass out from his drink before they finished. But they're good men. Barry and Gary. They truly are."

"You didn't tell me you was coming to church today."

"I didn't know I was until I did."

"Thing like that," I said, "you got to tell me. We always been careful, Micky. We ain't never been in the same place in town except for school and the ball field. But those times I know you'll be there and I can get myself ready. So hard acting like you're just some-body else I barely even know. You should of said something."

"I know. I'm sorry."

"You want to tell me what that was all about? Coming in there and walking down that aisle the way you did? Because I left you last night and . . ."

And what? I left you last night and *thought nothing had changed*? Left you and *figured everything would be fine from here on out, whatever happened out there in Brutal Simpson's field was a thing so fraught with questions better unasked and unanswered that we would come to silent agreement to never speak of it*?

I dropped my chin. Micky drew her leg over mine and ran a hand down my arm. Goose bumps prickled in the dappled sunlight.

"You ever take that biology class with Mister Mosher?" she asked.

"No."

"Well, I did. It was about the dumbest thing ever. I never could get good grades in school. Momma always said I got her looks but Earl's smarts. Didn't much a what old Mosher said make sense, but one thing did. About the butterflies."

"What butterflies?"

"There's these monarchs. Every year they start out all the way from Canada to Mexico. Like a migration? But it's such a long ways that it's more than any a them can live. So they lay eggs along the way. One generation flies south, the next north. On and on forever. But when them monarchs fly over Lake Superior, they don't move directly like they should. All they should do's go straight south, you know? Like a line. But they all swerve east first, then south. Mister Mosher said ain't nobody knows why. But he said there's some think way back a million years ago or something, part a that lake might've been taken up by one of the biggest mountains in the whole continent. It got worn away or destroyed over time, but them butterflies, they somehow remember it. You imagine that? A mountain there taller than any, ageless rock, standing unmoved while everything lived and died around it. But them butterflies keep right on flying. Swinging on around where a mountain once stood."

"I don't get how that's got to do with you goin' to church."

"You got a mountain and you got some frail little butterflies, which one you think'll last? It seemed like a miracle to me first time I heard that. Made me think maybe I could last longer than my days, too. That somehow even after I'm old and dead and gone from here, somebody will be around to remember me for the things I done. I think all anybody ever really wants from life is to know they counted for something and it all wasn't to waste. That's why I went to church. Because I ain't a waste now. I was gived a miracle."

"What miracle?"

"What'd you see last night, Owen?"

"Us almost die."

"That ain't what I mean. I mean the other part."

"Weren't no other part."

"Don't tell me that. You seen something. I need to hear it."

"You answer my question," I said, "I'll answer yours." Her leg stayed over mine. I laid a hand to her kneecap so I could touch her, but mostly because I was afraid she'd run off and try to jump in front of something else. "Clancy knows, by the way. I seen Brutal out on his porch last night when we left. I don't know if he called the law or if those men on the train did, but Clancy knows and so does my folks. I think Mom's mostly just worried about you. 'Specially after this morning. Daddy's mad."

"I didn't mean to cause no trouble."

"Why'd you do that, Micky? Go up there on them rails? I can't figure it."

"What did you see up there, Owen?"

"It don't matter what I seen or didn't."

"It's the only thing matters." She tilted her face and smiled as the wind played at the fringes of her hair. "Because I seen something. I can't tell you why I gone.

Travis was up there acting like the fool he is, mockin' everybody. I knew he was drunk. Shoot, by then just about everybody was. But it was the way he stood, I guess, all cocky and sure of hisself, and what got into my head was it weren't fair Travis Clements could act such a way. Weren't fair he had a rich daddy and a nice house and good clothes and I didn't, or Todd Foster, or anybody out in the Pines. That's why I went up there. So I could feel for a minute like Travis does and think the world's too small to hold me. You understand?"

I didn't want to, but I did.

"But then when I got up there, I seen that train bearing down on me. I couldn't move a muscle. It was like it tranced me. Then you was there. That's when I seen it. It was like everything stopped right there at that last second and then . . . *bloomed.* It was so beautiful I can't put words or feeling to it. All that fear I'd kept locked in me, every bit of sadness, it all runned away. And then I looked at you, Owen." Tears filled her eyes even as the light in them remained. It was as if Micky saw me not only as I was but as I had been along those tracks. "I *seen* you. Not just your hair and your face, but you. It was like my eyes weren't big enough to see it all but I did, because it wasn't my eyes

181

that were doing the seeing, it was . . ." She shook her head as though she was not unwilling to speak but unable, as if mere speech wouldn't do. "The men in the train, I seen them too. And everybody standing off down in that field, screaming and hollering. And you were all so beautiful, Owen. So beautiful I really did want to die because I didn't think I could stand it. Beautiful and precious and needed. Loved." Her mouth swelled. "That's the word. Everything was so loved."

Micky's head dipped. Her hands grabbed on to mine. It was like she felt embarrassed to say more, or unworthy of it.

"I seen myself too, Owen. And I was so beautiful and loved. I think that was the most terrible thing of all, because I never seen myself that way before. Not onced. 'Cause I'm a Dullahan and that's all my family is, just dirty skin and sad stories. But what I seen in that light? That said I was more. We're all more. More than the things we love and hate about ourselves and each other. And I knew then if we could all just see ourselves that way all the time, we'd just about have the perfect world."

"I love you like that," I said. "That way. Never thought of you as just a name."

"It ain't like that. It was more, Owen. So

much more."

I took my hands from hers and sat there wondering what that meant.

"That's why I come to church this morning. Why I walked down that aisle, or tried. I was doing pretty good until I got about halfway. It was like a weight pressed down on me, like these big cement blocks made up of all the things I ever worried over and feared, all strapped to my back. And I knew if I turned away and walked right out of there past your daddy, that weight would go away some but it would come back. But if I kept on a little ways more and got to the reverend's feet, that weight might be gone for good. So that's what I did. I had to crawl, it was so heavy. Stephanie's folks was asking me all these questions. I didn't know a thing to say other'n my name. Dullahan. But my name didn't sound so bad up there, because I knew I was loved. And I guess I just need to know you seen all that too, last night."

Micky lifted her head and stared out over town. A smattering of homes set in silhouette against early evening, pinpricks of porch lights signing their welcome. I wondered if she sat facing that way on purpose — if what she had seen the night before had changed her such that not even the rolling mountains and silent pines held so much beauty to her now as plain people. She had not spoken a word of what she'd seen exactly, only the feel of it and whatever meaning she'd gleaned.

"I didn't see nothing like that," I said.

"But it was something. I could tell. You looked . . ." She paused as if searching for the closest term. *"Full."*

The dance, that symphony.

"This don't sound like you," I said. "Talking this way. Going to church. That ain't you, Micky. That's somebody I don't know."

"Don't you say that, Owen."

But I had, and I meant it.

"You seen my bat? That black one I use? Daddy bought me that when I come up my freshman year. Took him a whole week's pay. First thing he did to it was change the grip. The tape on it was too thick, he said. So he took it off and put other on to make the handle thinner. First thing I did, though? I cut out a picture of Ted Williams from some old book and taped it where the handle flares to the barrel. They called him the 'Splendid Splinter.' You know that?"

Micky said she didn't.

"Know what he said once? Said that all he wanted from life is to be walking down the street one day past somebody and hear them say, 'There goes Ted Williams, the greatest hitter who ever lived.' That's all he craved. Didn't want no money. Didn't care if he was famous. Just wanted to be the best ever. I think he was. Daddy too. He thinks it."

"Owen, I don't —"

"Every time I go out to the plate I got to rub the dirt off it. I'll wear the same socks so long as I'm hitting good. We got four batting helmets but I only use one. This one time we had the bases loaded and I was up. That pitcher wasn't nothing. He couldn't throw and he seen me coming up and I knew he was scared, but I couldn't do nothing because I didn't have that helmet, Travis did and he was on first. So I called time and made him switch me helmets, then I doubled off the fence in left center. Ain't nothing so superstitious as a ballplayer."

"Why you telling me this, Owen?"

"Because that's what we do. What everybody does. My daddy. What you did today. I don't think puttin' a Ted Williams picture on my bat'll make me hit better or rubbin' off the plate'll make me catch. Don't really matter what helmet I wear. But that's what we do to keep the baseball gods on our side, which ain't real but which everybody on our team says is legion. But we do it anyway,

185

just so we can have something we think is solid to carry around in all that chaos. Might only be some picture, some old hat, but it's power there because we give it power. We do it because deep down we know the game's so big and we're so small. That's how it is in life too. That's why I can tell you I didn't see nothing at that train. Why you didn't neither."

"Reverend Sebolt said the scales fell from my eyes. He said I was blind but now I see."

"I don't know nothing about that."

I felt her watching me. Micky reached and touched my chin with her fingers, tilted my head to hers. "What's wrong with you?"

"Momma was so happy, seeing you there."

"And you?"

"Scared. I don't know why. All these years we been coming up here. Now it feels different."

"Because it is. Reverend's right. The scales done fell from our eyes, Owen. Everything we ever thought turned out to be not so, and I ain't never been so glad to be wrong. It's so wonderful. And I got to tell everybody."

"Tell everybody what?"

Micky kissed me. "The truth."

6

When I come out of the tunnel it's like time has gone wobbly, because Mussina is back on the mound and it's Mike Bordick up, our shortstop, and that can't be because Anderson struck out for the last out in the top of the fourth. Then I look out to the scoreboard and see it's not the fourth at all, it's the top of the fifth. I've missed an entire half inning. Worse, Mike Singleton turns from his spot and stares at me, arms crossed over a widening gut, his face stoic but accusing. Bordick flies out behind third base as I move past players who do not acknowledge me save for moving their spikes from my path. Aiming for the end of the bench where I belong as Richard lines a single to center, his third hit of the game. I see him pump his fist as he rounds first, then look to find someone else has taken my spot. Sitting there grinning at me with the handle of his bat set against his left thigh. Motioning me over with the curled fingers of his left hand, saying, "Come on over here, son. They call you Hillbilly? They call me Country."

1

"Don't mind none, do you?" Country asks. "Me taking your seat. Way you been clinging to this spot, figured I'd look see if somebody'd done put your name here." He grins. "They're apt to do that. Mess with a rookie."

I take a minute before sitting beside, one seat closer to where I can feel Mike eyeing me from the dugout steps, and am embarrassed to catch myself thinking, *Country Kitchen's right here talking to me.* Not like it's the first time I've crossed paths with a major leaguer; plenty come through Bowie for their own cups of coffee either getting healthy from injuries or working their way back to the Show after being traded or getting their outright release, trying to squeeze a little more from their aging bodies and prove they still belong. But this isn't one of those players, this is Bobby-freaking-*Kitchen,* and Country's got an MVP and six All-Star selections in his twenty years of being in the Bigs and an outside shot at Cooperstown. And all of this comes out as, "Nope, don't mind."

He doesn't make room. I sit as close as I dare and make sure not to edge the bat against the inside of his left thigh. It's a black Louisville Slugger known as Betsy, thirty-four inches and thirty-five ounces, and I know this because it said so on the back of a baseball card long lost to all but memory. They've all been Betsy, every black bat Country has ever taken to the plate, and the story is he names them such as a way to honor the person who taught him the game. I idolized this man as a boy and now for one reason alone apart from his prowess: we are both from the Appalachia. Our only difference is it was my daddy who taught me to love baseball, and it was Country's momma.

"Hum, Conie," he calls. Looking out toward the field. Conine steps into the box. Mussina looks tired out there. Richard takes his lead off first, takes one more step. "Where'd you run off to?"

"Bathroom," I say.

"Uh-huh" — still looking out — "what I

189

figured. Ain't a finer place to hide than the toilet."

"I ain't —"

"Atta *boy,*" he hollers. I look out. Conine's stroked a liner to left; it skips through the grass and settles into Knoblauch's glove. Richard stops at second — a little one-out rally. Country waves me off with the hand not holding his bat. "I ain't busting your chops none. Spent about the first three innings of my first game in the can. That guy up there too."

He points to Mike, now studying the field. David Segui is next up. He sees Mussina faltering, has that hungry look in his eyes I know well.

"Two kinds a rookies," Country says. "That's it. Ain't never met a third in all my years up here. First kind's the ones got a burr in their pants. Think they *deserve* bein' here. Wearin' that uni. Come right out and jump right in. You know? Pace up and down the dugout, slap players on the ass when they ain't even fit to clean their jocks. Then it's ones like you and me and Mikey up there. Get here and know they don't deserve nothin' 'cause it ain't *you* who got you here, it's all the rest. It's a life unspooled." He smiles, maybe at the picture in his head. "Yeah, that's what it is. You get up to your

190

first big league game and got it all planned out in your head what you're gone do and how it's gone be and it ain't never like that. 'Cause it ain't the game you think about a-tall, it's all that brung you here. You tell me I'm wrong."

"You ain't wrong."

"Well then, that's why I'm sittin' here. Might as well get it all out now, son. Because let me tell you, our boys look pretty good up there at the plate and Mussina pretty bad. It's that swole moon. This game gets a little more out of reach for the home team, might be me and you both find ourselves out there before the night's through. Might mean you need to start gettin' your head in the game a little. So talk, son. Get it all out now, because Mike, he's watchin' you."

2

I played my last game of college ball against Cleveland State at the old Cleveland Stadium a few weeks before graduation; 1994, that was. I can't remember much from it. What I carry from that day is more impressions than memory, seventy-four thousand seats and so much history you could hear the ghosts whicker past you on the field, and how I'd all but accepted that was maybe the closest I'd ever get to the majors.

The draft had come and gone. A few teams showed interest but my phone never rang. I'm not sure who was more upset over it, me or Dad, but I know Mom was the only unworried one among us. In her mind it was as if I'd been spared some great misfortune.

Cleveland Stadium had been home to the Indians from the Great Depression until around '93. It was a relic when the team walked in there, but still a thing of beauty. The groundskeepers warned us the field was the sorriest in the majors, and we all nodded from the dugout and looked out on that grand vista with the same thought — *If this is the worst, none of us is worthy of better.* We all ran toward the outfield and sank into grass as thick and smooth as carpet. Rolled around in it, then lay there looking up at the sky. You would have thought we were at play in the Elysian Fields.

The crowd wasn't big that night, but there were scouts in the stands. The clearest memory I have is my last time at the plate. Punching the weighted donut off my bat and walking toward the box for what could have been the last time in my life. Taking my time, knocking the dirt off my spikes. I looked off toward the mound where the pitcher waited but couldn't step in until I took one last look at the stands and the fences and felt the wind off Lake Erie. Soaking as much of it in as I could. Taking what baseball gives you, because it never gives you enough.

3

Segui lines one up the middle, scoring Richard and getting Conine around to third, and between yells I hear Country say, "Cleveland Stadium? Hell, son, that guy was right. Sorriest place in all a baseball."

But I smile, oh yes I do. Because it wasn't. Not even a little.

4

Mom and Dad made the trip to watch me walk across another stage and help clean out my apartment. Everywhere buzzed with efforts to prepare for graduation. That whole last week of college felt like life, or like life should always feel — as if you're about to be lifted up and carried off on a wave of anticipation. I felt little of it. My sights were more set on the next scouting bureau tryout than on being handed a diploma that meant not a thing to me. A degree in physical education made me a glorified gym teacher and nothing more. Someone like Coach Stevens back home, driving around some godforsaken little backwater town.

It was Thursday the nineteenth of May, and the only thing left in the apartment was a sofa I didn't want, a half gallon of milk in the fridge, and a telephone plugged into the wall. Dad said he wanted to patch a small hole in the living room wall I didn't remember putting there. I took a last look at everything and found Mom at my bedroom window. The bare glass acted as a filter for the afternoon sun, making her look almost ethereal. The shine hid her thinning figure and graying hair. I didn't think it possible anyone could have suffered more than me in the wake of what had happened back home. Standing there proved me wrong. She looked a shell of the woman she had once been, stoop-shouldered and weary in spite of the soft smile she bore. My parents had not argued once during their visit; their tone was cordial, even something close to loving. But apart I could tell something in each of them had shifted, and why wouldn't it? Some wounds lie fresh long after they are inflicted. Sometimes healing never comes. More than anything, that was why I'd kept far from Camden. It wasn't only the fear I believed going home would kindle, but the guilt.

"Taking one last look?" I asked.

"Can't say I'll miss it. Have to get used to a thing before you can miss it, right? I never got up here to see you enough, Owen. I'm sorry for that."

"Don't be. Doubt I'll miss it much either, to be honest."

Her arms were crossed when she turned, like a chill had run through the room. Dry riverbeds formed across her forehead and down her cheeks. Sometimes I wonder if the first cells inside my mother's body had already begun to shiver and groan against the cancer that would eventually kill her. Or maybe those thick lines were a product of the doubt that killed her first.

She said, "I scrubbed your toilet."

"You didn't have to do that, Ma."

" 'Course I did. Found this by the sink. Didn't know if it was worth holding on to."

She reached out a fist too wrinkled for a forty-two-year-old woman and unfurled her fingers. The phone rang. I heard Dad give a quick "Hello?" that barely registered. Resting against Mom's palm was the piece of white quartz gifted to me on a hilltop when I was twelve.

"Thanks."

She waited, puzzling over the care with which I took the rock and studied its facets.

"What is that?"

"Called a rock, Ma."

She tapped me on the arm. "You're so smart."

I heard Dad talking.

"Is it hers?" she asked. "Did Michaela —"

"Owen," Dad said. He came into the room dragging the phone and cord behind him, face twisted into a look of pained ecstasy. He pushed the receiver into my hand. "For you."

"Who is it?"

"Orioles," he said. And then my father smiled. "Go on. Only been waiting about twenty years."

I held the phone to my mouth. In a spot near my right kidney that I hadn't thought of in years, a dull tingle formed.

"Hello?"

"Owen?" came the voice. "Carl Norman, Baltimore Orioles. How you doing, son?"

I knew the name. Coach Solis had introduced me to Carl Norman before a game not three months prior.

"I'm good, sir."

"Carl's good enough. You ready to get out of Youngstown?"

Dad shifted his weight from one leg to the other, waiting. Mom dabbed an eye.

"I am."

"Good to hear. Listen, anybody talk to you yet?"

"No, sir. Carl."

"Well, I'm talking to you right now on behalf of the Orioles. I been looking at you for a while now, always a place for a good catcher. You got a good arm and a steady stick. Head for the game. But it's more than that. Seen you play up in Cleveland."

"You did?"

My hand tightened on the receiver. Dad's eyes begged me for anything, the smallest hint of information.

"Your last at-bat," Carl said. "Way you stood there soaking it all in. Heart, Owen. You got heart. And your heart's gonna get you somewhere. What'll it take for you to sign a contract with the organization?"

I said the first thing in my mind: "A plane ticket and a hat."

"We'll give you both. What you say to that?"

Well, what was there to say but yes? You wait so long for a thing like that to happen, that thing you worked at and bled over all your life, though you know in the back of your head might not ever come at all. That dream you have. But to me, baseball was more than that. Four years I had spent acting like I faced toward the future. All along,

197

I lived in the past. But on May 19, 1994, I chose to set myself free. I would forget yesterday and start living for today.

I signed my first professional baseball contract over the phone at the age of twenty-two for a plane ticket, a hat, and a thousand dollars, and then I hung up and hugged my family. It was a miracle, nothing less. And on the heels of such a wonder came another: my father weeping, his hand at the back of my neck, saying, "I'm proud a you, son.

"I'm proud a you."

5

Country won't speak on what I said. He's got his eyes to Mussina and saying how the Yanks will get their bullpen up soon, they ain't got but a choice now, even when Melvin Mora strikes out swinging to bring the inning near to closing. Jay Gibbons, our left fielder, comes up. I see Fordyce on deck and try to imagine that's me loosening up with my bat, shin protectors on because it's two down and it just means less he's got to put on should Gibbons end things.

Country says, "My daddy died in a coal mine when I's seven. We lived down in Kentucky. My momma brung me up. Swore I'd never step foot in a mine. And I didn't ever."

"Sounds like a good woman."

"She was." His left hand inched down the barrel of the bat against him. Almost like Country was embracing it, holding her. "She was," he says again. "Where'd they send you to A-ball?"

"Bluefield. Appalachian League."

He smiles. "God's country."

"I'll amen that."

"Hard awakenin', A-ball. Even for the good ones."

"Hard for me. And I was good."

6

Bluefield, Virginia, was but a few hours' drive from Camden, and now for the first time I believe had I been older, wiser, I would have wondered if there was more to its closeness than mere geography. But nowhere in those first days of what Dad called my new life did I allow myself time for reflection. My thoughts ran no deeper than what possessions I needed and which I could leave behind. At no time did it occur to me that I had run all the way to Ohio in order to escape my past, only to all but return home to embrace my future.

The Bluefield Orioles was largely the first stop for every player signed from either high school or college — the lowest rung of the ladder so far as professional baseball goes. Yet it was a rung nonetheless, something Mom repeated in the weeks after my contract was made official, an upward spot upon which I could place my foot and begin climbing. She tried sounding happy. I could tell she wasn't. As for Dad, he was quick to say the rookie league may sound a small thing, but it was big enough that few players were ever granted such an opportunity.

We both agreed I would be in Bluefield only a short while. I think I believed that even more than Paul Cross. It was arrogance that fueled me back then, this notion that a twentysomething boy from rural Virginia could stand out in such a crowd. That thinking became my first mistake among many. College ball taught me there were far greater players than what western Virginia could produce, though I still rose above most. Rookie ball taught me I was no better than anyone. The boys in Bluefield were bigger, stronger, faster. Their minds were just as sharp. Pitchers threw seeds; every one I faced was a Junior Hewitt and more, fastballs that cut and jerked and off-speed pitches that would disintegrate halfway to the plate before putting themselves back together inside the catcher's mitt.

I struggled those first weeks in spite of the

wonder that permeated the everyday. We were thirty-seven players from as far away as the Caribbean thrown together by dreams and hunger, speaking different languages and adhering to differing cultures and ways, yet to a man we were united in the sheer joy of being paid to come to a ball field. The ballparks were slivers of paradise set in the midst of run-down towns, stadiums rather than simple fields. Bright lights. Press boxes. Stands rather than bleachers. Crisp lines of white chalk and grass that looked like emeralds. The infield dirt was smoothed so not even a pebble could be found. Crowds numbered in the low thousands, which was more than any of us could ever fathom.

Mom and Dad often made the drive. They'd sold the house and transplanted themselves in Charlottesville. Dad confessed their moving was the only way he knew to start over. He found work keeping things up at the hospital. Mom parlayed her library experience into a nice job at UVA. They would arrive in Sunday clothes for a Saturday-afternoon game and find seats close to home, sitting unmoved until the final out. Cheering me in their separate ways, Mom with her shouts of encouragement and Dad with his silences broken by a nod or wink. He never took up a spot near the dugout in Bluefield as he had in Camden. In those days, my father stopped being a coach and simply became a fan. I think in his mind he'd done all he could; there was nothing more to teach me. He was wrong.

I hit .267 those first months of the 1995 season — fair for the majors but not for rookie ball, and woeful for me. The skipper said it was nothing to fret over, a catcher hitting anything above .250 would be considered good enough for the big team. It was the pitchers I needed to worry over instead of my average at the plate. The hitting coach swore my swing was fine and counseled time as the best remedy. I believed time more poison than cure. A baseball player has but a small window of years to succeed. The average age of a major leaguer is twenty-six. He will enjoy approximately six years in the Show. Most will be out of the game by their midthirties, either retiring or receiving their outright release. I was a boy but felt old inside, like something was gaining on me. In a lot of ways those first months in the minors were the hardest of my career. Were it not for Dad they would have been the only months.

He drove down alone one morning in late May. Mom couldn't make the trip. Not feeling good, he said, though I wondered then if it was more that he wanted to speak to me alone. We met at the stadium long before game time and walked the outfield grass. Dad didn't say much the whole time. He didn't have to say why. That stroll was the closest he ever came to the majors.

We were standing near the batter's box, me on the left side and Dad the right. I told him I was pressing. Worried. Scared. Things I'd never felt on a baseball field. What happens if I wash out? Make it all this way only to have everything taken? What if I'm not as good here as I was everywhere else?

Dad looked out over that wide space of green field and that fence in the distance. He nodded, then scuffed the toe of his shoe at the edge of the plate.

"Need a new one a these back home. Fella took over for me at the high school called to let me know. He didn't know where to get one. I probably should of took care of it before I left. It was all bowed up and nasty looking. But I didn't. Couldn't, I guess."

He shrugged and gave me a little look that scared me because it was embarrassment in his eyes. I looked away to save us both.

"You touched that plate, Owen. More'n anybody ever has at that school. Crouched behind it. Spent your years there. That plate was yours."

Dad toed the plate again. He bent down with a terrible cracking in his knees and ran a hand down the center as if stroking a living thing.

"So this fella wants to know what kind a plate he needs and where to get it from. And I says it don't matter. Only one size, so any'll do. This plate here? Same's the one in Camden. Same's the one in Youngstown. Shoot, this plate here's same as the one we used in our backyard. Seventeen inches across. You see? Don't matter where you go, son. Game don't change." He ruffled the plate with his knuckles the way he used to do my hair. "Because this don't change. It's the fundamentals you got to keep straight. You take the ball to right with a man on second and less than two outs, you bunt the ball down the third baseline for a sacrifice. You hit that sacrifice fly to get a man in from third and take the extra base on a ball in the alley. You call your game. Trust what brung you here. Do your job. Let the game come to you."

I went 3–4 that night with a homer the Bluefield paper measured at 430 as Dad sat alone in the bleachers. By the end of summer my average was up to .335 and I was on my way to winning the Appalachian

League batting crown. Because of my father, the man I'd spent my life trying to impress.

7

The crowd groans as Mussina delivers a fastball that rides too far in, clipping Gibbons in the elbow. He jogs to first. Bases loaded, Fordyce up. With two outs and our catcher at the plate, I start putting on the spare set of shin guards. However much I wish my teammate all the best, I admit aloud a secret desire for a little groundout, a weak pop fly, if only to sway Mike's gaze back to me. Country says don't worry about it, Fordyce is a good guy and he's a pro, and part of being a pro is always looking at the guys coming up behind you.

"Guarantee he's thinkin' more about you than you him."

I wonder if that's true as Mussina settles down enough to get our catcher to strike out on five pitches. Country nudges me. I wonder.

"Sounds like a good man, your daddy."

"He was," I said. "In his own way."

"Turned it around your first year. That's good. I known many didn't."

I leave it at that. I did turn it around, thanks to Dad. But there was more to my first year than a slump, and I won't tell

Country any of that. It was a fine summer, maybe my best, and while I hit and caught and threw like never before, I also forgot that logic can sometimes fail you because we live in such an illogical world. I'd considered the phone call from Carl Norman and my new life in Bluefield as a sign of forgiveness — permission to begin anew. I knew different on an August evening near the season's end.

We had a kid — Garrett was his last name but I can't remember his first, so many have come and gone — who the Orioles signed for near to a hundred grand. Lightning arm. Proof, though, that Dad was right when he spent all that time saying about the only reason a pitcher can do what he does is he has a catcher to babysit him. He wasn't as bad as Travis about shaking me off, but he was close. Garrett's problem was every time he'd walk a batter (which he did often; half the time when the ball left his hand I had no idea where it would go and neither did he), it was the end of the world. He'd get down on himself. Slump his shoulders. Act like he'd never throw a strike again. It was up to me to keep him confident, because that's what a catcher does. He keeps the hitters off balance and the pitcher upbeat and the home plate umpire happy, and if he does it well he remains in the shadows, barely ever seen. He is equal parts therapist, strategist, and ghost.

Garrett had started off the fourth by walking the first two batters. I'd gone out to calm him down, you're pitching good and that last ball was a strike the umpire missed. Trying to get his head where it should be. On the way back to the plate I took my mask off to wipe the sweat from my head and that's when I saw her, walking up an aisle toward a concession stand. Same corn-silk hair, same bronzed skin. I stopped, so shocked I was, and heard the umpire say something about getting on with the game. She passed behind a family working their way to their seats and disappeared. But it was Micky. I could swear it.

She had followed me after all.

BOTTOM 5

1

Fordyce shakes his head and walks toward the dugout as the Orioles take the field, Johnson, our pitcher, among them. As it will take our catcher a bit to get his gear on and Johnson needs his warm-ups, it falls to me as the backup to fill in.

"Hey, rook," Country says to me. "Don't look like no idiot out there."

I walk toward Mike at the head of the dugout and up the steps, fighting the urge to pause at the edge of the field as before. Around me the crowd moves in tiny waves back and forth, stretching their legs and hollering out for dogs and beers. They pay me no mind. No one does, not the umpire standing away from the plate or Johnson waiting for me to crouch, not the players, and that is as it should be.

It is an easy thirty seconds until I spot Fordyce coming out of the dugout with his helmet and mask tucked under his arm. Johnson throws three fastballs and a curve. I'm nothing but a backstop of flesh and bone, my purpose to catch the ball and throw the ball and nothing more.

Fordyce offers a "Thanks, buddy" to relieve me. I jog off toward the dugout steps. Mike pays me no mind. At the end of the dugout I find Country still grinning. He is an old man of forty-two who looks in better shape than any twenty-year-old I've ever seen. Blue eyes twinkle out from a scruff of graying whiskers.

He jokes and says, "Might be you're cut out for more'n menial work after all."

2

I had a job lined up my last summer in Camden working for Travis's daddy down at the Auto World. Extra cash for college. Dad helped set it up. Bubba Clements was a deacon at the church and maybe the richest man in town, and he had a soft spot for me since Travis and I were friends.

Keeping the inventory on the lot shiny was about the best Bubba could offer. Travis told me it was easy work (*charity* was the word he used and I did not doubt it; I couldn't think of any dealership paying somebody just to wash cars, and three bucks an hour was a whole thirty-five cents over minimum wage). My scholarship would go a long way so far as room and board, but having some money set aside would help get Micky settled when she left with me for Ohio.

With baseball season done and graduation only a few weeks off, I'd told Bubba I may as well start work after school right after prom weekend, which turned out to be the Monday after Micky took the sinner's walk up the aisle at First Baptist. It was to be Travis's first afternoon on the job as well, training for his soon-to-be position as salesman — the first step of what promised to be an uninterrupted ascension to successor of the Bubba's Auto World empire.

That morning Mom packed me an early supper in case I needed it. I kissed her on the cheek and ruffled Dad's thinning hair ("Don't let Bubba push you 'round," he'd said, followed by something about having to pick up a part for the mower after school, so maybe he'd check on me) and walked out thinking the day would come out as any other. But then I got to school and found Micky wasn't there, and all the talk I heard was of what had happened out in Simpson's field after prom and the Shantie girl who'd embarrassed herself at church the next day.

I waited all day for her to show. Cut my eyes out of classroom doors every time someone walked by. Even grabbed a bathroom pass and snuck down to the cafeteria when I knew Dad wouldn't be around, to drop a quarter into the pay phone and call Micky's house. The number was still disconnected.

Worse was I couldn't go to our hill right after school. My new job waited, and Travis was insistent I not miss the first day. I drove through downtown, past the grocery where Jeffrey was already working and the church that had already claimed Stephanie as worship director, until I reached the seven paved acres that made up Bubba Clements's kingdom.

A Shantie working the garage pointed me toward a bay in back where the tools of my summer trade waited — a bucket, a hose, and a sponge. First up was Bubba's Corvette, which retailed for about what Mom and Dad had paid for our house.

I kept to myself for the first hour or so, my only friend an old radio hung from a rusty nail on the wall. Around four thirty I went to grab a drink from the machine in the showroom and check on Travis. I pulled a Coke from the machine and watched Bubba himself stroll across the showroom floor. He was a tall man, thick-gutted and suited, sporting slicked-back hair and a ready smile. Bubba always looked like he was about to ask if you were interested in a warranty.

He steered himself toward a glass-walled cubicle where Travis leaned in a leather chair behind a desk that appeared to be carved from a single block of cherry. A phone sat there, stacks of manuals. Already Bubba had made up a placard bearing his son's name in gold letters. Beside it rested a baseball on a pewter stand — Travis's own souvenir from the state championship game, I reckoned. He had brought a change of clothes from school, a suit that made him look older than he was. Travis seemed more a banker now, or an adult, talking in an easy way to a man in frayed jeans and a denim shirt who was probably his first customer, even if Bubba would be signing all the forms and taking the commission. Bubba looked on like a proud papa. Standing there, it looked as though Travis had leaped back in time from the future to glimpse his former self.

As he stood to shake the hand of the thankful man in front of him, I was struck with a sense of envy so strong it left my feet stuck to the waxed floor. I could not reckon my jealousy. This was no more than a spoiled rich kid whose aspirations reached no higher than the corner office of Bubba's Auto World in Camden, Virginia. I was the one going off to play ball. I would get drafted someday, reach the majors. But that was someday, not today, and today I could not dismiss the fact that Travis had found a thing I had yet not: his place in the world.

Travis Clements would sit in that little office until Bubba either retired or died and then take over the business, just as Jeffrey would the IGA. For years I had viewed my friends as chained to their futures, but as I watched Bubba lead Travis's customer out and Travis bend to answer his phone, none of their futures seemed like chains at all. For Travis and Jeffrey, their journeys had all ended. And though I held my own future as something greater than small lives set in a small town, I could not help but feel they had claimed something of exceeding value and I had not.

Travis saw me. He pointed my way, wanting me to wait. Head nodding. He hung up and stuck his head out of the doorway. "You doing anything?"

"Washing all those cars you're getting ready to sell."

"Take a break. Jeffrey said something's

going on down at the IGA."

"Something like what?"

"It's Michaela."

My face grew hot.

"Jeffrey said she's standing on the street corner with that queer. Said it's a show we won't believe."

3

Johnson makes his first mistake of the night when Paul O'Neill comes up for the Yanks in the bottom of the fifth and crushes a flat curveball over the right field fence. For the first time I hear the storied Yankee Stadium noise. We're still up five, but the game feels closer.

Country nudges me. "Don't worry 'bout it. We get that one back, still might find ourselves out there."

4

Downtown Camden looked less a square than broken spokes of a bent wheel. The town center comprised the oldest buildings, some dating to the early 1800s. From there the streets moved in more or less straight lines, some of which fizzled to little more than empty wooden buildings and over-grown lots — victims of one economic downturn after another — while others had grown from two lanes to three. Anchored there were the bulwarks of the IGA, flower shop, hardware store, and town government building. As Travis and I walked the quarter mile west from the car lot toward the IGA, one thought consumed me: that would be the best and worst place for somebody to make a scene.

"Jeffrey say what she's doing?"

"Nope, just we had to come see. He was laughing pretty hard, though, so it must be good." Travis's suit jacket was unbuttoned. His tie caught a little in the breeze so that it fluttered up and over his shoulder, giving him the appearance of Superman rushing in to save the day. "Tell you what, that girl says one thing about me being up on those rails, I'll kill her. You see me with that old farmer in there? Sold my first car. I mean I didn't really, Dad did all the signing and stuff, but I did all the talking. That used F-150 out in the back lot? Guy just wanted something to beat around in."

I didn't care. "That's cool."

"It's complicated, man. Not just the sales stuff. There's people I got to deal with, that's the main thing. Selling's easy, that's what I'll be doing for a while, but Dad won't be around forever, you know? Shoot, I'll be running things soon. The whole lot. I'll be the boss man — you believe that? Just me and some salesmen and a bunch of Shanties for secretaries and mechanics. Dad says they'll steal you blind. You believe that? You're the one gives them a living, then they turn around and think you owe 'em even more."

We were coming up on the bridge where the trains crossed. I could see the outline of the library and the sun glinting off the front glass of the IGA. People crowded the walks and skittered from one side of the street to the other. I couldn't see her from that far out, couldn't spot the corner where Jeffrey had said Micky was standing. Standing — what did that even mean?

The scales done fell from our eyes, Owen. Everything we ever thought turned out to be not so, and I ain't never been so glad to be wrong. It's so wonderful. And I got to tell everybody.

Nothing looked different. Just cars and folk, the occasional horn and wave. Maybe Jeffrey lied, one of his tricks. Maybe Jeffrey hadn't seen Micky at all, or Micky was already gone. But then out of the noise of all that human motion came her voice carried by the breeze. It felt like someone had set a candle under my shirt.

Rupert Davis's IGA grocery took up most

216

of the block where Pine Avenue intersected with Main Street. It was an ugly relic of the early forties, nothing but a white cinderblock square and a parking lot of fading lines and weeds sprouting from the cracked pavement. Customers streamed in and out through electric doors. More than a few had paused, their backs to me as they watched, women whose purses hung by a mere finger and men who stood with their weight on one leg. An abandoned shopping cart sat near the road. Across the street at the hardware store, old men with nothing better to do gawped. Faces appeared in storefront windows, their lips moving as though they were ghosts trying to impart some message through the veil between worlds. All of them staring at the same strange person who had claimed the corner sidewalk in front of signs reading *Watermelon 12¢/lb* and *Choice Ground Beef $1.56!!,* man and woman and child all bewildered at what Michaela Dullahan was up to.

She stood near the crosswalk atop an old milk crate turned on its side, blond hair twisting in the breeze each time a truck turned left when the light went from red to green. Her tennis shoes wobbled on her doddery makeshift stage. Todd Foster stood behind her in silence. The cords in Micky's neck strained with the words she spoke as she raised her voice over mufflers and horns. I heard, "This is wrong, what you're doing. It's all wrong . . ." and saw a pleading in her eyes.

"Freaks," Travis grumbled.

Some crossed the street to hear her, driven less by interest than by curiosity. More than a few of Rupert's customers clustered where a line of cars was trying to turn into the lot. A horn blew. Someone yelled.

I settled into the back of the growing crowd as Micky talked on.

". . . what I seen. I seen the truth of things, and the truth is every single one of you is more than you think. You think you're people, but you ain't. You think you're bodies, but you ain't. You were made for more than what all you're doing and saying and believing, that's what I'm wanting to tell you . . ."

Hands outstretched, head high. Long legs encased in denim shorts and bronzed arms reaching from the sleeves of a plain white T-shirt. Micky looked like a countrified Statue of Liberty calling for our tired and poor, our huddled masses that yearned to breathe free, talking of souls and worth and a dignity common to all.

"Quit giving yourselves over to things that

don't matter one bit. I'm sorry I don't know how to say it, it's just so big in my head."

The line of cars now lay a dozen deep. One tried to turn but was stopped by a wall of flesh that refused to move, which only served to tie up traffic in two directions rather than one. Micky kept on as a look of terror crept across Todd's face. Men streamed across the road from the hardware store to gawk or help. A flicker of blue and gray — my father, carrying a lawn mower part in a brown paper bag. I ducked before he could see me.

The glass doors of the grocery slid open. Out came Jeffrey in a pair of khaki pants and a chambray shirt (his own uniform now, no different from my father's) and both Harper boys. Jeffrey's hands shot out, palms up, making a *What the world?* gesture. Travis answered with a shrug.

Micky was deep into the "I saw everybody as they truly are, and in greater eyes than mine own" portion of her sermon when her sight fell on the future proprietor of the Camden branch of the Independent Grocers Alliance.

He said, "What the world y'all doing out here?"

I thought he'd stumped her, because Micky fell quiet. But then I saw her silence as a way of looking, of *seeing,* rather than confusion. Micky held her back straight and her shoulders square. Her eyes carried the glint of something I could not figure.

"Todd's helping me. I'm just trying to say something is all."

"Well, you done blocked up all this traffic," Jeffrey said. "People trying to get their groceries."

Down the block and across the street, my mother appeared from the library doors.

Micky said, "I don't have long."

"I know you don't, 'cause my daddy's done called Clancy over here."

"You don't understand," Micky said. "None of you *understand,*" her words carrying over all the ones screaming and chuckling and shaking their heads. "I know who you all are, but you don't. You don't know it yet." She settled on the Harpers and pointed. "Gary Harper, I know what you are. Barry, you too. Do you know how precious a thing you were born to be? Do you know you are loved?"

The Shantie twins looked upon her as we all did, like this was a girl in the midst of losing her mind.

A siren called in the distance. Horns blaring. It sounded as though every law enforcement officer in four counties was on its way, even though it was but one old Crown Vic traveling a little over two blocks from the sheriff's office. Clancy stopped the car at an angle to the sidewalk. He parted the crowd like Moses, calling each man and woman he passed by name.

It was of course not Clancy's first introduction to the Dullahan family. He said to her, "M'chaela Dullahan, what fool thing you think you're doing upsetting the whole of downtown this way? I oughta haul . . ." What steam and bluster our sheriff wanted to sputter faded as Micky looked down at him. In that moment I believe Clancy knew himself as seen and seen truly, and I believe he had not an idea what that meant.

"I'm sorry, Sheriff. I am. We didn't really plan all of this out, Todd and me. I just had to come down here and . . . talk, but nobody's . . . I'm the one stood in front of that train Saturday night."

All went quiet. Travis took a step forward.

"I'm sorry for all that trouble. But I was saved, you see, and now there ain't no scales over my eyes. I seen everything. The truth of everything, and . . ."

Micky looked out over the snarl she'd created, all those vehicles and grimacing people, ones mocking and disgusted. My heart broke for her until she saw me cowering.

Words unsaid passed between us, a pleading in our eyes for each to help the other. But what I needed from her just then was silence, to keep me out of things, while all Micky needed was a friend. All the years and rules between us, having to keep silent on what we felt and knew. So many times I'd wished we wouldn't have to hide anymore. Now all I wanted was for the two of us to stay hidden.

"Owen."

I saw my father inch closer, spotted Mom coming across the street and cutting in front of Clancy's car.

"Owen, you were there. You saved me. Tell them. Tell them what you saw."

Clancy looked over his shoulder. "Owen, you know any of this that's going on?"

And I said, "No. Maybe she got in Earl's drink is all."

Chuckles rose. Clancy shook his head. Rupert Davis came out to say the milk crate upon which Micky stood was one kept on the loading dock out back of the grocery, which amounted to theft, and he demanded charges be filed.

Clancy silenced him with a simple "Shut up, Rupert."

The crowd was thinning, yielding to the turning cars. Old men shook their heads and went about their business. The women looked on with a measure of pity, as they will when happening upon a child lost through lack of care. Shame filled me.

Clancy took Micky's hand and eased her down off the crate, then motioned for Todd. "Come on," he said. "Let's get you two home."

He placed them in the cruiser's backseat. Travis walked past and clapped me on the shoulder, saying he'd see me back at the car lot, his Camaro needed cleaned. Over his shoulder, my mother walked off toward the library and stared over her shoulder.

Clancy started the car and left the siren off. He came alongside me as he pulled away. Micky stared through the glass. Beneath her expression I withered. Not because she offered me hurt or betrayal, but because her eyes carried a look of forgiveness, Micky's blue eyes soft against my own.

I followed those eyes until the car cut through the last of the onlookers, a man wearing a pair of blue work pants and a gray shirt. That man turned and walked on as though the boy before him was a stranger.

5

It's a single bump in a single game, Country says, nothing more. Johnson, he still looks good out there. And as this is a man who's seen more pitchers than I ever will, I can't disagree. O'Neill is barely in the dugout after rounding the bases when Johnson gets Brosius on a ground ball to first. Ethan moans from the other end of the dugout. One down.

6

I'd have given about anything to get out of supper that night given what was bound to happen, but eating together was Mom's rule. Didn't matter if I had a game or Dad had to stay late to get the football field in shape or Mom got held up at the library, supper came only once we were all home. Though I'd grown to loathe those thirty minutes or so — what teenager in his right mind wants to have dinner with his parents? — I endured them as best I could. Not for the company (which was minimal) or the lively conversation (which was nonexistent), but for the look of contentment on my mother's face. From the time I'd signed my scholarship, that sense of ease inside Greta Cross seemed limited to whenever she pulled a roast or an apple pie from the oven and laid it upon a table bearing three plates.

It was near to six that evening when I got home. Three cars that day, Bubba's and Travis's and one off the lot. My shoes and socks were soaked through with water. The skin on my hands was a bright red that promised to crack in the following days. My pores oozed soap and tire polish. I wasn't about to worsen Dad's anger by saying supper would have to sit until I walked around in the woods awhile. Micky would have to wait, if she showed up at the hill at all.

Dad sat at the head of the table, newspaper spread before him like a curtain. The kitchen smelled of brown beans and ham and buttered corn bread from the skillet — my favorite meal, made for Momma's little working man. She kissed my head as I sat. Dad moved the edge of the paper and cast me a grin through two knowing eyes, as though they said, *Ain't much fun, is it, having to spend all your day in thankless toil?*

We prayed.

Mom passed the corn bread. "How was work, Owen?"

"Wet. Boring. Felt more like Bubba's personal assistant than anything else."

Dad grunted. Mom sighed. I could fill a book talking of my parents, but those few words are a good enough summary.

She said, "Well, it's money well earned and money you'll need."

"Yes'm."

"Got that blasted mower fixed," Dad said.

He ignored me. Mom did not. I could talk to her of Micky. Mom would maybe understand. Would be thankful, at least, that I'd climbed atop those rails and saved the girl I loved. She would wait. Would listen. But before then I would have to get through supper, and I would have to get through my practice with Dad in the backyard after.

He suggested soft toss once the food was gone and the table cleared. That's when I knew I wasn't getting off easy. Whenever Dad was serious about practicing, we went through pitch calls and game scenarios. When he wanted to see some real work, he'd stand in the yard and have me block balls in the dirt. But when Dad wanted to talk, it was always soft toss.

He grabbed a bucket of balls and a bat from the shed and walked both to the net strung between two spruces in the backyard. Dad made me use a wooden Louisville Slugger for soft toss, thirty-three inches and thirty-four ounces. Planning ahead, as was his way, for that someday when I reached the minors and aluminum bats were no longer allowed.

I took my stance. Dad poured the baseballs out and turned the bucket over. He sat
directly to my side and lobbed the first ball
in underhand. I waited until it reached the
zone and swung, sending a liner into the
net in front of us.

"Weight back," he said.

I adjusted and garnered a "That's it" on
my next swing.

"Dad?"

"No," he said, and tossed another. I
swung. "Don't want to hear it. Knew you
was up at Brutal's. Knew it soon as Clancy
told me on those porch steps. You're a fool
boy just as all boys is. Thinking they invincible."

Another ball.

"I didn't mean for any of that to happen.
She went up there playing chicken."

"So you decided you was gone run up
there and get her away?"

That felt like a trap. I said, "No one else
was gonna."

Another ball and then another. It was like
neither of us would have to say anything
more so long as Dad kept tossing. Or maybe
he only wanted a hard talk made softer by
the sound of my hitting. I think of the wind
upon our hill, how it always sang. Micky's
voice and Mom laughing and that one time

my father said he was proud. None of those sounds ever brought so much comfort as solid contact of ball meeting barrel. It resonates. You feel it deep.

"My job's protect this family. It's my only job, and I do it well. Don't you think?"

"Yessir."

"No fool boy can think for hisself. Doubt a woman can neither. So it's to me. My responsibility."

He tossed another and five more, letting those words hang until they seemed to fade against my swinging and his tossing and the crack of the bat and the swoosh of the ball as it came into the net.

"Baseball's got a rhythm. Like a slip-stream. A current in water. Most people don't know that. It's hid unless it calls you. But if you find that rhythm, it's like leaving this world altogether. You sink down in it and it takes you on, and all you can do is take hold of it. You become somebody greater than you are. You don't see it as a thing you *play*, you see it as beauty. Like a web that connects everything."

He sat on that overturned bucket with a ball in his hand, browned by constant use with swollen stitches and a deep gash in one side. Holding it like that ball was an answer to everything. I guess it was back then, for us both.

"Words can't tell it," Dad said. "But I don't need to tell you anything on that, do I? Because you know, Owen. You know that rhythm. You slip into it ever' time you pick up a bat the way them other players slip into a uniform, and that's something can't be taught. You got to be born with it. That's a gift ain't but a few have. It's the Lord's given it to you, and you dishonor Him when you go against it. Like jumping out front of a train to save some poor broke-hearted girl you barely know. Anything could've happened to you the other night, and I ain't even talking about dying. Could've got hurt permanent."

He touched his right shoulder in a way that made me think he didn't even know he was doing it, that right shoulder that had once made him a man of promise.

"I know what you think of me, son." He picked at his blue pants. "Know times you felt shame at seeing me work. But least I work. Lord give me it. But I got to ask forgiveness every morning when I go off to earn a meager wage. I ain't thankful in my heart having to do what brings neither joy nor purpose. You found that out today, didn't you? Got yourself a little taste of it. Bubba Clements told me he's got a job all lined up for you if college don't work. Said pay's good. But pay's nothing if you don't find no love in it. You won't find no love selling cars. You were born to play ball. It's a hole inside you nothing else can fill, same as me. Baseball's gone from me now but that hole's still there, and I'll always be empty for it. I still feel that rhythm, every time you play. It's like a . . ."

The rails flashed through my mind, the sound of it and the peace, that glimpse of something true and holy.

"Symphony," I said.

"Yeah." He watched the next ball he tossed sail into the net and judged its degree off my bat at twenty degrees. Fifteen was Dad's ideal. Fifteen degrees off the bat was a liner no one could catch. "It's just like that. Why you play? Shoot. You're a conductor. George Solis knows it. Why he signed you. Everybody knows it." Dad shook his head. "That's why I want you to understand. What you got is a precious thing, Owen. I worked hard to give you a good home and two folks who ain't split up, but you're made for more than what I give you. You're made for *greatness*. And so long as I draw breath, I won't never let anything come between you and that. Not your momma. Not Bubba Clements. Not no

Shantie girl can't keep her head on straight long enough to get out the way of some train. Not one single thing."

My father meant those words as a promise. They sounded like a threat. We hit through a dozen buckets that evening, three hundred swings, leaving the calluses on my hands bloody and my side aching where the bruise still lingered. We walked back through the yard under the shadows of the moths flickering in the porch light's glow. We were all right. Dad seemed better. And though he said he appreciated me being honest in telling him most of what had happened in Simpson's field, I knew then I could never be honest with my father again.

7

Micky wasn't waiting at the hill that evening. She'd left no mark. A worry I had not considered settled over me: What if she wasn't coming? In my mind I saw her perched upon a faded plastic milk crate, the tip of her dirty tennis shoe digging into the corner to keep her upright as she spoke my name, only for me to call her a drunk like Earl.

How much harm had I done us? How much simply to keep my father from an anger he had felt anyway?

Shantytown's pines lay like a darkened ocean. I stood facing them and would not move. Willing her to appear, even praying for it, until from the line of trees came a small darkened dot and I wiped tears I had not known were falling. She moved in slow confidence along the worn path and up. Head high and unmoving. A hand reached to graze the tops of flowering weeds.

Though it was such a simple thing, I still cannot give an account worthy of how Micky came to me that night with such beauty and presence. All those times before it was as though she owned the land. Now she seemed a part of it, no less than flower and wind.

I yelled down, "I'm sorry. I didn't know what I was supposed to do."

She expressed no measure of hurt or sadness. There was only a slight upturn of her head as she navigated the narrow path to our hilltop. Can it be said that a single look can pierce you in such a way that you are made bare yet still pleased to be seen? That was how Micky saw me.

I took her hand as she sat and said it again: "I'm sorry."

The way she spoke was like water over rocks. "You didn't know any of what I was going to do. I didn't either, I guess. Until it happened. I woke up this morning feeling about like I'd explode if I didn't tell nobody. Earl said there was maybe some work out Mattingly way at somebody's farm, but I knew it wasn't no work, he was just gone off drinkin', and I didn't even think of goin' to school. School seemed a small thing before the train. It's smaller now. I took a walk. People say Shantytown's the ugliest place there is, but it ain't always. The way the light comes through the pine trees, all them woods and the mountains nearby. Anyway, that's when I come upon Todd."

"And what? You two decide to come to town preaching?"

It was the most ridiculous thing I could say — my small attempt at bringing levity to what was not funny at all.

She said, "Fosters live way around to the end of Shantytown, off by themselves. His momma works evening shift for Rupert at the grocery. Don't think Todd's dad does much of anything except take the walk out to the mailbox every afternoon looking for his draw check. But when I walked by there, it wasn't his daddy comin' for the mail, it was Todd. I tell him hey and we get to talking, and then I say, 'What's the one thing you love most, and where's that got you?' "
She held out her hands like it was some

magic trick and a rabbit was about to appear. "Todd asked me about what happened up in Brutal's field and it all come out, I couldn't stop once I got started, and Todd drank it like it was water and he the thirstiest boy in the world. Then before I knowed it we'd come to town and I'd gotten a crate from the back of the grocery and there was about thirty people standing around, horns honking and people yelling. I didn't even know what I was saying. It was like I'd been asleep and then got scared awake, and the first face I saw was yours."

"Travis and Jeffrey thought you'd gone nuts."

She let out a high, hard cackle that made me wonder if they'd been right. "All them is the ones crazy." She shook her head slow but in an understanding way, like how Dad did when he helped me with algebra. "I had it all wrong, though. I figured all I had to do was go to town and start talking. Never occurred to me nobody'd want to listen."

"Listen to what?"

"To the truth of what we seen at that train."

"We didn't see anything at that train."

It wasn't a laugh this time, only a frown.

"You can say so, Owen. I get why. I didn't when you wouldn't help me this morning.

Only thing I thought when Clancy shoved me and Todd in back of his car was I couldn't believe you'd ever hurt me that way. All these years of telling me none of what we got should be secret, then the first chance you get to tell folk even a hint about us, you pass off. But then Clancy took me back there" — pointing down off toward the Pines — "where he said I belonged. Then I understood. He's right."

"That ain't true."

"It is. Always has been. Shantytown's my home. I learned that today. Came clear as a bell while I was standin' on one a Rupert's old milk crates and lookin' down on everybody. Seeing y'all for what you are."

"And what are we?"

"Lost. It's what everybody is. Me too, though I guess me less now. I'm the one who seen."

"You didn't see anything."

Micky said nothing to that. "Clancy dropped me off home, I just went on talking. Todd come with me. Wasn't no street corner I could go on, but there's porches. There's living rooms and windows wide open and people milling about. I spent all day talking and half the night, and now here I sit talking still. Telling everybody what they need to hear. Asking them that question's most important of all. And now I'll ask you."

She looked off down the slope and back up it, following where the greening grass rolled in waves brought by a sweet wind to where our legs lay and our clasped hands atop them. "What do you love?"

"Micky, I don't —"

"Understand? I know. I don't expect you to, Owen. Not anymore."

I wasn't sure how she thought I was to take that, whether she'd meant those words as a sign that we should move on to another topic or that she didn't want me asking more questions. I only knew it made me feel stupid.

"Don't do that, sit here and say I'm the one don't understand. You got up there in front of a *train*, Micky. And now you're what? Some street-corner preacher? That make sense to you? It's like you lost your grip on things. You're not even you no more —"

"— I'm not —"

"— and I don't even know what to do to help. You're shaking me off. I'm calling pitches but you're throwing what you want."

She grinned again.

"What it always comes down to for you, isn't it? A glove and a ball can explain all the mysteries of the world. Maybe they could before, Owen, but not no more. You want me to forget what I seen? You want me to set all that aside and keep going on with the awful life I had? I can't do that. What I seen was so big it made me think everything I always thought was real weren't. You can say you didn't see nothing, I'll believe you, because I know you'd never lie to me."

I pulled my legs toward my stomach.

"But you can't tell me what I didn't see," she said, "and you can't tell me what I should and shouldn't do about it. This old world is just a big hole filled with ignorance, and all we spend our lives doing is digging it deeper. But sometimes there's folk decide they're gone climb out, and what they see is a thing so wonderful it changes them forever because it's truth. That's what I seen at that train. I am loved by something that will never not love me. And not just me; that love touches everybody. How could I run off knowing something so wonderful as that? I got a look at what's beyond. Not so I could go there yet, but so I could jump back down in the hole and tell everybody I can." She looked off beyond the mountains. "It's everybody in the whole world. They all lost, Owen. Looking for the wrong thing."

"And what you think everybody's looking for?"

Her hand tightened around mine. The other settled on my arm. She asked me again: "What you love most, Owen? More than anything else in the world?"

"You."

"Be for real."

"I am."

But Micky kept her gaze. It was like she gave my answer back to me so I could study it hard and know that wasn't right, not really.

I said, "Had this picture in my mind ever since I-don't-know. You in the stands of some stadium in some big city. Your chin's up all raised and proud, listening as fifty thousand people holler my name. That's what I dream. That's what I love."

"And you think if you get that, you have that single moment, it'll make all your life worth something?"

"I know it will."

"It won't. Won't nothing make you happy really. It's a hole in us all we keep pourin' stuff into but never gets filled. That's all I wanted to say at the grocery. Nobody listened, and I didn't know why until Clancy dropped us off. You townfolk got too much is all. Got jobs and nice houses, money or at least a little of it. And all y'all go chasing off for some dream or other, whether it's a big one like yours or just a little one like Travis taking over the car lot someday. Even me, Owen. I chase too. Chase something to love and love us back. But we don't ever find it, and ain't that sad? My momma never found it, and it killed her. And what none of us know is we don't ever have to chase it at all, not that real love. That real love's right there always."

"You talkin' like the reverend."

"I'm just telling you what I *seen.* Town-folk cain't see it. They're too lost. But us Shanties?" She shook her head down over those pines. "We're more apt to believe, Owen. And do you know why? Because we're poor. We ain't got nothing to lose."

I plucked a blade of grass and split it down the middle, let it carry to the wind. "You need to set all this aside, Micky. It was just one night. Shoot, everybody'll forget about it in a couple weeks. Clancy'll ask some questions, but won't nobody tell him anything. We almost died on those tracks. I couldn't even move. Thing like that happens, bound to mess with your brain or something. Like people seeing tunnels of light or dead relatives."

"You really think that's all it was?"

Her eyes met mine. I looked away.

"Something pushed us out of the way, Owen. I told them people you saved me and I believe it, but not 'cause you the one shoved us both from those tracks. We was supposed to die up there, but we was given something instead. Like another chance. It ain't much time left for me. I got to make it count."

"We'll both make it count," I said. "Won't be long, we'll be out of this place."

"You don't understand. I can't leave here now."

"What?"

Micky's hand tightened in mine. "I can't go with you. It ain't what's supposed to be. Maybe it was once, but things is changed now. I got to stay here and help people."

"Help them what?"

"Know. Understand."

"Well, Micky, *I* don't understand." My voice cracked with its rising, making it echo off the hill. Our hill. "You saying you don't want to go away with me now? That all we talked on since we was sophomores is all of a sudden over just because you think you seen something in some stupid train lights?"

"What'd you see, Owen?"

"Nothing."

"What'd you see?"

"Nothing," I screamed, lips trembling as I let go Micky's hand. My face hot, wet from the tears that fell there. "You ain't coming to Youngstown with me?"

She leaned with her arms outstretched and took hold of me. "I want to more than anything, Owen, but I can't. There's something more I got to do while there's time left. And I want you to keep here with me."

"Keep here? You mean don't go off to college?"

Micky leaned back, measuring her words. She brushed a bit of golden hair behind her left ear. "I seen it. What comes of you if you keep to the road you're on. It was in that light along with everything else. It's your love. Your love's all wrapped up in a thing that can't love you back, and you'll only come to harm because of it."

"So I got to choose now? Baseball or you? Why? So I can turn out like my daddy? That what you seen? Me and you gettin' married and having us a few kids? Maybe I'll get me a son, how about that? I'll shove a bat in his hands as soon as he slides out of you, start him out right. Raise him up saying, 'Let's go out back so I can throw balls and you can take a hundred swings, because your granddaddy's a failure and so's your old man, but I'll be *damned* if I let you be one.' "

Micky did not flinch, did not back away. She only looked upon me as she had earlier that day at the corner of Main and Pine, with a measure of pity and love.

"I'm only trying to save you, Owen."

"You lie," I say.

8

Country looks at me. "Ain't lyin', look at 'em out there. Johnson's still on. Little homer ain't gone ruffle him."

I blink, trying to place what Country said and where I am and how it is that Brosius is jogging behind the mound on the way back from his groundout to first while I've remembered most of an entire day ten years gone.

"We got this game," he says. "Don't mind calling it. Been in this old barn of a stadium twenty years, ain't never once seen a ghost. Not once."

Top 6

1

There comes a time during a ball game such as this, say in these long middle innings of the fourth through the sixth, when one team settles for grinding things out. That's where Mike is now. We're up five and to the sixth inning. The Yanks only have four more innings at the plate, twelve outs to score six runs. Time to play things safe. Put the outfielders a little deeper so a ball won't reach the fences. Get Johnson to throw strikes. Keep the ball low. Don't walk anybody. Make sure the players are loose and focused. Grind it out. That's so much of what baseball is.

Down by five, Mussina's night is finished. Brandon Knight has taken over on the mound for the Yanks. I don't know much about him. Country fills me in on Knight's pitches. He keeps his spot but he's looking at Mike more than me as Hairston starts off our inning at the plate. Country waits to catch our manager's eye, give a little nod. As if wanting Mike to think, *Might as well give ol' Country a couple innings in the field, maybe an at-bat. Keep him fresh for when we maybe really need him next game or next week.* It is a sorry thing to know. A man like this — a true baller maybe bound for the Hall of Fame — riding the pine and waiting for what scraps are thrown to him.

"You should be up there," I say. "Getting ready to hit or out there in center. Ain't never seen a guy hit like you. I remember sitting with Dad in the living room once watching you and the Dodgers play the Mets. You hit one off Gooden . . ." I shake my head. "Anything goes that fast should come with four wheels and an engine."

"And when was that?" he asks.

I don't answer, knowing Country's point is made.

"Long time ago. Shoot, Gooden's done now." He nods toward the other dugout. "Yanks cut Gooden after spring training. You imagine that? Guy has his problems, don't get me wrong, but in his prime? Wasn't a better pitcher maybe ever. Then he gets old. Gets cut like some rookie. No offense."

I wave off the words.

"This game will humble you, son." As proof of that, Hairston strikes out on five pitches and makes the long walk back to our dugout under a cloud of quiet. "It will raise you up and set you down. You know that."

"I do."

He gripped his bat and lofted it, the barrel even with his nose. "How old are you?"

"Twenty-nine."

"Twenty-nine years, catching in Double-A. Makes you about as much dinosaur as me. Still holding out hope. Am I right?"

"Well, I'm here, ain't I?"

"Yep, right here in the Bigs. But let me tell you something, whole other mess of problems to deal with up here in the Show. Got the media always on you, got people trying to hook you into any sort of crazy deal. Injuries to play through, and that long unending season. Takes a beatin' on you. You know that well as anyone. Never understood why anybody in their right mind wants to be a catcher. Not when you can be out there in the outfield in all that soft grass, looking at the pretty women between pitches."

"Ain't all bad. You're out there calling every pitch, lining up the defense. Jawing with the ump and the hitters. Good way to keep going on in the game once you're done. Plenty managers used to be catchers."

"True enough. Ain't many twenty-nine-year-old rookie ones, though. I'm forty-two. *Forty*-two years old. Makes me a relic. Tell the truth, I feel like one sometimes. Hell, half these kids was in diapers when I come up. Wife keeps telling me it's time to quit and come home. Got us a horse farm near Bowling Green. Know what I tell her?"

I don't.

" 'One more year.' Been saying that for the last seven. 'One more year.' I got three hunnert sixty homers in the Bigs. 'Nother forty'll give me four hunnert, and that'll punch my ticket to Cooperstown. That's why I keep. Because all I want's something that'll outlive me. It's why all these guys is out here. They say they love the game or they're making good lives for their families, but most why they're out there every day playing through sore arms and knees is because they want to be great. They want to be remembered. You get that, don't you?"

"More'n you know."

We watch as Anderson comes to the plate.

"You got a girl?" he asks.

"Not no more."

"She get jealous?" He stares at me, nods like it's from experience. "That what it was? 'It's me or it's baseball' thing?"

"You could say that. Pretty much."

Country leans to me, interested. "You pick the right one?"

"Guess that don't matter now."

"Why's that?"

"Because she died."

2

I traveled north once more after spring training in 1996, though not to Bluefield. A batting title was enough to convince the Orioles I had talent enough to match the heart they signed me for, and they sent me to the Bowie Baysox in Maryland instead. Double-A, the Eastern League, which meant one step closer to the Bigs.

More, I left Sarasota no longer your average minor leaguer. The organization labeled me a prospect. That designation is near as cherished as a ticket to the Show when you're a busher. It means more of everything: money, status, future. I signed with an agent who got me a contract making $2,500 a month from March through September. I was twenty-four years old and clearing more money in seven months than my parents made in a year. I wasn't just playing ball. I was earning, and earning meant more to me than anything.

Dad couldn't have been happier. Mom tempered her congratulations with a plea to lay aside as much pay as I could. Given my home was a room in our third base coach's basement and I didn't have a car, that turned out to be quite a bit. I lived as much a king as I ever would, and I relished every minute.

You learn early on to take even the smallest victory baseball hands you. It's easy to watch a game in person or on the TV and think it's a bunch of men at play. Even the ump says it at the start of each inning: *Play ball.* But I never knew a guy went about his business on a baseball field and thought "playing" was what he did. It's work, day in and day out, and behind it all is a fear you cannot know. Every time you step onto a diamond can be your last. One awkward step will blow your knee. One too many throws can snap your elbow or tear your shoulder. Could be you're sitting dead red for a 3–1 fastball grooved down the middle and it's in your jaw instead, hundred-mile-an-hour gas that knocks you cold and bloodied, and after the surgeries and rehab you realize you can't even bring yourself to stand in the box again. Could be a thing so simple as the manager asking you into his office and telling you to shut the door and how he calls you "son," and you know your playing days are over.

That's what you live with. Doesn't matter if you're pulling in ten million a year in the Show or riding the pine in the rookie league. Doesn't matter if it's Bobby "Country" Kitchen or me, the fear stalks you. You accept it as what comes from loving a game that likely won't miss you at all when you're gone. Baseball is beautiful because it is so big, and it is terrible because you are so small.

In what was becoming something of a ritual, Mom and Dad made the trip to help me settle. Dad looked his same strong self. Mom looked older, more frail, yet peaceful in a way she'd never been. They say the passage of time can heal all. I say it soothes only the wounds we allow to show. Their move from Camden to Charlottesville went a long way in repairing the damage done both to and by them. Mom held to near the end that Micky wasn't really gone. Her belief faltered in her last days, but it burned hard during my years in baseball and brimmed over while with me in Bowie. She would never speak of Micky in Dad's presence, but she felt no such hesitation when we were alone. It was always rumors of Earl and recollections of all that had gone on that summer, much of which my mother continued to call miracles, related to me with adoration. Tears would gather at the corners of her eyes as she spoke the same words over and again: "The mob will always crucify Christ, won't they? That is the sadness of this world."

I hated my mother's faith then, as any unbeliever would. It seemed unnatural even as my own faith in a game of sticks and balls felt so true. Belief came so easily for Mom, though she had only Micky's words to drink. Yet I had beheld true wonder that night at the train, and not even such magic as that was enough to make me yield my own selfishness. Micky was right about so many things. None more than that faith comes hardest for those who have much to lose.

Mom and Dad left for Charlottesville after the first week of the season, though not before watching me hit my first home run and throw out my first base runner as a major league prospect. Prince George's Stadium was a basilica where upward of ten thousand people a night came to watch me work. I signed my first autograph there and sent home my first baseball card. You should see that picture, me in my stance grinning like I was seven. You take what baseball gives you.

Days spent under a sky so blue it hurt to look into it for a ball popped high behind the plate. Nights I would pause for an instant before tossing a ball back to the mound so I could look at how the moon sat above the stadium lights. Crowds cheering and booing. The smell of hot dogs and popcorn. The feel of fresh-cut grass. Those are the things I remember. They were what kept me grounded.

Ballplayers will talk of the long season. April and May pass in a blur. You're strong and healthy and still have those winter months of rest to draw from. June and July are harder. August can be hell if you're struggling or your team is out of contention. By September, all you want is rest. You still love the game, but you come to realize the long season demands more than heart.

I hit .267 my first year in Double-A and have never matched that in my five years since. Played years with guys who got the call up to Triple-A and the pros. Played with guys on their way out. Sometimes I've wondered why the organization keeps me around. There are days when it's so hard getting out of bed and nights when I wonder if this is what it feels like to be thirty, all broken up and sore. But I play on. I work like no one. Not because I have a dream, but because somewhere along the line I realized a dream was all I had. I'm a twenty-nine-year-old catcher, and my time is low.

That fear burns as bright and hard as any faith my mother could summon.

3

Brady Anderson takes a fastball over the right field stands and sends about a third of the crowd walking toward the gates. Another third follows as Bordick homers to right center. We're up big now, getting late, and I see Country starting to fidget a little next to me. He's gripping Betsy like he's already up to the plate looking to inch closer to his four hundred dingers.

"Might be out there," he says. "You too, Hillbilly. This might be our time."

Richard flies out to left and Conine follows with a little pop-up to Soriano at second base, ending the half inning. We both look Mike's way now. Our manager is looking happier, a little calmer, and Country says that's a good sign.

He says it's a good sign indeed.

Bottom 6

1

You could call it the middle innings during that early summer of 1990 as well. May dwindled in a succession of warm days and moonlit nights. There was nothing for us at school but to take our final exams. I kept washing cars for Bubba in the afternoons and telling myself it was money that would be put to good use when Micky and I left for Youngstown. Told myself that over and over not as a reminder but as a lie I could come to believe through repetition. I scrubbed Bubba's cars under a metal roof that left me sweating and tired, had for years worked at a game that had already left me sore and worn, but I'd never worked so hard as I did trying to convince myself nothing had changed in my life.

We met every evening. By then, Dad was so used to my walks through the woods after our backyard practice sessions that the only thing he said to me was to make sure I mixed in some talking to the Lord. Clancy had all but forgotten how a bunch of Camden kids had evidently gotten drunk enough to near derail a train, but my father never would. To him, it was a warning sign I could veer from the path he and God had labored to lay out for me. Our trips to church on Wednesday nights and Sunday mornings became more fervent. Like Dad was leading us into battle. Him and Momma went up one Sunday to rededicate their lives to Christ and dragged me with them. Dad wanted Reverend Sebolt to baptize me again as though the first time hadn't taken.

Micky was always waiting. And though she seemed happy to see me and eager to speak on all the wonderful things going on in her new life, I will admit it was sometimes difficult for me to make the trip to our hill. It was as if it had grown somehow, gotten steeper, and its top no longer offered a wide view of the world. All Micky talked about was how the Shantie folk were taking such interest in all the things she had to say and how needy they all were, and all the while she never once spoke of me or our future. She'd quit school. Said there was no time for it now, which made me believe there was also no time for me. Yet my anger remained no match for my loneliness, and that was what brought me to the oak again and again. I told myself I'd rather have some of Micky than none, even if the some of her left me seething.

Every night she held the same sense of urgency, reminding me of the work needing done and the short time to do it and always, always bringing our talk around to what happened on those railroad tracks. Analyzing it from one side and another. Poking holes in every excuse I gave.

"It wasn't you," she'd tell me. "You was too scared to move. And it wasn't me. So who pushed us, Owen? Or I was and you weren't, but you got caught up in it. I think you coming up there changed things. But only for a while."

"Wasn't nothing at that train, so you stop it."

"Remember the first day we met? That snake? What'd I tell you back then? Sometimes a snake quivers because it don't know it's dead yet. Maybe that's all we're doing, Owen. Maybe you and me's just quivering too."

2

She never did ask me to stay in Camden again. Never once said I should give up baseball because the train had made base-ball as worthless to me as school to her. But in our parting Micky would always take my hands in hers and kiss me soft and deep, say she loved me, and ask what I loved most of all. I never did know what to say. Some-times it was nothing. Other times I said I loved her and loved baseball and our future most of all, and she would smile like a momma will when hearing a child too in-nocent and ignorant speak of the truth of things.

It was as though in the days after her first appearance at church Micky knew she would not have to work as hard convincing me as I did convincing her. She believed other forces were at work on her behalf. Sometimes I could not help but believe the same. Those small weeks before graduation were a blur of activity. But in ways more fundamental it felt like the world had become a stranger to me, or I a stranger to myself. There were times in the backyard with Dad when I would grow obsessed with something as insignificant as a leaf or a corner post of the shed, moments I could hear Dad telling me I needed to change my stance for those college pitchers and feel myself nodding in a distant, noncommittal way because I wasn't listening to him at all.

I was staring at that leaf. That shed corner. Trying to remember how to see as I had in Simpson's field

(breath not breath, a mist golden and silvertipped stoked into tiny suns that explode and shoot, soft noise of joy wedded to bliss beating beating, symphony guided by a great Source)

and know things as they truly were, worlds within worlds turned such that they bent toward some far but near well-spring that Micky called Love. I spent one whole day at the Auto World on my hands and knees trying to see an ant as I had the moth that had fluttered between me and the train. At none of those times did I ever see anything. It was always a mere leaf or post. Some insect. That night in Simpson's field had done more than alter Micky's life. It was as though she'd been remade. Yet to me, all of what happened on those tracks became little more than a dream left faded in the middle and fuzzy at the edges.

3

My quiet struggle could not last long. There lay an empty place inside me, like Micky had gone somewhere else even as she remained close. Travis and Jeffrey noticed it. Dad too, though he gave it over to those long summer months when there was no baseball to play. But I could not keep the truth of it from my mother. Moms always know. Even the bad ones, but the good ones especially.

Dad was away at a deacons' meeting one week before the turn of June and graduation. I was struggling with the notion of not going to the hill at all when Mom said to me, "Something preying on you, Owen. You want to talk to me?"

Though I didn't, I knew I must. I had no one else then. Travis and Jeffrey were friends but in the male way alone, that teenage boy way in which all things were open for discussion up to a certain point. I could go to my father for nothing but a hitch in my swing. My nights on the hill with Micky had turned to something I could not reckon. It was like a gulf had formed between us, like I spoke to her as I would anyone else in town, talking but never saying anything. That was the worst of it, the emotion those weeks had birthed in me — I felt alone.

"I'm taking Michaela away with me," I told her. "When I go to Ohio. We'll find her a place close to campus and a job somewhere. I'm giving her all the money I'm making at Bubba's this summer. We'll make it work."

"Sounds like a bold plan."

"We've been talking about it for a while. I have to get her out of here. Shantytown."

"Been hearing talk of Shantytown. There's some Shantytown girls work evenings at the library cleaning up. They say things is changing in the Pines and give Michaela the credit. To hear them say it, the Lord's speaking through that girl."

"Don't know who's doing the speaking."

Mom sipped. I studied my hands.

She asked, "All this comes from what happened after the prom?"

"Didn't nothing happen. Travis thought he'd get up there and play chicken and I don't know why. Michaela followed him and I don't know why she did that neither. I ran up there to get her off. That's it."

"You sure?"

"Why you ask that?"

"Because I seen her. Yesterday down at the IGA getting her and Earl some groceries. She was talking to the Harper boys and then she got to talking to me —"

"She's talking to you?"

"And I seen a change in her. Yes, she's talking to me." Her eyebrows shot up. "That okay, ain't it?"

I didn't say either way.

"Michaela told me you saved her. She give

all the credit to you. Said she'd of never heard from the Lord if you hadn't been up there with her, she'd just be dead. She said she seen the truth of things up there, and she thinks you did too."

"Didn't see nothing but death coming at us. You don't think she heard from the Lord, Ma. Tell me you don't. I love her and I'm taking her away to give her something better, but I still know she's just a Shantie."

The word was out of my mouth before I knew it, stinging me with a measure of shame.

"I didn't mean nothing by it," I said.

4

She said she was going to build a church. Said it with the very conviction with which she'd once said we would someday be married and she would be walking down inside some big stadium wearing fancy clothes and a smile to sit in the wives' section and cheer me on. She was going to build some place where everybody in Shantytown could come to hear her speak, and she wanted me to help because she couldn't do it herself. When I told her I couldn't because I was too busy working to give her money enough to come to Ohio with me, Micky only acted as though she knew better. As if she'd seen the long days of our future and knew our single road diverged into two, one only some shorter than the other.

"We're growing down there, Owen." She looked off toward where the pine trees lay in fading light as though they were something of her own creation. "You wouldn't believe it. People are changing. It ain't like the old way of doing things anymore. They believe what I tell 'em. About that Love, and how they're more. They're giving up their drugs and drink. It's wonderful."

The Shanties began wearing dandelions, tucked into the brim of their hats or pinned to their threadbare clothes. Flowery ones, fat and yellow as the sun. Mom said when Micky would come to town she'd have a handful and give them away as though they were something precious. There was even an article about it in the *Record,* a picture of her handing one to Louise Townsend, our sheriff's wife. Dad read the piece aloud over supper. Two hundred words about the strange girl who was taking it upon herself to champion the plight of Camden's poor. The writer called her "a voice in the Appalachian wilderness." Dad huffed and set the paper down. Mom read in silence.

"It's for you, Owen," Micky said that evening. "Dandelions is what you always left as a marker. I never even knew how perfect they are. Like a symbol, you know? They're so pretty, but all folk seem to think of them is they're weeds. Like folk think of us" — meaning, I supposed, Shantytown — "and even like how we think of each other. Like we all think of ourselves deep down."

5

And through it all, drifting at the fringes, was Earl Dullahan. In truth it pains me to think of him even these many years later, given his role in all that would happen that summer. His face more than any other is the one that has haunted my long nights. Earl became the reason I kept in contact with Camden once Dad and Mom took across the mountain to Charlottesville. Looking for him. Waiting for him to be found. A part of me hopes he's burning in hell for his sins. But much of me — too much — despairs at the thought of Earl Dullahan sitting at a bar down Mexico way with a suitcase full of money at his feet and a pretty girl on each arm, still with those spindly legs and that bushy white beard, laughing at it all. It is rare that things are made right in this world, and that has always been a sticking point between me and the Almighty.

Earl was there all along, hovering in the shadows and trying to make sense of the peculiar thing that had overtaken his daughter-that-shoulda-been-a-son. When he figured out what Micky was doing (or figured enough of it), he pounced. Wasn't love for his daughter that spurred him toward the light so much as wanting a piece of that newfound attention she was getting.

It was Earl who took to building Micky's church, which involved nothing more than fixing up some old abandoned barn deep in the Pines. He even came up with a name for it: The Fellowship of the Lost, seeing as how that's what they all had been. Telling everyone in town who'd listen that he'd "sought the Lord and changed his ways." Earl who came up with the idea of how best to help everyone in Shantytown "on the economic side" since his precious child was tending to their hearts. Since most had nothing and only a few had some, he called it the Christian thing to have everybody share everything. Most in Shantytown lived by some sort of government help (one hand holding an upraised *Don't tread on me* flag, the other held out to demand their fair share — that explains much of the Pines back then). Micky bought into it all. She told every Shantie it was up to them all to see to the general well-being of those in the Pines, especially since the people of Camden never much cared what went on in the hills. People started taking their welfare and disability checks to the bank and depositing them straight into Earl's account. He got to strutting around like he was blessed. Like it'd been him up there on those tracks right along with his little girl, getting a word from the Lord.

Micky told me all of this one night on our hill. I was running out those innings, thinking of graduation and the summer and how by August all of it would be back to normal. Some nights I left early, unable to bear the growing distance between us. Other nights Micky was the one who parted first, talking of all the work needing done. Time was short, that's what she would always tell me. She would say that and then say, *We should be dead already, you and me, but we been given a little more time.*

But that night I didn't hear much of what she said. What I was thinking about was Micky's feet and all that money coming in to her and Earl. How that money was supposed to have been getting spread around but some of it had somehow found its way to Micky's feet in a pair of New Balance high-tops so fresh from the box that the toes had yet to be scuffed.

And I remembered this as well, other words Micky had once spoken to me that were not so holy and wise as the ones falling now from her mouth. About how all she'd ever wanted was to leave her mark upon the world, any way she could.

6

Mom got to working late nights at the library to get us more money, leaving Dad and me to fend for ourselves when it came to supper. Micky started asking me to come to the hill later so work on the church wouldn't interfere with us, though I believed it otherwise: she didn't want us interfering with her church. I took to waiting until my parents had gone to bed and sneaking out of my window to see her, wondering how long it would be before Dad found out.

We had hot dogs off the grill and a Braves/Cubs game on the TV a few days before graduation. Dad always was a Cubs fan. His governing philosophy of baseball centered upon the conviction that whatever joy the game granted you would at some point turn to bitter disappointment — a lesson he had well learned. Whether such thinking played a role in his allegiance to a team whose last World Series championship came before the invention of sliced bread, I do not know. To Paul Cross, there existed a certain honor in throwing your support behind the perennial loser and constant underdog. Dad stuck with the little guy because life had made him one. In that regard he likened baseball to God and its adherents to a mass of long-suffering Jobs who lamented their fate yet held enough faith to appreciate the sheer beauty of a 6–4–3 double play or a sacrifice bunt that hugged the line.

We never could merely watch a baseball game. Every pitch was considered the result of a decision that must be analyzed, every defensive position a thing to be dissected and studied. Yet on that night entire innings played out with no comment. Dad's two hot dogs and bottle of beer remained untouched on the small table beside his chair.

"Seen Earl Dullahan today."

"What's he doing?"

"Stopped by the Ace on the way home, he's there buyin' up wood and such. Nails. Said they got them a church to fix up. Had them Harpers with him and some I didn't know. Paid cash for it all, and I did not wonder where he got that money." He shook his head. "That girl and Earl got them Shanties living like Communists."

"Won't last," I said.

"Shouldn't matter if it does or doesn't. Shanties always been a different sort. They live their own way and we live ours. We provide them jobs, feed them, give them money to spend on their drink and drugs, in return they do as they're told."

It sounded funny the way he said that, like Dad counted himself a pillar of the Camden community. He was right about our hill people. Those of them who bothered to work did so doing the worst jobs for the smallest money. But at least the janitor down at the high school wasn't no Shantie, was he? No sir, he was not.

"Rupert's there," he said. "Him and Jeffrey come in to get some floor wax for the IGA, and Rupert's up at the register paying. Earl butts on in front of him like Rupert ain't even there. Them two got in it so bad I thought I'd have to get a bucket a water to throw on 'em both."

On the TV, Andre Dawson sent a 2–2 fastball that caught too much of the plate high into the Wrigley air. The Cubs were up 1–0. Neither of us noticed.

"What's a girl like that know of love?" Dad asked.

"Who?"

"Dullahan girl. All her talk. Thing like love's good for the young alone. Like them"

— pointing at the television — "and you. Get on in life, you come to know different. You get old, you'll find love don't get you far. It only costs."

I could have said something smart to lighten the mood, like how that sounded a fine thing coming from the man married to my mother. But Dad only watched the screen. He made no mention of how the Braves pitcher took too long a stride or how the Cubs would never win so long as they lacked plate discipline. It was as though he saw nothing but the young men playing and how one sore shoulder had kept him from playing it the same. Love had nothing to do with it. Love had only cost him. All those years I resented my father for the man he became. That night was the first I wondered if he ever looked upon me with something of the same — if Dad resented me for the man I would become.

He asked, "How's Bubba?"

"Guess you could say I'm making a difference in the world one coat of wax at a time."

"It's work. Makes you appreciate things."

"More work than Travis does."

"Travis is different," he said. "Always has been. There's little folk and big folk. Travis got born big. Like you, Owen, only different. Like me once upon'a." He reached for the beer then and tossed it back in a long gulp, washing away the taste of what he'd said. "Them boys on that field's the winners, son. They get to play for a living what I'd do for free."

Mom rushed in close to nine thirty, going on about the books she'd shelved. I went to bed and out the window soon after, though I had no heart in it. I didn't want to see Micky that night. It felt strange to realize that, like how you spend your whole life a kid only to wake up one day and decide you're not supposed to play with toys anymore. It did not matter. I reached our hilltop and found beneath the oak a small stack of river stones, nothing more.

7

On a cloudy Saturday afternoon in early June of 1990, Camden High School bid farewell to its one hundred and forty-third graduating class. There were cheers and laughter and the sense of things both ended and begun, one speaker I doubt any of us can remember now, and enough pictures taken to keep the King Photo store on Waverley Avenue busy until the next Christmas. We were all there. Even Todd Foster. All but one. When Principal Taylor called out the name of Michaela Constance Dullahan, only silence answered. All that was present of her that day in the school gym was the growing sea of yellow weeds scattered along the bleachers and seats of those who called Shantytown home, every one worn with pride.

8

It is a quiet half inning that comes and goes in little more than a blink, Knoblauch and Justice grounding out to second, Jeter between them sending a line drive caught by Gibbons in left. Beside me, Country is growing nervous. The sixth ends with us up 8–1, bringing the final innings. A sense of panic starts in on me, a notion that something is drawing close. I stand and stretch my legs as our guys come in from the field. Mike cuts his eyes to me and seems to pause in thought. I look away and don't know why. I should want to be out there, right? That's all I've pined for. Get up to bat or take an inning or two behind the plate. Show my worth. Prove I belong.

My hand reaches into my back pocket. I feel the piece of rock there. Knight comes out of the Yankee dugout to take the mound. His head is down. Only Jeter and O'Neill are jogging out to their positions with purpose. The rest carry the bearing of ones who merely want the night over at this point. Grind through these last innings and get home, get some food and a good night's sleep, come back ready to play tomorrow. In the Bigs, there is always tomorrow. But as I look back over at Country, standing from his place to welcome Segui in from first base and trying to conceal the desperation on his face, I realize it is the same in the Bigs as it is anywhere else in the world.

There is always tomorrow until there is not.

TOP 7

Country says to me, "Be right back, gotta put a bug in Mike's ear." He takes Betsy along. Moving down the narrow dugout path between rail and bench, tapping the bat's barrel against a knee of every player he passes. Country saying, "Look good out there, Bubba" and "Got 'em on the ropes, don't we?" and "Big ol' moon's on our side tonight." At the end of the dugout he lays the bat to his left shoulder, says, "Mikey" — I can't imagine any other Oriole can do that except maybe Ripken — and I watch as the two of them slide into conversation. David Segui walks from the on-deck circle to the plate as the Yanks throw the ball around the horn and back to Knight on the mound.

Caldwell, that hotshot rookie who flew past Double-A in Bowie like it was a rest stop along my own interstate of dreams, sits beside me. He's looking at our manager and shaking his head as he smiles, says, "Does that every game. Goes up there begging to have one at-bat, get out there in the field. Gotta get that four hundredth dinger. He don't care how it looks neither. But ain't nobody gonna say a word to him about it. Ol' Country. Love that guy. Sorry again I spiked you."

"Don't worry about it."

"You up from Bowie? I see you when I went through?"

I nod. "Hit right behind you."

"That's right." He taps me on the leg. "That's right. Got a decent stick, Hillbilly." Now Caldwell leans back, appearing to stretch but really trying to read a bit of my name on my jersey.

"Owen Cross," I say.

"Right. I've seen so many faces I can't keep them all straight in my head. But I'm here now. Not going anywhere. Mikey" — that's what he calls Mike, and I cannot believe it — "says I could be starting next year. Got some old guys out there need to get out of the way. It's a young man's game, you know."

"I know."

Segui takes a curveball by night and pops it behind third base. Caldwell says it could fall but I know it can't; Brosius is out there and he can handle the leather. My guess is proven right when Brosius calls off Jeter and makes the play. Segui makes the turn at first and heads back to the dugout. It's one out at the top of the seventh in a game that will count for nothing in the end, yet Caldwell is grinning like it's Christmas Day and he's got a stack of presents taller than himself.

He says, "Man, I love this game. All I ever played. You know? Ever since I was a kid."

"Where you from?"

"Cali. You?"

"Virginia."

He chuckles. "*Hillbilly.* No wonder you and Country get along so well. Two of a kind."

We look where Country has gone. He's standing beside Mike but they're no longer talking.

"They bring you up to babysit Fordyce?" he asks. "Or is this your shot?"

"Little of both, maybe."

"Good on you, man. Always need a good catcher. Brook's good. Can't much hit. Lopez neither. Could use a stick like yours."

Melvin Mora faces Knight. He's had a tough night at the plate so far but redeems himself with a liner to left that ends up bouncing off the wall, putting him on second. Caldwell leaps atop the railing with a cry of "Atta boy."

When he settles down beside me once more, he says, "No place like the Stadium. I love Camden Yards, don't get me wrong. It's about as nice a ballpark as there is. But it ain't got no ghosts. You know?"

"I heard about them ghosts."

"It's crazy, isn't it? You gotta watch. My dad always said baseball's a living thing, you know? Like it's *real.*"

"Mine always said much the same."

"He here tonight?"

"Depends. You believe in them ghosts, maybe. I ain't got no family anymore."

"Send my bats back home every once in a while. For real. Dad bundles them all up and takes them down to the church. Priest blesses them. Then he gets them back to me. Been doing that since Single-A. Because you gotta watch. You know?"

"Yes."

Gibbons steps up to the plate and promptly calls time, trying to throw Knight's rhythm off on the mound. It's a good tactic.

Caldwell says it again: "I love this game. Used to play all the time when I was a kid back home —"

"What's that?" I ask him. "Last year?"

"You're funny for an old man. But I'm serious. All year long. Out there every morning in the summertime, and I'd play straight through till the streetlights came on and my mom called me home. It's crazy."

"Guess we all did that. Probably a big part of why we're here."

"But it's the same game. You know? Doesn't matter if it's Yankee Stadium or the sandlot out by the county dump back home, it's still the same game. Only difference is I used to ride my old bike down to that sandlot, now I drive a Porsche."

"Got me an old truck down in Bowie. Don't think I'll ever get me nothing fancier'n that."

Gibbons shoots an easy fly ball to right that O'Neill catches after taking a few short steps. Two down. Country is pacing.

"Shoot," Caldwell says, "you've still got time. What are you, twenty-five, twenty-six?"

"Twenty-nine."

Caldwell pauses. "Twenty-nine's not old, even for a catcher. It's you they called up here tonight, not some Triple-A catcher. Must be something to it."

I appreciate the kindness, even if it is from a cocky utility infielder who calls me *sir* but our manager *Mikey,* but that's not the point.

"I'm slumping," I tell him. "Been in a funk at the plate for a month now. Think this was my skipper's way of getting me out of it."

"You give me your bats, I'll send'm home to my dad. Put the Lord in them."

I chuckle.

"Seriously." Caldwell nods at Fordyce, who looks lost stepping up to bat. "Brook is good, man. For real. But he's not having such a hot game tonight now, is he? Oh-for-what? Hear me? Got three Ks already. Could be Mikey puts you in."

"Mike says I'm to babysit."

"Go talk to him."

"I ain't no Country Kitchen," I say. "Talking to the manager ain't my place, 'less it's after he says something to me."

"Better make it your place. You want your chance, you gotta make it known. Could be that's what Mikey's waiting on."

Fordyce lets two strikes get by him before flying out to Knoblauch in left. That leaves our catcher with an oh-for-four tonight and Caldwell punching my rib with his elbow. Our guys head back out onto the field for the bottom of the seventh, which may take a few extra minutes to get started since it's stretch time.

"Twenty-nine," Caldwell says. "Not getting any younger, Hillbilly. This here's a young man's game." He stands and moves off to visit Ethan at the bat rack, turns and gives me a wink. "But hey, least you're not as old as Country. Am I right?"

Stretch

1

Things were never the same once Micky started with her church. What made it worse was so often the house held Dad and me alone. I'd get back from the Auto World around five, Dad would arrive soon after from the school. Mom still worked nights, leaving us to fend for supper on our own and leaving no one to cover for me when I took my trips to the hill. Not that there needed to be. On those evenings when I did manage to arrive early, I often found only the oak waiting. I'd sit there an hour, sometimes two, before Micky eased her way from the pines. Always looking tired but beautiful, always smiling even though I hardly did. Not even seeing her could lift my spirits. Not even talking. I was made more miserable by the fact that she was not miserable at all.

It was all about the church by then. Every

little thing. How they'd fixed up that old barn to make it a proper place of worship and how all the Shanties were pulling together. All the money Earl was taking in and how it was getting spread around so nobody went without. Always sitting down beside me with a peck on the cheek and an *I missed you today, Owen* that I found difficult to believe, because if she missed me so bad then why were we apart so often? Why did the girl I loved feel such a stranger?

The only time Micky would fall silent was when I talked of college. Never a word to that. She would only look off toward the ridges or to a darkening sky and ask me what I loved. I said the same every time — *It's you I love, and what we'll soon have.*

And I believed it, and I was a fool for believing so.

But what are any of us but fools, always chasing but never finding? And what are any of us but lost when we cling even to broken dreams, because we have nothing else?

2

That first Sunday after graduation — that's when even the lies I told myself seemed to hold no more. That was the day Micky returned to Reverend Sebolt's church, this time bringing a few of her Fellowship along.

The day I believe I lost her for good.

The funny thing is, I doubt it would have happened had my father been handing out the bulletins at the front door. Dad would have put a stop to it before it started. But it had since come to Reverend Sebolt's attention that his daughter, Stephanie, and Jeffrey Davis were turning into something serious, enough that even the reverend's wife, Abigail, was beginning to speak of a future wedding. Folk in the Appalachians tend to fall in love once and early. It wasn't uncommon in Camden to have a wife you met in grade school or a husband who was once your homecoming date. That would be Jeffrey Davis and Stephanie Sebolt. I did not go to their wedding, though I received an invitation forwarded to me by Mom. My answer was a polite no. Mom knew why. After Micky, I swore I'd never go back to Camden again.

Whether by Stephanie's prodding or his own desire, Reverend Sebolt decided Jeffrey should begin manning the front door every Sunday morning. My father was happy for the break, having been stuck having to listen to the sermon from the chair inside the church foyer for years. And Jeffrey, he was happy for easy work that consisted of merely smiling, offering everyone a good morning, and handing over a Sunday bulletin.

That's why it was Jeffrey rather than my father waiting at the doors when Micky and the first of her flock paid their visit. It's also why they were not turned away but let right on inside with nothing more than a flash of surprise. The way Jeffrey told me later, "I didn't think nothing was gone happen. I mean, it's just church, you know?"

Jeffrey didn't even bat an eye at the rest of them, Todd Foster and Earl and both Harper boys. He never even stopped to wonder why Todd had his arms full of dandelions cut fresh from the wastes of the Shantytown fields.

Most of the work had been completed by the time I showed. A dandelion waited at every place in every pew from the back of the sanctuary all the way to the front, including the pulpit, the organ, and where the choir would stand. The Shantytown delegation sat in a phalanx at the back, Micky serving as its center. In her new white dress she looked like a cloud surrounded by dust. My mouth went dry at the sight of her.

Her eyes flitted to the others streaming inside, some from the back where Jeffrey stood pale and trembling as though he had begun only now to sense trouble. Others entered from smaller doors that led to the Sunday school rooms. From these came Jeffrey's parents, Rupert and Irma, who took one look at the Shanties gathered and all but made the sign of the cross. Then Mom and Dad, she freezing in place until he took hold of her elbow and steered them both to where I sat. Dad's only words to me were "You know anything about this?" I shook my head and wondered if Micky had seen that, if she was staring.

Sheriff Townsend and Louise. Abigail Sebolt and Mayor Henry. Bubba Clements. Travis, who stared at Micky and all of a sudden seemed genuinely happy to be at church that day because something funny might happen. Stephanie entered and sat at the organ. She stared at the dandelion waiting for her like it was a spider and then struggled through the first bars of "Shall We Gather at the River."

The murmur that had groaned through the crowd at the sight of Micky became a buzz. Some smiled as they twirled weeds in their fingers. Others tossed their dandelions on the floor to be trampled. A few of the more righteously indignant tossed theirs in Micky's direction, which garnered no response other than one of the Harpers leaping from his place as if seeing those flowers as foul balls to be grabbed. I watched Earl gently pull the big twin back into a sitting position. Micky's eyes were shut. I wondered if she was scared or praying.

Reverend Sebolt entered last. Preachers must develop a kind of sixth sense regarding their Sunday-morning flock, because he stuttered his steps a little as soon as he breached the doorway. His smile puckered and then flashed to life once more, gaze darting. He strode up the steps to the pulpit and laid down his Bible. His hand moved. A dandelion twirled in his fingers.

The service proceeded with an abundance of caution. Stephanie stretched the last notes of the opening song. The prayer seemed designed to mention every need and want — the reverend grinding out the innings no less than me, until he could no longer.

"Does anyone have any announcements?"

You could hear necks turning, skin rustling against linen suit coats and cotton dresses. I kept my eyes forward to the wooden cross hung above the baptismal pool, those two straight pieces of wood resembling a moving figure by the sunlight cutting through the stained glass. Dad faced forward as well. As did Mom, until Micky spoke.

Her voice came so soft that it barely

cleared the back of the room — "Hello, Reverend" — before gathering up. "I don't know if I'm the sort can give an announcement, seeing as how this is only the second time I been here. But when I walked up there a while back you said I had a home here now, so I thought I could maybe speak. For only a minute."

Reverend Sebolt rubbed his lips. He looked an imposing man up there above the rest of us, gray-haired and wise. Dad cleared his throat from the front pew. I could not decide if that was meant as a signal.

The preacher lifted his own dandelion. "Michaela Dullahan, I believe you have already attempted to make a report this morning, though I cannot reckon its meaning. I am happy to see you here again — and those you've brought along. I am happy as well to hear of all your doings out in Shantytown, however strange some of them may be. I'll let you talk, child. But this is the house of the Lord. It is a holy place and a holy time, not one for hubris."

"I don't reckon I know what that word means, but I ain't come to start no trouble. I only want to talk is all."

A soft ripple of laughter rolled through part of the crowd. A dandelion lay on the gray carpet at my feet. I gathered it in my hand as Micky went on.

"Guess about everybody's heard what we been doing down in the Pines. Maybe you're thinking what's got into me. I can say I really don't understand it all myself. Things is happening." She chuckled. "I even got my pitcher in the paper. That ain't never happened to a Dullahan before. 'Less it was a mug shot."

When Micky spoke again it was clearer and more direct, as though she was no longer trying to speak over and around all those bodies but to them. I used the reverend's face as a kind of weather vane and concluded she had stepped out into the center aisle.

"It was me caused the trouble in Brutal Simpson's field. I won't get into all the wheres and how-comes of it, I'll only say that when you're a girl like me, life can sometimes get to slipping away from you. Well, it slipped so far from me that I wound up standing in front of a train. I was on the wrong path, I guess. But I was saved."

My fingers closed upon the flower in my hand.

"And I was gived something." Her voice sounded closer, no more than a couple pews back. "I don't know why. Surely I didn't deserve such a thing. I got a vision is what

286

you might call it, though that don't do what I seen justice. Things like that ain't supposed to happen to no Shantytown girl. No Dullahan girl 'specially. Ain't that right, Daddy?"

Earl said in his gravest tone, "You right, child."

"But it happened." Her shadow fell across a square of carpet in the aisle to Dad's right. "And that thing changed me whole from the inside out. Made me new. What sort of thing you think could do that, Reverend Sebolt?"

The preacher didn't say.

"I don't know either," Micky told him, "other than a miracle. That's what I call it. Because I got shown all the errors of my ways. I seen what we truly are and all the beauty that makes us. But you know what I seen more than anything else?"

She let that hang over us so long that Louise Townsend actually said, "What?"

"Love. Purest, fiercest love you ever imagined. Love that never ends."

Reverend said, "That's fine now, Michaela."

"I ain't done yet, if you please. I'm coming to the good part. That love changed me. It made me see all the living I ever done was backward. My whole life was one mistake after another because I didn't know that love."

Every face pointed Micky's way. Only mine and my father's remained unmoved.

"I know what y'all think a me, if you ever thought a me at all. You'd be right to say I ain't nothing but another Dullahan from Shantytown. You'd be right saying all us Shanties struggle. We always have. But you know why? It's 'cause we always been looking someplace else for that love we need. I didn't even know it before, but we were. Like you all are."

She came forward past where I sat.

"What is it you love? That's all I'm asking." It was as if she looked at every face there, studied every soul. "Any you ever asked yourself that? I never did, and I suffered for it. Because if it ain't that single thing I found on them train tracks, the thing that'll always love you back regardless, then you ain't never gone be at peace. You'll always be looking and always end up hurt."

She studied the cross hung over the baptismal pool. "I don't know what to call that love by. I reckon you could say it's God or Jesus or any these names you got hanging on the walls I can't pronounce. They're good enough because it's all that love we're able to hold, but I'm telling you it's more than some word or name. More than we can ever know on this side of life. You can't be chasing after things that don't matter. They're all empty. I know. I chased them too. And I just don't want anybody here suffering the same as me. I know it don't sound right saying this, 'specially here, but my momma always told me a church is a place of truth. That's why I gotta say the truth. This here's supposed to be a place of sinners and whores, and you know why that is? Because that's all we are deep down."

Irma Davis shouted, "Heavens," as if the Spirit had laid hold of her.

The Reverend Alan Sebolt flared. "That is quite enough, young lady. Jeffrey, you come show Michaela out or to her seat, I don't care which."

But Jeffrey didn't move. All he knew was to say good morning and hand you a bulletin. My father never covered with him how to get a demon out of their midst. Besides, I guess Jeffrey knew Micky could whup him in a blink.

Micky turned to the preacher and asked, "What do you love, Reverend? Them words you say, or the One you're supposed to speak for?" And then to Stephanie, "What truth you find for yourself, or only the sort somebody finds for you?" To Jeffrey she

289

asked whether he loved the short life he thought was his or the eternal one this life pointed toward. She said to my mother, "We have so much love to give, but only because we're loved first."

On she went, passing person to person, tailoring each entreaty and question as though she knew their deepest wants. Many of them found they could no longer look at their accuser at all. My father was spared, and me, though in my case it could be said whatever wisdom Micky felt led to offer had been given me at the hill.

"I tried telling y'all this, though I don't think I been too good at it. But the Shantie folk know. It's easier for poor folk to hear the truth of things. They ain't got as much to lose. We got a new church out there called the Fellowship of the Lost, since that's what we was. And I want to invite y'all. Don't matter to us who you are, you're welcome. I guess I'll be the one to preach. You'll hear much of what I told you today."

Micky cleared her throat to make a final push.

"Those dandelions you got is our mark. We wear 'em to show even the weeds of this world is loved beyond measure. I guess I come here to tell y'all that too. We might be poor and got nothing. But what we carry inside is something the world can't take away, and that about makes us as rich as a body can be. It's a reminder, these dandelions." She stroked the one pinned to her dress. "It tells us we ain't gone be pushed down by Camden folk no more. There's too many a us workin' for y'all and gettin' treated bad. Gettin' ignored. It ain't right. So I'd like you each to have a dandelion too, if only to remember that. Remember you ain't no better than anybody else and we're all loved. And I want y'all to know you're always welcome down in the Pines. Can be an expensive venture," Micky said, "starting a church. We won't ask for your money —"

"Love offerings will be gladly accepted," said Earl.

"— but maybe if you're led to do so, what tithe you aimed to put in the plate here could be put to better use. You just save that money, give it over to me or Earl. Give them dandelions you got to the preacher maybe. I guess that's it."

She gave an awkward curtsy to the reverend. She didn't return to her seat. Instead, the first members of the Fellowship of the Lost met her in back where Jeffrey stood and left en masse. I relaxed my hand. The dandelion inside was crushed, my palm stained yellow.

I will give Reverend Sebolt credit. From there onward he made certain our Sunday service deviated not once from the usual. He barely flinched when the plates were passed and brought forward to the altar. Those silver trays sat there for all to see, holding piles of white envelopes with *First Baptist Church* on the front. Some checks poking out here, some cash there. And a whole lot of flowers and stems.

3

It is a subtle thing yet very present if you know to look for it, how this space between the top and bottom of the seventh is made longer by a mere matter of an extra warm-up pitch and one more grounder rolled to short, or how the ump behind the plate lingers a bit longer while talking to the ball boy. Fans inch their way down the aisles with little hurry. Their hands carry fresh nachos, one last cold beer, a tub of popcorn to see them through the ninth and the trip home. Kids jockey for new positions in the vacant seats nearest the dugouts. It's as if they know time is growing short to catch that stray foul ball or snag a broken bat some player may find in his heart to relinquish. A baseball game is a beating heart.

And as with all things that live, the beauty lies not in the beats themselves but those small moments between. It is a pitcher toeing the rubber as he gets the sign; the batter gently rocking; a catcher digging heels into the dirt over which he squats, ready to move right or left to receive the pitch. These are the moments that set baseball apart, the small gaps in which nothing happens yet everything takes place, when you are given time to reflect and remember.

4

It took an event as extraordinary as that morning at church to grant my family something we had never before experienced: a silent dinner. Only the plinking of glasses and the scrape of silverware over plates rose above the soft whir of the fan. I studied the clock and convinced myself those hands moved, there were still sixty seconds to every minute and eventually I would be excused to get on with my day. Dad took small sips of his tea and stared toward the backyard and freedom. Mom looked at nothing at all. Were it not for Dad's prayer and the amen spoken in unison, one would have thought we were a collection of strangers thrown together by happenstance.

But that was what we were, strangers, and

had been for years. I had no doubts my parents loved me and each other. We kept to our assigned roles — Dad the provider, Mom the supporter, me the dutiful son. I suppose that's what a family is. People all over Camden looked upon us with respect. Those Crosses are a good family, they would say, Mayor Henry and the Davises, the sheriff and our preacher. They look after one another.

We did. But what I hadn't known then and what none of us realized until later was all of that only served as the soft skin of our family, the bones beneath being brittle. We talked, but rarely of anything important. We shared, but only what we each first deemed safe. Our silence at the table that afternoon arose not from a lack of something to share but an abundance, all of it so personal that to speak it would lay us bare one to another, which made our quiet like an arrow to the heart. Micky had confronted us all. We were each too afraid to say anything.

It was Mom who broke the impasse as she dished dessert, whether because the silence had grown too great or she believed its greatness her own failing. She spoke simply and to the point:

"I believe something has happened to that girl."

Dad's reply came with equal economy, meant to settle the subject before it could begin. "Something did happen. Girl come into the world a Dullahan."

"That isn't what I mean, Paul."

He shook his head.

Mom wouldn't back down. "That isn't what I mean," she said again. "How many times I seen that child before? Thousands? Knee-high to me, roaming the grocery aisles or standing at the bank or at the post office for stamps, hand in her momma's, looking lost and dirty and ashamed. Every time looking the very same except for the height and age of her. But that was not Michaela Dullahan in church today. That was some-one new."

Dad took a bite from his wedge of pie. "That was nothing new, Greta. I'd lay it on Jeffrey Davis's shoulders for the whole thing. Girl should've never been allowed inside those walls, much less Earl Dullahan. It's disrespect, pure and simple. What they doing down in Shantytown, it ain't the Lord."

I doubted Mom had any idea how to define what had happened in church, and my own idea of it was likely no better formed than her own, but I believed we could at least agree on the fact that it was certainly new.

"Earl Dullahan come to see me at the school a year ago. June or July, I don't remember, but it was summertime. Said he's got to talk to me since I was 'the one in charge.' Well, I knew soon as he says that he was up to no good. Had himself an idea on reseeding the football field." He rolled his eyes my way. "You believe that? Said he's got ahold of this special seed grass gets used by the Packers — 'genuine Green Bay ones,' Earl says — and he'll sell it to me for cheap. Best seed grass there was, guaranteed to make Camden High the envy of the county. And Earl's gone help me out."

"You didn't tell me that," Mom said.

" 'Cause it come to nothing. I took one look at that fancy seed and knew it stole. What fool steals grass seed anyways?" Dad shook his head. "Earl's so dumb he don't even know we use sod on the football field. Point I'm trying to make, Greta, is all that girl done today is try to sell us some seed. Been working too. You notice them shiny clothes? Seen that girl at school four years, never knew her to wear such finery. Where you think that money come by? You think Earl's gone and found himself proper work?"

I set myself to eating, wanting no part in this.

"But you must have some sympathy for the child," Mom told him. "She's been through such upheaval. First Constance passing and then no longer having school. There's holes in her life, Paul —"

Dad snorted. "And she's fillin' 'em only way a Dullahan knows. She's a crook just like her daddy, playing all them poor Shantie souls."

"How do you know that?" I asked.

He wiped his chin with a napkin. "You get a batter stand in and he's holding his bat low in his stance. Say the knob's resting at about his hips. What do you call?"

"Fastball up."

"Say pitcher throws a high one in, batter swings and misses. What's the next pitch?"

"Same."

"And why's that?"

"Because you got to throw that pitch until he stops trying to hit it."

"Yes," Dad said, and here came the first bit of a smile from him all day. " 'Cause folk don't change. They don't change for nothing."

Mom said, "That's a poor way to look at the world."

"I'd rather see the world as it is than what

I'd like it to be, Greta. That is our difference."

Yet Dad did not know Micky as I did, nor Mom to some point. I had been made privy to a part of her kept hidden from all but her dead mother. The years have proven much of what my father said of people to be true, but he was wrong in that. People could change. If they could not, then what hope was there for anyone? And no matter my father or anyone else inside that church knew it, Micky had changed as well. What confused me was which of her selves had been transformed — the Dullahan part of her, or the part known only to me.

Mom whispered, "I heard the hint of truth to her words. I will not believe otherwise."

"You will." It was a yell choked down, a fury barely quelled. "I will not have my own wife giving credence to such falsehood. That girl will bring ruin to an already ruined place. Michaela Dullahan asks for trouble she cannot reckon. It's one thing to try selling what you stole, another to steal in religion's name. This Shantie church, you think any good'll come a that? Robbing the poor in God's name. She'll get struck down. It'll be the Lord's hand or someone else's."

Dad rose. He placed his dishes by the sink and crossed back toward the living room, laying a hand to Mom's shoulder. "She speaks of loving, but the only loving Michaela Dullahan has ever wanted is the sort that gets pointed straight to herself."

5

The Fellowship of the Lost took in near a hundred dollars that day. It had been Earl's idea to spread out over town once church was done ("Don't make no scene, just be seen," Micky said, chuckling over the breeze) and let the good people of First Baptist find them. Those good people had obliged. They snuck Earl cash as he stood in front of Rivera's and Micky checks as she loitered in front of the 7–11 to catch people coming out with their Sunday papers. The others who had accompanied the Dullahans collected similar. The Harper boys managed a windfall.

"Must've been a whole pile of dandelions for the reverend to gawk at. All that money's gonna come in handy, Owen."

I studied the ground beneath us.

"What's the matter with you? You mad we come to church?"

"Seems like I shouldn't be surprised anything you do now. You made some folk upset today, Micky. Don't think Reverend Sebolt appreciated it. I know my dad didn't.

Him and Mom got in a fight."

A worried look fell over her. "Your mom?"

"It wasn't bad. Bad enough. People don't know how to take you. They're saying stuff."

"Don't matter what people talk on." And after a bit, "What they saying?"

"That you and Earl got yourselves your own little kingdom down in the Pines. Got money stacked up everywhere. They see Earl coming to town to put some in the bank and take more out. Him strutting around like he's somebody. They see you wearing all these nice clothes."

"That money's for church. It's to help people. We're taking care of our own."

"No, they're taking care of you. And in return you rile them all up about how special they are and how loved, how they're getting mistreated by folk who pay them wages and give them a livelihood so long as they ain't too lazy to go looking for anything but some government draw, which I guess now they just cash and hand over to you and Earl. So don't you sit here talking about that stupid train and a hole people can't crawl out of. I won't listen to you say how you want to make things better. You ain't on no street corner here. You ain't standing in some barn. It's just me."

"You ever know how little us Shanties get?

300

They're worked to death in town. Want to talk about how those people at the library treat their cleaning folk, or how Bubba is so awful to the hill folk who depend on him? Think it's right he cheats his mechanics out of pay they earned so he can line him and Travis's own pockets? People in this town get what they have off our backs. My people are hurting, Owen. They been hurting a long time now. There's always poor folk. But people like ones in town do more than keep money out of Shantytown, they keep dignity away too. I can't say how all we are is Camden's fault. It's ours too, for giving in to everything gets said and done to us. I hope you at least understand that. You didn't come up here. You got to be born somewheres else. Not us. You only had four years to see how some a those people down at the school treat your daddy because of the job he's got. You live in Shantytown, that's every day of your whole life."

"So that's what all this is then? This preaching you're doing and all this church talk? All to get even?"

"No. It's to change things." Micky tugged at the collar of her new shirt. Ran a hand along the folds of her new skirt. She did those things and yet said, "I'm trying to make things better. That's my only aim. And

I thought you'd be helping me."

"Whatever made you think I would help you in this?"

"Because you were at that train. Because you seen something."

"How many times I got to tell you about that? Why won't you let that go?"

"You think I can let something like that go, Owen? Do you really?"

"You think I should let baseball go."

I yelled it, couldn't say the words otherwise. Micky took her hand away from mine. She backed away from the oak to where the limbs reached down, drowning herself in moonlight.

"That's what you said, ain't it? That I should quit and stay in Camden? Why would you say such a thing to me, knowing all you do? Knowing what we spent so much time up here talking about? And now . . ."

She whispered, "And now what?"

I searched out her face, wanting my next words not to be true, but they were.

"Now I don't even know who you are anymore. It's like you're not even you, Mick. I can't understand what you're doing or why. *It don't make sense.* I come up here every night thinking maybe this is the time you'll just stop all this, just stop it so we can go back to the way things used to be.

But it never happens. All you want to talk about is some church or that night at the train, and I don't want to talk about that. I don't want to hear any of it. What I want to hear is that everything's going to be okay with us and that nothing's changed, but it has. It has, and I hate it."

Micky kept where she was. The space between us may as well have been worlds. I wanted to go to her. Hold her in my arms. Make her understand. But that was not Micky sitting there. It was a stranger with me.

"I'm so sorry," she said.

"It's like you don't even have room for me no more. Or that you don't want me. Is that it?"

"Of course not."

"Well then, what is it?"

"I'm trying to help —"

"Stop. Don't say that. You want to help somebody, help me. You say you love me, then show it. Ain't nothing been done in the Pines or any place that you can't turn away from, Micky. If you want to help the Shanties, that's fine. Help them all you want. But when it comes time for summer to be over and I got to leave for Ohio, I want you to come with me. I want it to be what we always said it would. You made me

303

choose, now I'm making you. I love baseball. I always have. There's sometimes I think all people do is go from place to place trying to figure out where they belong, but I know every time I step on a field. I was made for it, that's all. And I was made for you. So please. Tell me we're still good. Tell me all of this we have ain't done, because I don't think I can bear it."

She stood, smoothed her skirt. Said, "What do you love, Owen?"

"You. I love you."

"I'll hurt you."

"I don't care."

"Yes, you do, because you love what can't love you back the way you want. The way you need. Not even I can love you like that. It's the same way baseball will hurt you. You can't sit there and tell me otherwise. Things fade, Owen. Nothing in this world lasts. Not some game, not me. Maybe once it was supposed to be the way you want it. That's all changed now. Maybe things would've gone wrong anyway, or maybe it was because I went up on those tracks. Maybe it was because you wanted to save me. If it's that, then I'm so sorry. But there's no going back now. I don't have much time. That's the only reason I want you to stay. I don't have much time, and I want you to be with me through it all. Every second of it. Because I love you."

"But not enough. That right? You don't love me enough. You'd rather stay here and wear nice clothes. Rather tell people how much they're loved when you don't love at all."

A tear gathered at the corner of her eye and went tumbling. "That ain't true."

"True enough for me."

I turned, making for my side of the slope. She called to me but I ignored her. Called again, and I turned.

"I can't be here no more," I said. "Go on home, Michaela Dullahan. You go take care a yours."

BOTTOM 7

1

Country meets Caldwell coming up the dugout, and the two eye each other grinning, one saying, " 'Scuse me, Gramps," and the other, "Outta my way, you snot-nosed kid," the veteran seeming to slap the rookie upside the head with a bat more famous than any of us will ever be, and now they clap as our guys take the field to start the last innings.

"Caldwell, man," he says as he sits. "Keeps us all loose. He didn't talk your ear off, did he?"

"Wasn't bad. Seems to think he knows everything."

"That age, they all do." He shakes his head. "Was I ever that young and cocky? Don't answer that. I tell that boy to calm hisself down, he never will. Game'll do that to him enough. Game takes us all down a few notches."

Johnson still looks strong on the mound, though with the score 8–1 I get to wondering how long Mike will keep him in. Best to save those starting pitchers' arms when you can, especially this early in the season. As if to signal a tired that isn't yet showing, Bernie Williams leads off for the Yanks with a double off the left-center wall. What crowd remains in the stadium erupts to cheers. It is a muted roar, though, as if most here believe not even the ghosts that linger in these rafters are enough to score seven in three innings. Tonight those spirits may remain quiet.

"You talk Mike into letting you in?"

"Didn't take much twisting." Country grins and turns his head to spit a rocket of tobacco juice into the drain set along the floor. "Mikey'll give me my at-bats this season. He'll get me out there in the field a few times a week. Going out next inning."

"Think you'll get a bat?"

He grips his black Betsy. "Nawp. Not tonight. He offered. Said that ball's flying with that moon. I told 'im give you a shot."

I scrunch my shoulders like some schoolkid who's just learned his secret crush likes him back. Tino Martinez is at the plate. Johnson pitching from the stretch as Williams takes a few steps off second. I care about none of this. "You did what?"

Country shrugs. He's got that grin still, the one that sells all the cars and deodorant on TV, the one that's gotten him on covers of *Sports Illustrated* and a pretty little country woman waiting on a farm in Kentucky.

"Ain't a ballplayer alive don't deserve a bat in Yankee Stadium. You gotta take somethin' from here, am I right? Anyway, Mikey's saying Fordyce is in for good. Might be some other spot for you to hit, though. Just you get your chance, make sure you show'm something. Mikey's watchin'. Always a need for a good backstopper in the Show."

Martinez flies out to left, stranding Williams at second. Even with the big lead, it's good pitching by Johnson. Outside, outside, outside. Don't let that ball go to right and get a runner at third with nobody out.

"You didn't have to do that," I said.

"We was all rookies once, bud. Don't matter anyways. I'll play the field tonight, ain't no problem. Mikey says I'm starting tomorrow at DH. That's the game I want. You think them balls is carrying now? Shoot, you wait till then."

"That's right," I remember. "Full moon."

"Ain't just any full moon. Tomorrow's is strawberry."

It is as though Country's words are spoken through a tunnel of wind, like he himself is the ghost of this place. His lips move in the slow ease of that long-ago train as it approached Micky and me. Like time itself has caught in a bubble. I cannot feel my own reaction. Only the look on Country's face tells me something of my secret self is showing. He allows that look to pass.

"It's the strawberry moon tomorrow?"

"One and only." His eyes bore into me, wanting to know more. "You know this game's such a beautiful thing words can't say it? Hell, feelings can't say it. They try to say it with numbers. I heard once that numbers is the language of God, which I hope ain't the case since I got trouble enough puttin' two an' two together to make four. But it makes sense, don't it, that there's so much numbers to baseball? Shoot, they got a number for everything. Half of it don't even make sense to me. But I had some front office guy tell me onced that in all my years a playing pro ball, I hit more dingers on the full moon in June than any other time. I'm tellin' you, them balls fly."

Paul O'Neill is up. I look out long enough to see Johnson watching Williams back at second. They look like spirits out there, as unreal as the crowd and the lights. O'Neill grounds out to Segui at first, who waves off Johnson and touches the bag himself. Williams advances a base to third. Two down.

I say it again, slower this time: "Strawberry moon."

Country leans my way. He takes his left hand from the bat he cradles and nudges me.

"You okay, boy?"

I'm not. I'm not.

2

I could not keep away from her. My heart would not sanction it.

All that next day I swore I would allow Micky what she most wanted — not me, but her beloved vision. Her ruined pines and ruined Shanties. I scrubbed Bubba's cars and kept to myself. Each hour that passed I vowed to go home and not to our hill. Spend the evening with Dad. In the end, I couldn't. I'd heard it often said the truest love lay in setting free what you loved most, but whoever came up with such drivel had never loved at all. I had to go, it was that simple. I had to walk the hill that night if only to say I was sorry, for everything.

Micky would suffer under no obligation to forgive me. My only hope lay in her feel-

310

ings for me — for us — which may not have been love anymore but were surely still strong enough for us both to lean upon. But she was not on the hill when I arrived, nor did I see any mark beneath the oak. And though I waited until I could no more, I knew I would wait all night and still be alone. Micky was not coming. It was foolish to think otherwise given the things I had said to her, and yet that night proved I was not the only fool. My father, too, had deceived himself, along with so many others in Camden. They all believed what had sprung forth in Shantytown was a thing soon to fade, but were Dad and the rest with me on the hill that night, they would have known different. They would have stood as I stood listening to that warm wind swooping down from the mountains through a vast sea of pines, bringing with it not only the sounds of night but of worship and song.

3

Three days I waited. Three nights in bed while soft voices leaked through the crack at the bottom of my door, muffled whispers and disjointed sounds that made me feel as though I shared my room with two grieving ghosts. To this day I do not know what my parents spoke of as they talked and argued over Mom's long nights at the library and her continued insistence that Michaela Dullahan spoke truth. Never once did either speak of those late-night conversations beneath the covers of their darkened bedroom. And while the words themselves leaked through my bedroom wall only some, the passion with which they were spoken always did. I can only imagine my father missed his wife, missed her simple presence, and the only way he could ever express such heartache was in anger. The only evidence of that given me was Mom's worried and wearied face and my father standing at the edge of a muddied puddle in our backyard, a watering hose in his hand.

My trips to the hill became more than escape. They were cries for a bit of sameness in a life that had changed so completely in the space of a month. I found myself caught between the universes of youth and adulthood, past and future, Camden and baseball. The sense of isolation bared its teeth with every walk I took up the slope to find nothing but the wind my company. There were no marks left by Micky. Not a single river stone or shiny rock. The only bit of nature out of place was the growing collection of bundled dandelions left as evidence that I had come and waited. That I was sorry.

For two of those nights I sat facing the Pines as an echo of song washed over me much like the whispers of my parents, cloaked in a muted language I could not know. The last night greeted me with silence alone. I did not know which I preferred.

Then on a Wednesday toward the middle of June, Bubba sent me on an errand down to the hardware store for new sponges to replace the ones I'd already worn out. I'd come down Main Street along the sidewalk past the library where Mom's car sat in the lot when I spotted Earl Dullahan's old truck at the bank. He'd parked by the entrance and left the driver's side door open. My first thought was he's in there robbing the place, though that consideration did not last. Micky's father no longer had need of blatant criminality. Not when there were so many Shanties to pillage.

Micky wasn't with him. As I moved forward I saw that someone else occupied the passenger seat. A few who passed lingered to stare, but Todd Foster paid them no mind. His expression remained as one who looked upon the world with newness, as though there wasn't a thing he did not mind.

His eyes found me, and his face lit with a smile I could not reckon. I walked from the curb into the lot and around to his window.

"Owen," he said.

"What you doing here, Todd?"

"Come with Earl. He's gettin' some money for the church. Church needs money right now."

"That ain't no church down there, Todd. It's a barn."

"No."

"Michaela not with you?"

"She had other things to do. What you want Michaela for?"

I looked away. "Don't want her for nothing."

"See her tonight if you want. Anybody's welcome. Church is right through the woods a ways a bit from their house. You should come, Owen. Lots a people do." He spoke the next in a way I saw as filled with secrets. "More'n anybody in town thinks."

"I know what y'all are doing up there. It ain't right."

"What ain't right? That we're all coming up in the world? That we take care a ourselves now 'stead a depending on townfolk to do it? You go on then, Owen. You ain't gotta believe. You tell me all you want about how we're so evil, I don't feel your words. And you know why? 'Cause I'm loved. I'm loved more than anything, and I'm special."

314

The bank door opened. Earl Dullahan walked out holding a bag that looked filled to bursting. His white beard dangled in the breeze, and his pants, stained by sweat and unwashing, carried a stench that backed me away. He eyed me.

"You that boy what hit that ball. My girl speaks a you."

I did not know which of that to focus upon, that Earl had called Michaela his girl or that Michaela spoke of me, and so chose the only thing that remained.

"What you got in that bag, Mister Dullahan?"

"That ain't none a yours to mind, son."

"How many families' money you got in there? What you do with all that?"

Earl stepped forward, letting the bag dangle. It did not seem possible how a man so small in both size and honor could back me away, but he did. "Listen here, baseball boy. I ain't no Shantie you can step upon. I am a man of repute now. You best not forget it."

He moved toward the truck. Todd regarded me with a measure of pity.

"You must be so tired from your hating," the boy said. "It costs so much. You don't have to be that way, Owen. You are loved, but you don't know it is all. You go looking

315

for it every place but where you is, and that's why you won't never find it. I feel sorry for you."

From somewhere out of sight, he produced a single dandelion. Todd held it through the open window like an offering.

"I don't want that," I said.

Earl sputtered the engine to life. The weed fell between us as the truck pulled away and into traffic. Just before they disappeared, Earl threw up his hand and waved. I could hear his laughter even from that far away.

4

I finished up the day's row of cars and got home to find Dad's truck already in the drive and him on the porch. One hand balanced a can of beer on the rocking chair's arm. Beads of sweat gleamed from it against a downing sun. A ring of sweat had formed where his work shirt was buttoned against his neck. Set atop the small table beside him were four empties and two Arby's bags wilting in the sun. He did not bother to raise his head as I came up the sidewalk and onto the steps. Did not even hear me call to him and ask how he'd managed to get away from the school so early. His gaze was instead on the thing he held in his right hand — twirling it, as I had seen so many others do in the early days of that summer. My first thought was that somewhere between the high school and home he'd run across Earl and Todd — that would explain where my father had gotten the dandelion he held. Then I saw the others scattered in a pile around his cracked brown boots.

"What you doin', Daddy?"

Still he did not look at me. Only twirled that weed and said, "Got these things ever'where this year. I didn't spray the yard when winter broke. Always do that, but this year I didn't. Said it wouldn't matter. Farmers said it'd be a dry summer and dry it is. We ain't mowed but what? Twiced? That sound right to you?"

"I guess."

"Whole yard's gone brown already, ain't even July yet. But these things," he said, holding that dandelion up, "they still growin'."

"They'll dry out 'fore long and turn to seed. Won't even notice them after that."

"Turn to seed."

"Yes."

"Turn to seed and spread. That's what they do. World ain't never be rid of them."

He dropped the flower from his hand and let it land atop the others, then scooted them all with his boot toward the edge of the porch and off. Where they had lain was now a streak of green and yellow.

"That our supper?" I pointed to the bags on the table.

"Eat it if you want."

I said I'd wash up and turned to the door. I was partway inside when Dad spoke again: "Went to see your momma little bit ago."

"You did?"

"Got off work early. Thought I'd go down get us some food, take it to the library. We ain't et supper together in a while. 'Less it's Sunday."

He slurped at the beer in his hand. I wondered how many he'd had that evening. My father was never a drinker but for during a ball game on the TV and occasionally after working out in the yard. It was not a sin doing so. Saint Paul, he always said, advised the use of drink to calm the stomach. Of course that was wine. According to my father, if Budweiser had been readily available in the olden times, it would have been the apostle's preferred drink.

"Why'd you bring it home if it was for you and Mom? She too busy to eat?"

"She weren't there."

I stepped back out onto the porch and let the door close. "What you mean she weren't there?"

"Car weren't there. That's what I mean. Didn't see it in the lot. You know anything about that?"

"No. I was by there today to the hardware store for Bubba. It was there then."

"It's her usual hours. Weren't there when I come by. I took them bags a food in there anyways. Like a fool. Ast the woman at the front, 'Where's my Greta? I got her and me some supper.' Know what I get told? 'Greta gets off at five. Don't you know that, Paul?' That's what she says to me. Like I'm some idiot don't even know what time his wife gets off work. So I says, 'She's been workin' late, ain't she?' And that woman tells me, 'Late? Ain't none of us work late 'round here. Overtime ain't in our budget.' That's what she said."

He let those words settle. A robin sang from the roof of the house and another answered from the pine trees in the backyard. I let them finish while I tried putting together what my father was saying.

"Then where's she been?"

He looked at the smear by his boots. In words as flat and dead as any I had ever heard my daddy speak, he said, "I think she been down at that Shantie church."

"Momma wouldn't do that."

"Wouldn't?" His eyes cut to me. "You

been a party to the things she's said ever since that Dullahan girl come back to church and brung her hill folk along. Your momma's heart's bent toward the things them people preach. Talk a love and peace and worth and whatnot. Like syrup, it is. Yessir, that's just what the poor and broken pine to hear. They'll even pay money they don't got to hear such a thing. It's a weak mind thinks a hard world can be overcome by gentleness. That's your momma. Always has been."

I said, "She ain't down there," but it was not a statement of fact. It was more a wish, I believe now. More a pining of my own, as though even then I knew my father was right.

"I'm goin' down there to see."

"You going to Shantytown?"

"I am."

He stood, wobbling as the rocker shot forward to clip the back of his knees.

"You ain't driving," I said.

"Then you drive me."

"We can't go to the Pines."

He came toward me stammering like the fool I always knew he was, the loving fool who wanted nothing more of life than for his son to be more than he himself had become. I saw in my father's eyes the bloodshot red of hurt and despairing rage. He shot a finger forward, which landed in the center of my chest, backing me against the door.

"You will not stand in judgment of me," he said. "I've enough a that from your momma. This is my family. Do you know what I've given? What I've endured? I will be called to testify in front of the Lord's throne, boy. And what will I say then? That I allowed my own family to stray from the path laid out for them? That I did nothing?"

He pushed past me and fumbled at the knob, forgetting that it turned, then pushed open the door. His hand swiped at the hook inside. I heard the jangle of keys falling and saw him stumble once more. A hand to the doorjamb was all that saved him.

"Let me," I said. I took him by the back of his gray pants and eased him out of the way. Dad walked off toward his truck. I picked up the keys and locked the door behind me, but only before glancing at the chipped and fading sign above the key rack. The one that had in so many ways guided all my father had done and given in leading us down the crooked and overgrown path of our lives:

As for me and my house, we will serve the Lord.

I had only Todd's words to guide me. The Shantie church lay through the woods just a ways beyond Micky's house, which offered me little in specificity. The road Momma and I had taken only a few weeks prior remained as unchanged as it had the day of Constance Dullahan's burial, less an artery clogged with potholes and dust than a pathway into some backward time. Then, I had been greeted with blank expressions and mistrustful eyes that served as a warning I had intruded upon a place not my own. Now I saw no one. As the sun dipped to the caps of the pines along the steep ridges above, I met not a single beast, whether mongrel dog or feral cat. It was as if Shantytown had been emptied through some merciful rapture, leaving behind only the refuse of lives ill-spent and the brittle husks of shacks and trailers.

We stopped at Micky's house. Earl's truck rested at an angle to the porch. Dad pounded upon the door but there was no one to answer. Through the living room window we glimpsed a mass of canned food lined against the wall. Diapers and cans of formula, bags of potato chips and boxes of cereal, whole pallets of bottled water. The single window around back held the same layer of grime as the wood siding. Dad's balance failed him, leaving me to stand on my toes and peer inside. Micky's sheets lay in a tangle. A new dress hung from the knob of her closet door. Her drawers hung open by several inches like she had fled. Then I looked closer and saw those drawers too stuffed with clothing to shut. On top, running the dresser's full length, were stacks of money bound by thick rubber bands. Piles of them, dozens upon dozens. It was more money than I had ever seen in my life.

Daddy slurred, "What's in there?"

"Cash. Earl could open his own bank with what they got in there."

The sun dipped behind us. Long shadows crept from the woods like oil leaking from some unseen crack in the machinery of the world. We walked back to the truck. I told him we should go home, that wherever the Shantie church was we'd never find it, not out here with dark ready to fall. And I meant those words. It would come to nothing good should my father find that barn. Even if Momma wasn't among them, Daddy's fury would not be quenched that night. It was as if all the hardness of his life and all those shattered dreams had come to a final boil, and rather than grieve or lay down his brokenness at the feet of the God he swore he served, what my father did was make Micky the cause of it all. I said we were going home. Told him to sleep on things. Maybe he'd wake in the morning knowing the foolishness in his heart.

But then in that waning light we heard something rise up from that spoiled land. Creeping from the trees and tangles toward us like shadow as well, only of light rather than dark. My father held still as Shanty-town began to sing. He moved off as the noise came louder, leaving the truck and me as he crossed the road and into the far trees. I called to him, though he did not turn.

The path beyond lay too wide and straight to be a game trail. Through gray evening I saw light not far ahead, pulsing with the soft thunder of melody. The path yielded to a glen. In the middle rested a leaning structure that blended so well with the weathered oaks and elms that it looked a place of spirits.

Dad stopped. I came alongside.

It is said every house of prayer takes on the character of the god worshipped there. First Baptist rose tall and stately from Camden's ordinary ground and sported a cross-topped spire at the crown of its roof reaching heavenward but never far enough.

Its clean angles and pristine grounds were symbols of a holy separation. If I held to any deity, it was that. Yet there in the ruins of Shantytown I beheld evidence of another God, no less holy, who reached down in full knowledge that we could not reach up. A Lord not from wood and soil, but of them and among them, as He was of and among us all. A dweller of the broken places.

Upon sight of that crooked building of gaps and rot, I was overcome by a sense of transcendence. I had been churched ever since our arrival in Camden, dunked in the river and told I was forgiven, but in my secret heart I held Beauty as no more than what we ourselves fashioned to give our lives meaning, and Truth nothing more than the sore reflection of those ideals by which we navigated our darkness. To acknowledge a Source beyond those things was something not even Simpson's field could persuade. Yet bearing witness to that patched barn, the fresh boards, the sturdy nails, the burning lamps from within and a music like defiance spilling from every crack, I nearly believed. Nearly. And perhaps I would have had I not first stumbled upon Micky's horde of goods and cash inside their home.

The doors were shut. "We'll go around," Dad said.

We kept inside the tree line and moved off in a wide arc before cutting across to the barn's right side. Dad pressed his hands against the wall and pushed his face to a hole between the boards as though he were a little boy denied entrance. Another gap formed lower to the ground. I took to my knees and peered inside. Night had nearly fallen, giving us cover enough. Above the clearing, bracketed by pines, stood the growing outline of a moon nearly swole.

A throng of hill people danced or stood swaying inside, each shadowed among bars of lantern light. Bales of straw served as pews. They were stacked along the walls in the shape of a great ring with a wide empty space in the middle. In the center I spotted both Harpers blowing into what looked like the plastic recorders we learned to play in the fifth grade. Beside them stood Todd with his guitar, trying to lead them all in a broken rendition of "When We All Get to Heaven." Earl sat near them on the floor, his hands keeping the music's time by tapping the bottom of an overturned oil drum.

And there among them all danced Micky, her lithe body shrouded in a dress so white it gave her the appearance of one visiting from heaven. She moved in seamless rhythm with the great shout of singing around her.

Hair golden and breeze-blown. Her hands moved low to raise the hem of her gown as she leaped and charged, revealing two muscled legs. My heart pounded at the sight as I allowed myself to let go the longing I had felt at the path's end in order that I might be swallowed by another, deep and primal and hungry.

"You see her? Where's your momma?"

"She ain't here."

The song ended. A cheer rose up before dying with the sound of gasping lungs. Micky balanced herself on a bale of straw so everyone could see. The lanterns burned hard against the day's last light. I waited. Hoped. Not once did Micky separate herself from her followers long enough for me to capture her attention, nor could she have even if she'd seen me watching. It is hard to tell what I saw through those boards. It is near impossible to tell what I felt.

Yet as I kneeled in that Shantytown dirt and inhaled the earthen smell of a hundred seasons and ten thousand rains, I could not help but think that if these services in the Pines were a mere cloak drawn down over deceit, as my father held, it was the finest performance I had ever witnessed. The way Micky moved. The command in her voice. The sureness of her every word left me convinced she believed in what she preached, and more — that she would die preaching it.

And you were all so beautiful, Owen.

Beautiful and precious and needed.

Loved. That's the word. Everything was so loved.

And I was so beautiful and loved.

The train. That had changed her. While that was no insight, until that moment I had not known the depth of it. Our night in Simpson's field had altered Micky Dullahan such that she was now the hub of some great wheel of spirit turning over the muck and mire of Shantytown, carrying all who joined her away. The image of her and those faces and lanterns blurred to a memory of standing inside two iron rails that shook and thrummed, glowing rocks and wooden ties that were everything wood could be, spirals within spirals and a symphony so beautiful it hurt. I mourned not that night nor even what I beheld. No. I mourned that it had not changed me at all.

There was no structure to their service. Song and prayer, confession and preaching, ran as one seamless act. A metal bucket was passed among the circle. It ended as a pile of money and vials of pills in Earl's hands, baggies filled with white powder. The pills (some in the plastic amber vials gotten from the pharmacy, many in clear plastic baggies) were carefully set aside and guarded as Earl began counting the bills. It was every drug I knew and many I didn't.

"This is the devil's den," my father said. His fingernails dug into the wood wall. "This is a place of iniquity, just as I knew."

Voices called out above the quaver of singing. They asked for help in their debts and pled that jobs would be spared, petitioned for healing for the sick and comfort for the old, and many were voices I knew but could not place. Each of them Micky answered.

She said from atop her pulpit of chaff and hay, "I hear you all. I do, and I promise I ain't the only one. I know all that's happened to you. You're beat down and struck with worry. Lives spent caught up in a way you never meant and didn't deserve . . ." Her voice trailed off to almost a whisper, one laced with a grief Micky looked unable to name. "But you're free now. Free a all that, and that's where your comfort lies." Her hand reached out. Earl glanced upward before thumbing through more bills. Micky looked like Reverend Sebolt about to give a blessing. Then she said, "Louise, give me that you're holding."

The name caught in my throat. Dad

pressed harder against the wall. The board gave way with a creak. Through those empty spaces we watched Micky being handed a tattered Bible by Louise Townsend.

He whispered, "That's Clancy's wife."

The old woman held a look of near adoration as her fingers brushed Micky's own. Micky held the Bible and began flipping the pages.

"I been trying to read this a lot of late. All these stories and sayings in here. And I confess some a them don't make much sense to me, though plenty does. The parts that don't, I got some help on. But you know what all these words come down to? Only one word it all means? Love. That's it. Love."

Beside her, Earl offered a simple call of "Amen."

Micky shut the book. "I'll amen that too, Daddy."

That's the word she used for the man who beat her, the man who drank what meager money Constance Dullahan possessed and who had helped put her in the grave. He wasn't Earl anymore. He was *Daddy.*

"I don't know some a those words. They're awful fancy and reach a place my head can't go. But I know the last is truth. I seen it. I been telling you all a time is coming when

330

I'll have to put off this my tabernacle. I got a debt needs paying. Sooner or later, that paper's gone be called in. Cain't run from it. I'll be taken."

Todd's voice: "We won't let nobody take you, Michaela."

The calls from Micky's sheep rang in anger rather than song. She stilled them with a raised hand.

"I thank you. I ain't thought much on it really, having too much to do in the now. But I ain't scared." She stepped down from the bale. "And I'll say this. I ain't scared for you neither. Daddy says there was once wolves in these woods long time ago. He says they gone now, but that don't mean y'all are safe. There's other wolves in this old battered world saying you ain't nothing. They mean to keep you penned and quivering like you always been, but you ain't like that no more. You got a power now called truth, and nothing of this world can stand against it. Who will lead us in our words?"

I saw her nod. Saw Micky look off toward her right at a shadow near the far wall and saw her smile, and I knew the voice that shadow made.

My mother said, "We are made of love, from love, for love."

I felt a chill over me. In that darkness, I

trembled.

Daddy turned from the wall. He said, "No. No more."

I faced him. He shoved me to the ground and all but ran toward those two big doors in front. Even as I followed I knew myself too late.

6

Dad took hold of the rusting metal grip and pulled with a strength unknown to me, sliding one side of the doors open with a squeal that brought a silence down where the noise of worship had reigned. By the time I reached him, he was already inside. Those who faced him could not meet his rage. None could stand against him.

"Whore. Whore of Babylon."

He waded past the Shanties nearest, scattering them as he upturned bales of hay and any instrument in his path, and I have no doubt that in my father's mind he was Christ Himself, overturning the tables of the money changers. My mother screamed. Earl shot forward not to protect his daughter, *his little girl,* but so that he might place himself between my father and the pile of money.

Earl said, "You got no right here. This is a peaceful assembly."

Micky looked at me in terror, though she did not yield her place in the center of the barn. She merely moved two steps leftward, where my mother stood cowering.

"Mister Cross," Micky said. Voice even and untouched even by this. "I'm glad you've found us. Won't you take a seat for a spell? Owen?" She looked at me. "Owen, would you like to come up here and help your daddy?"

Dad refused. "Don't need no help from you, whore. Spoutin' your words. Poisonin' these folk. And for what?" He looked over Earl's shoulder and moved the small man out of his way. Set his boot where all that money lay, and those pills. "For this? You people think this here's who the Lord is? You sicken me." He looked at Mom. *"You. Sicken. Me."*

I could not move from my place. There stood a few inside that barn who looked willing to fight should things come to it, yet even those appeared nervous to challenge my father. Not then, not that night. On that night my father looked as he must have once to all those batters he faced, right before he set them down with a fastball unseen but heard.

"We're going home, Greta," he said.

My mother looked a frail thing against the

lantern on the wall closest to her. Beaten and defeated.

Micky said, "Greta, you ain't got to go."

"She does." Dad stepped forward. He reached to take hold of Micky's arm.

I called out, "Don't you touch her."

He turned to me, eyes burning. "What you say to me, Owen?"

"I said don't you touch her. Don't you ever touch her."

The way he stood there. It was an expression beyond hurt and past disappointment. It was a look of humiliation.

"This girl got her claws in you too?" he asked. "That what it is? You shame me. You shame my name more'n her" — pointing to Mom. He looked at all gathered there, strangers he did not know, and I believe my father knew them as witnesses against his own life, himself the persecuted. "I ain't good enough? That what it is? You and your momma look at me and see a failure of all I ever wanted, that what makes you both run off to some harlot what promises you better? I done all I could. Gave her everything. Gave her you. She mocks that by taking up with false prophets? You hate me for wanting more for you than what I got. I drove you out of love."

"Love of what, Daddy? Me, or you?"

Were I a good son, I would have done what my father could not. Gone to him and knelt at his side, touched his arm or head. I would have embraced him and said, *Yes, you are good enough, and whatever pains we both give and receive in life are born of a thirst this world cannot quench, and that is why we strive and suffer and fail.* But I was no good son, and the space between where he stood enraged and mourning and where I kept silent and broken felt as far to travel as the years from birth to death.

He moved around the place Micky stood and into the faint shadows. I heard a scuffle beyond the light. When I saw my father again, it was my mother he touched, dragging her out by the arm. He reached me and let go of her with a small shove, sending my mother into my arms as I had so many times run to hers as a child.

He turned and said to them, "You're all done here. You hear me, Michaela Dullahan? Earl? I'm going straight to town and calling Clancy down here. All that money you got in your house ain't enough for him to charge you with something, all them pills you got laying here will be. Will be an' more. Let's see how your words of love go over in jail."

My mother wept.

Dad took her. To me he said only, "Come on or walk home, I don't care which."

Micky called to him, "Please, Mister Cross," but even she looked to understand there was no use. All of them did. The barn emptied in a rush, some in a flat-out run, knowing that within the hour Clancy and his deputies would invade Shantytown. Earl cried out the service was done. He leapt onto that pile of money and all those drugs, shoving them into what pockets he had as Micky ran forward to plead with them all to stay, don't fear.

I took hold of her and said, "You got to get away from here."

"I ain't leaving. I can't —"

"Go," I said, and then to Earl, "Clancy's coming. You know he is, and he'll know Louise was among you. What is that? Heroin? Cocaine? What you think the sheriff will do?"

Earl remained hunched. "He's right, girl. I'll go the house, get what we need. You finish here and head up the cabin."

"Cabin?" I asked.

"It's an old place up along the Saint Mary's," Micky told me. She took my arm. "One mile east of the waterfall. Owen? One mile east. Take the dump road to the turnoff and follow the trail. Meet me there tomor-

336

row. Promise me."

"I promise."

"Promise."

"I will."

"I'm gone," Earl said. He had all that money, every bit of those pills and powders, and he left without a word. Nothing to me. Not a word to Michaela. His daughter, his little girl. That man walked out of the barn that night with all he needed, leaving behind all he believed could be spared.

There was a time — at that summer's end, in the long years that followed — when I believed had Micky run off then, had she taken off with Earl and left her life behind, things would have turned out different for us all. I somehow doubt that now. Things are written. That is all I can say. The stories of our lives are not our own but are crafted by hands unseen for purposes often unknown on this side of existence. Let us believe otherwise. Let us hold that we alone are our own authors, masters of our fates. Let us believe that, as I once did. I hold different now. We can no more change what is meant than rip out our own pages, and we all live on borrowed time alone.

TOP 8

1

Brosius pops out to Hairston at second, ending the bottom of the seventh with a whimper and sending our guys in from the field. Country says he'll be right back, he'll be out in the field for the bottom of the eighth and he's got to go find his glove. Betsy goes with him. Half of me expects Country to take that bat out to left field with him. Carry it right along with his glove. It doesn't seem so strange. Hitters have such strange attachments to their bats. Like Caldwell down there at the end of the bench, shipping all of his lumber back home to get it prayed over. My own bats remain in Bowie. It doesn't matter what I use, I can't seem to hit anything anymore unless it's a fat batting practice pitch, but even during the years I could hit it didn't matter what I used. The power was in me and not some piece of wood. That's what Dad would say. Then he died, and I began to think maybe the power wasn't in either, but in him. In my father's undying will to see me succeed.

It'll be Hairston, Anderson, and Bordick this inning — three veterans who have all had good games at the plate. I cast an eye to Mike. He does not look at me. The game is winding down. If our manager is planning to use me like Country asked him, it'll have to be soon. The moon sits large over the stadium. Full moon tomorrow. Strawberry moon. I'm reaching into my back pocket before realizing it, holding Micky's first mark in my hand.

Country comes back with Betsy and a glove that's seen more seasons than I've been in professional baseball. He sits and says to me, "Goin' in for Mora in center. Means I'll be up second in the ninth."

"You see DiMaggio's ghost out there, you tell'm I said hey."

"I'll do that. Guess you'll be back in Bowie tomorrow."

"Need to be. Got a new kid on the mound don't know his head from a hole in the ground. I ain't there to catch him, he's like to set the record for walks in a game."

"That what you do down there? Hold a pitcher's hand?"

"What any catcher does."

Hairston digs in against Knight.

"How long you been stuck in Double-A, son?"

" 'Bout five years."

Country grunts. It's a low sound that I don't think he wants me to hear. "Double-A's good ball. Maybe the best ball the minors can give you. They say it's Triple-A, but it ain't. That's just a stopping point. Guys on their way up here to the Show or ones trying to get over an injury. Double-A? That's where guys are still hungry."

Hairston lines a single to center.

"Came up hot," I say. "Good stick, good arm. Arm's still there. And I got the smarts, won't nobody say otherwise. But I think my bat's gone."

"Didn't look like it earlier today. I's standing there watching you take BP. So was Mike."

"BP ain't major-league pitching. No. Bat's gone. That was my ticket. Catchers are a dime a dozen. Smart ones too. One that can hit?" I shake my head. "Ain't too many like that. Think they're keeping me around for my head alone now. You know, ease all those hotshot pitchers they got on up the ladder. I got to Bowie thinking that was my door to the Show. Turns out the only door is me, and all I can do is let everybody else walk through it."

Brady Anderson is up. He's got two hits in four trips to the plate, which means he'll sleep good tonight. Yessir, Brady will kick back in his fancy hotel room and lay his head on a fine silk pillow and wake up tomorrow knowing he'll go to work at Yankee Stadium.

"What happened, then?" Country asks. "Where'd your hittin' go?"

I smile a little, but it's an unhappy grin, and I give him one word: "Grave."

2

It was my second year in Bowie when Dad's stomach pain began. He passed it off as bad food and a cranky nature, which neither me nor Mom could argue against. Nothing to be concerned with. But it persisted off and on through the winter and got worse that spring of '98.

By late summer the doctors discovered it wasn't Dad's stomach at all. We talked at the least three times a week, him wanting to know how the season was going and how our pitching was holding up, me wanting to know how he was doing and never getting anything close to a solid answer. Dad always did protect me. Didn't matter I was a twenty-six-year-old man playing minor league ball and living on his own, to him I would forever be the little boy too small for the big world. I'd wait until his talking was done and then ask to speak to Mom, who would take the telephone into a quieter spot in their apartment and tell me the truths I needed. It was his gallbladder, and it needed taken out. The surgery had already been scheduled. No, of course I didn't need to take time away from the team. A simple enough procedure. Dad would be in the hospital a day at the most, and you know he'd be upset if you stopped playing ball just to come and sit with him, Owen.

We were in Trenton for a three-game set against the Thunder in early August. I called early that Friday morning to wish Dad well. Only some of me worried. He was Paul Cross, after all, the man who walked with a stiff lip and straight back even when he'd mopped those high school floors. I could not allow the possibility that someday his body would give out, as all bodies must. He moved our talk toward how I was playing. We were almost a dozen games out of first. My average hovered around .260. He told me not to get caught up with standings and focus instead on my average and handling the pitchers. The minors were all about making a name for yourself and that's what I was doing, so I was to worry about me and me alone. No room for any other concerns. I told him I'd work on that and left the number to the stadium in case anybody needed me, then I told my father I loved him for the first time since I was a boy. He said quit being a pansy, all he was doing was driving down to the doctor. I'd learned long before it was the tone of Dad's words rather than the words themselves that spoke for him. He was appreciative, and he was scared.

The surgery began at the University of Virginia Medical Center before noon on the ninth of August, 1998, near the time we began batting practice. Jim Blackburn was our manager and still is, a burly man we all called Skip. He'd spent a few years catching in the majors and had taken a shine to me, spent much of those past days sharing the story of his sister-in-law having her own gallbladder out and coming out on the other end of it fine, though as mean as ever and twice as ugly. He watched from behind the cage while I took my swings. I stepped out after the last pitch and took in the sparse crowd already in the seats. My heart stuttered.

Alone down the right field line sat Micky.

I stood there with a bat in my hands as the next guy jumped in, Skip saying, "Twenty's all you get, Owen, stop being such a hog," through what sounded like a tunnel of wind as Micky's face met mine. It wasn't her out there. Couldn't be, I knew, unless she had come back to me by means of the very magic with which she'd left. She did not speak to me from that distance but through her eyes, which were soft with sadness. I knew that sorrow as not her own, but for me. For my father. I knew.

By all accounts Dad's procedure started out as routinely as promised. At some point during the first inning he developed a circulation problem to his heart. A stroke resulted. Doctors did all they could. It was Mom who finally got hold of someone at the stadium at the start of the seventh inning. Skip pulled me from the game and said they'd induced a coma. I got on the next plane for Virginia, too late. Somewhere over Pennsylvania, my father passed from this world to the next. He was only fifty-two years old. I can only hope he saw a light at his last breath and not the darkness that always chased him.

I stayed a week in Charlottesville to bury him and keep Mom company. She mourned his passing as a loving wife would, the suddenness of Dad's departure leaving her in a shock borne out in a succession of painful reminders that she was now alone: making too much food for breakfast and supper, washing the dirty clothes he'd left in the laundry, the daily ritual of going through letters and junk mail delivered to their apartment in Paul Cross's name. His photos stared from walls and mantels and the tops of dressers. I would be cleaning the apartment and find bits and pieces of my father everywhere. Change fallen from his pocket into the cushion of his chair; a bit of whisker caught in the blades of his razor; how his smell lingered on his side of the closet, seeping into the gray shirts and blue pants he continued to wear in his retirement.

I found an old scrapbook tucked beneath his Bible and a pile of papers in his bottom bedside drawer. The cover was cheap cardboard washed in a fading and peeling red. Inside were photos and newspaper articles glued to the pages. Me in Little League, me in Babe Ruth and varsity, stories from the *Record* and papers in and around Youngstown, my baseball card. Among them I found a crumpled sheet of paper pulled from the trash. Written in Dad's hand was *440' measured. Harpers found it. Sign and take to Pr. Taylor in morning. Third deck Yankee Stadium.* An arrow was drawn from the bottom of the page that had once pointed to a baseball.

"He was proud of you," Mom told me over supper two days after Dad had gone, me eating a plate of spaghetti I knew she'd made for him. "He wouldn't allow himself to show it. Sometimes I think he didn't know how. Some men are raised to believe in only two emotions, Owen." She held up one finger, "Anger." Then another, "Happiness. The world can be boiled down to one or the other in their minds. The rest gets so muddled I guess they think it's better kept to themselves."

She hurt, and I knew she would for a long while. Yet there remained a strength in my mother I could not gather within myself, pain mixed with faith that Dad's passing was a link in a chain wound about all of our lives, anchored to a faraway point where she would meet him once more. Many times during that week I paused in awe of her faith, wondering where Mom had found it. I would think back to that barn deep in Shantytown and ask myself if my father's death would have broken her had she not found Micky during those few weeks in the summer of 1990.

I did not fare so well. Dad's passing served

as a reminder of those things we leave undone in life, and the many last times that pass without our notice. Once, when I was about eight or nine, my father picked me up and held me in his arms over some simple thing, to say hello after a day's work or to help me place the star atop the Christmas tree. He set me down and would never pick me up again. Inside a rundown campus apartment in Youngstown, Ohio, he said he loved me for the last time. We shared our last beer together when he and Mom helped move my things from Bluefield to Bowie. His final words to me were, *Quit being a pansy, all I'm doing's driving down to the doctor.* I still wonder how different our words would have been had Dad and I known what would happen. Sometimes I think we would have talked long that morning on things felt but never said. Other times I imagine our conversation going unchanged. The hardest things to say are to the ones we love most.

We buried him in a plot at the Riverview Cemetery with a clear view of the Rivanna. Many from Camden paid their respects. Jeffrey and Stephanie came, along with Clancy. Abigail Sebolt sat with Mom and me as the reverend gave the service. Rupert arrived. Coach Stevens. Principal Taylor. Mom spent much of the time turned toward the crowd rather than the casket she said held the bones of her husband but not his soul, searching all those familiar faces for the girl she believed had gone into hiding. Yet Micky did not make a return that day, not even to me.

I returned to Bowie and tried righting what was fast becoming a bad season. By the last of August, my average had dipped to .250. Skip waited another month and another twenty-five points shaved off my average before summoning me into his office. He called it a pep talk. To me it was more a come-to-Jesus meeting with a thinly veiled threat of doom underneath. "Batters are a dime a dozen," he said, "but good catchers ain't. You need to get your head right and show us something, son. It won't take much. Seen it happen to guys who've been down in the farm a few years. They get to losing their passion after a while, coasting along. You can't do that. Show me how much you want this, and I'll help you all I can."

I nodded through the whole thing, said all the right words. What I couldn't tell Skip was I still had that drive, had it stronger than ever, and whatever was wrong with me had nothing to do with my head being in the wrong place. My heart was what worried me, like something between Dad's dying and my return to Double-A had poked so many holes in it that I heard a whistle with every beat. I didn't want to let him down, though. That was the thing. Skip, but Dad especially. Those next weeks I went on something of a tear and got my average back up to a somewhat respectable .263 before I tweaked a hammy while trying to outrun a throw to first in Binghamton. Skip didn't want to put me on the DL. It would maybe be taken the wrong way by the boys upstairs. I sat for close to a week before he was left with no other choice, telling the reporters I was listed as "day-to-day."

Really, aren't we all?

3

It is a quiet inning in spite of Hairston's leadoff single. Anderson works a walk that puts two on with none out, but that is where our rally ends. Bordick pops to short and Richard K's on four pitches. Conine lofts a weak pop-up to Soriano at second. Not once does Mike turn my way. An inning and a half. That's the only bit remaining. One more Orioles bat and three more outs.

Country taps my leg with his glove. He says, "Time to go to work, Hillbilly. You keep an eye on Betsy for me? She's my ticket to Cooperstown."

He grins and sets the bat against me, rises and moves off to the dugout steps. Mora, the man Country replaces in left, winks at me as he passes. As he goes I see Mike take one stride from the spot where he's stood all game. He looks at me and ponders as if to speak, then merely turns and tells Johnson to go get 'em.

Bottom 8

1

It was silence that woke me from a broken sleep the morning after my father burst into Micky's church, early sun through the slats of the blinds and a weariness in my body I had never known. The house felt empty. I struggled from bed and eased open my bedroom door. The kitchen table lay bare. No smell of pancakes or scrambled eggs greeted me, not even the thick aroma of Dad's coffee in the air. It's the small things you take for granted that become very big things when they're gone. Beneath the unanswered questions and secret fears of our everyday beats the thin pulse of tiny rituals that serve to root us.

I had gotten home the night before to the noise of my parents arguing in their bedroom. That morning the comforter on Mom and Dad's bed was pulled too far to the right and a single pillow left crooked —

Mom had slept alone, and not well. A bit of her perfume lingered like a spirit. Dad's wallet and keys were gone from the dresser. Gone to work, I assumed. Dad doing all he could to pretend nothing in our lives had changed.

My first thoughts were of Micky, left waiting for me with her scoundrel of a father in some abandoned cabin somewhere along the Saint Mary's River where it skirted the outer edges of Shantytown. But I could not go to her just yet. Already in my mind I had begun to concoct a final way to bring her back to me, though it relied on the judgment of one person in town. And there was my mother to deal with as well. Mom would have to be first. I showered and dressed with the radio loud on my nightstand. At some point between songs from the rock station out of Charlottesville I heard the DJ mention something about the moon tonight, big and bright and the color of strawberries.

2

The fear as I drove to the library was I'd chosen the wrong place — maybe Mom had gone back to the Pines instead, and whatever meaning she had found there. But when I pulled around back of the two-story brick building I found her car in its accustomed place. It was sameness she needed now, no less than Dad and me.

I went through the back entrance. The break room off the checkout counters was empty, as well as the little closet where books were collected in bins before being reshelved. What people had scattered themselves among the aisles paid me little mind. Mom was nowhere. I was about to ask for her when I scanned the open stacks along the second floor and saw her standing by the railing next to a cart stuffed with books. I raised a hand and climbed the stairs. She met me at the landing. There were so many words for us to say. All the books around us could not contain them all. Yet we stood facing one another in gathering silence, each too afraid to speak first.

"You lied to me," I said. "To Dad. I can understand you not telling him where you were going, but me? You know I love her."

"Which is why I couldn't say." She touched the side of my face with her hand. The feel of her cool skin soothed me. "Michaela told me everything. Telling you I was going off to Shantytown in the evenings would only anger you more, Owen. You already think that church took the girl you love away. You'd only think it'd taken your momma as well."

"Ain't a church down there, Ma. It's a barn. And what you all were doing in there —"

"Was something you and your father can't understand."

She sighed and let go my face, then guided me away from the steps and the prying eyes of those below. Her gaze lingered over the stacks. The rustle of papers. How the early sun poured through the windows in clean white lines to lay squares of light on the floor.

"I've always liked working here," she said. "Don't think I ever told you that. It's a small job that don't pay anything, but that's okay. The people are nice, and it's quiet. But there was something more than those that I never could pin down until I learned what happened to Michaela. And to you."

"Nothing happened to me."

"Tell me that again." She sighed. "You never could lie, Owen. And besides, I know the truth. So does she. You're only too afraid to admit it. Michaela, though? That girl ain't afraid. She loves you. I always knew that but didn't know how much. Should make you feel good, knowing someone so touched by God thinks of you in such high esteem."

"You say that like she's some kind a holy woman. She ain't. You'd seen what me and

Daddy did at Earl's house, you'd think different."

"I wouldn't. All that they got is for others, Owen. Is that so hard for you to believe? That people are good deep down, that they can change? You speak of what you don't know and what you refuse to see. You want that girl to be who she was. You need her to be no different from her daddy, because that way you don't have to change. But it's not like that. They're not like that. Something wonderful happened to Michaela, and all she wants is to speak of it to all who will listen. Why is that such a horrible thing?"

"I'm trying to get you to listen to me, Mom. Micky isn't what you think."

"I'm trying to get you to listen. Your daddy won't. You know how many times I tried telling him? Or you? But neither of you'd ever hear it. Didn't matter a whit what I thought. It pained me to lie, Owen. It carved a gully right through me. I fought it for days until I could fight it no more. Something in me drew myself to that girl. I'd hear the women here at nights, the ones come up from Shantytown to clean. They'd talk of the most amazing things Michaela shared, and it filled my heart. It sounded so right. So after she and Earl come to church this last time, I went one night. I'd never felt so at home anyplace. Michaela told me her story. She made me see."

"So she speaks and everybody in the Pines listens? They just open up their pocketbooks and give over what little they got? How much money you give Earl, Momma?"

Her jaw clenched.

"I'm just trying to understand what's going on here. Why you did this. And Louise Townsend? How'd she end up there?"

"I told Louise. I told others, but they didn't come. Or wouldn't. But Louise did."

"Can you stand there for a minute and try to see things from our side? Not like you just up and decided to turn Methodist. This is something way past that. You snuck off behind our backs. You knew what Dad would say, the trouble it'd cause. But you still chose Michaela over your own family."

"Like Alan Sebolt chose his church over his family? Like Clancy chose his job over Louise? Like you and your daddy both chose some future that's not even here yet over me? Because that's what you both love, Owen. Over all else. Day in and day out ever since you were a boy, baseball and nothing but baseball. I watch you and your father from the kitchen window, and I'm glad the two of you have something to share. But what would either of you share with me? My family was my love. I poured my very being into caring for you and him and us, never to get a return."

"So what you did was all your way of getting back?"

"No, it was my way of salvaging what life I had left. Michaela showed me the truth. I can love my family hard, give them all I have, but only if my soul is bent toward higher places. The heart is a compass, and it only knows where it is if it can point true north. Mine never did. All that needle in me did was spin and spin. I got lost. Now I'm found."

She looked about the room before us and then downstairs, taking it all in.

"You know there's books in this building first written down in times so old we know next to nothing about them? Others so new the ink's barely dried on the page. I spent part of this morning downstairs shelving fiction and poetry. Now I'm up here with a stack of history books and science books and books on art. I'll put them all in their places and there they'll sit until the next person comes along and takes them home. One day not long after I started going to hear Michaela, I was standing close to where we're standing now and happened to look down on all those books. Tens of thousands of them. Any subject you can think of. You know what I realized? No matter what story they told or what thing they talked about, all of these books ask the same questions: Why are we here, what is this all about, and what are we all gonna live for? And then I realized I'd always been asking those questions too.

"What I'm telling you is Michaela Dullahan found those answers. We believe that with all our hearts. You, me, your father, everyone — we are here from love, for love, to love, and that love is what sets us free. She ain't Christ returned, Owen. But I will look to that girl for wisdom before I will look to anyone else made of flesh, because I believe in who she is. I will fight for her. And I know you would too if your courage wouldn't fail. She told me once your heart is divided. You want what you don't need and need what you don't want, and one day you will have to face it. That's what Michaela said. She said that day was far off for you but she still mourned it because she won't be there to help you. I told your father that story last night. He wouldn't hear it."

Nor would I on that June morning so long ago. But I remember it now these many years later as Country stands out in the left field grass playing toss with some kid in the right-center field stands, some boy in a Yankees cap who is having the absolute best three minutes of his life, having a catch with Bobby Kitchen himself, a man only forty good swings away from having his plaque in Cooperstown, and I remember Momma's words. I remember them well.

"You need to keep away from Shantytown, Ma. It's time you stay home and try to fix things with Dad. He thinks he's failed us."

"He's not failed anything. Your father is a good man, but so wounded. And for that he's got to know I'm coming back because I love him. I love you. But I'm not coming back the woman I was. I made my choice, Owen. I hold you both closer to me than any people in this world, and I know you both love me in the best way you can. But there is another love greater than anything you can give me. That is my true north, and there is where my heart must point most of all. I don't expect you to understand any of that now, you or your father. But I hope you'll both understand it someday, because she's right. Michaela is right. You'll have to choose, and that choice will mean everything."

3

We never did have what could be termed a modern law enforcement presence in Camden. It was Clancy, one secretary, and three deputies, one of which was the secretary's husband and the other two some sort of Clancy's kin, all shoved into a building near the mayor's office no bigger than Mrs. Hamrick's f lower shop. Things were hopping when I went in. Phones ringing, people waiting. The secretary said Clancy was busy but let me through anyway. It helps when you can hit a baseball 440 feet to win a state championship. It also didn't hurt that I had in my possession some information regarding some unfortunate events in Shantytown from the night before, which the sheriff would find valuable.

Clancy's office was a glass cube near the cells in back. I found him behind his desk with the phone against his ear. His uniform shirt was a wrinkled mess, one collar pointed straight up so it brushed against a snarl of white uncombed hair. He waved me in and hung up the phone. I stood in the doorway instead, not wanting to be there long.

"Know you busy," I said.

"More tired. Long night. Reckon you know something about that, according to your daddy."

"Need a word is all, Sheriff." That's what I called him — not Mister Townsend or even Clancy, though either name would have sufficed. I'd known him for all my years in Camden through either church or baseball. Shoot, him and Louise had been over to the house for supper more times than I could count. "How's Louise?"

"Bawling. What you think? She leaves the house last night saying she's off to play bingo at the VFW, next thing I know your daddy's callin' me in a panic to say Louise is down in Shantytown worshippin' with the likes of Earl Dullahan. And *more,* Earl's got him a mess a illegal drugs down there right in the middle of 'em all." He leaned back, making the chair beneath him scream for mercy.

" 'Course it wasn't nothing there when me and some deputies got there. No drugs, just a few Shanties along with Louise, milling about wanting to explain it all. Wanting to say how it was all your daddy's fault. But it was some pills there, Owen. Earl'd run off, and Michaela, but they didn't manage to get everything. And what them pills was wasn't prescription. They's illegal through and through, and I can't keep it quiet neither. That's the thing. I know your momma's drawn up in it, and for that I'm sorry. But for the Cross family this is all naught but an embarrassment. For the Townsends it's a scandal. I'm the *sheriff,* Owen. And to hear what some is saying, my own wife's mixed up in some hillbilly drug ring."

"That ain't what was going on down there. You know that."

"Don't know that. Not until I round up the people I mean to. Louise won't say a word against none of 'em. I got everybody I can out looking for Earl and Michaela both, but they done holed themselves up somewhere nobody can find them. Or they both in somebody's woodshed or closet out in Shantytown getting protected. I got to bring them in at least for questioning. It'll cost me so far as Louise goes. That woman says Michaela Dullahan's some kind of Second Coming of Christ Almighty. But it's a line I dance between town and home, Owen, and I got to end up on one side or the other."

"Know you're right." I leaned a hand to the door. "Louise have such high regard for Earl as she does his daughter?"

"What you mean?"

"I mean maybe you should leave Michaela alone, Sheriff."

"It'd be hard to do. To hear most talk, that girl's the start a this whole mess."

"Not the church, though. That weren't her doing, not right off. All Michaela did was want to talk to folk. That barn's been out in the Pines for how many years? Sitting there falling down. Who bought the wood and nails to fix it up?"

"Earl did," Clancy said.

"Who comes to town every week to get out all the money those Shanties put into an account from their welfare and disability? And whose name's to that account?"

Clancy went quiet. I'd made my point with more ease than I knew I was able.

"Comes to that church, Sheriff, it's Earl Dullahan's fingers all over it. What's Louise say about him?"

"Says Earl's changed," he muttered. "But it's shades, not colors."

"Talked to my mom this morning. She said not a word of Earl, but she spoke of Michaela like a saint."

"You believe that?"

I shook my head. "Nosir, I do not. I don't think Michaela ever meant harm in anything she's done. But I know about that money. She aims to share it all with everybody. That way no one in the Pines gets left out."

"Sounds like communism to me."

"Whatever it is, it's a pile. And it's in Earl's hands."

Clancy's eyes narrowed. He asked, "How you know that?" and nearly caught me.

"Mom said. Shanties get what checks the gover'ment sends them, they cash it at the bank, then turn around and deposit it into Earl's account. Earl gets the cash and keeps it at the house. Michaela divvies it up."

"Makes her just as liable. Just as guilty."

"I understand there needs to be an end to all this, Sheriff. And I know justice needs met. But you got to leave Michaela alone. Them Shanties think she's touched by God. Some in town too. Your wife. My momma."

Clancy made a face like he tasted something sour. "Touched by God."

"Truth is that's how they see things. You bring Michaela in, you'll stew a war. Bring in Earl, that might be enough to settle things."

"Earl's gone."

"You ain't looked every place."

"You know something you ain't telling me, Owen?"

"Nothing more than anybody else. We were all friends enough. Hung out at school in a little group. Things get said sometimes that pass over until something happens that causes you to remember. Call it a hunch."

"Then you need tell me. This ain't no youth group scavenger hunt. It's a law enforcement matter."

The phone rang. Clancy didn't pick up.

"All I want's to keep everybody safe, Sheriff. Same as you. Maybe I can find Earl and maybe I can't. But if I do, I get Earl here or I call and tell you where he is, you got to promise you'll leave Michaela out of it. It'll be a hard enough road for her as it is, momma in the ground and daddy in jail."

"Could be you're right on that one. Keep me outta Louise's rage, leastways."

The ringing kept on. In the clamor of voices and bodies out front, I heard his secretary say, "You gone get that, Clancy?"

I waited for our sheriff's answer.

He said, "You let me know you find him. Pass word to Michaela if you can. Tell her Earl's all I want, but she'll have to help me get him. Deal?"

"Deal."

Clancy sat forward and pulled the phone free, barking into it once more.

4

The bottom of the eighth starts out well enough. Johnson gets Oliver on four pitches, sending the Yankees catcher back to the dugout with his bat on his shoulder. But now the Yanks are beginning to rally. Soriano steps up and doubles to right center and Country can't flag the ball down, lets it roll all the way to the wall. Knoblauch follows with a shot to near that exact place. The ball looks like a rocket off the bat. Country's caught on his heels. He takes off too late and lays out in a dive, but the ball misses his glove by a good two feet. Richard tracks it down from right field and fires the ball in, but not before Knoblauch is standing at second. Soriano has scored, it's 8–2.

Mike looks worried enough that he tells the pitching coach to get on the phone to the bullpen. It's ghosts that's got into our manager's mind and ghosts I'm thinking of now, but it's Country I'm seeing. That man of forty years, young for the world but ancient for the game, getting himself up off the grass and limping back to his spot in center. Shaking his head like he should have gotten that ball. Knowing he would have if it was ten years ago.

5

How I would find a single cabin away in the hills and hollers beyond Shantytown was a question I didn't entertain until I reached the wilderness. I had only the general description Micky had provided the night before to guide me: it was along the Saint Mary's River, and it was approximately one mile east of the waterfall.

The problem was I had been to Saint Mary's exactly once in my life, this when I was all but kidnapped by Reverend Sebolt to attend a "youth spirit camp" that involved little more than a lot of sitting around and praying.

No hint of a waterfall presented itself in my fuzzy memory, meaning I'd be all but going blind into that stretch of wilderness, which only added to another complication that loomed even greater: I never liked the woods. Sounds crazy, a boy raised up among the Blue Ridge with no desire whatsoever to go tromping through every square foot of it, but those tall sapphire walls and all they held never brought me an ounce of comfort. It wasn't so much the ghost stories told me by Travis and Jeffrey when I first moved to town, haints and witches and angry Indian spirits doomed to walk the hollers. Was the breadth of it all, dark forests and wide meadows that stretch on for miles in the hundreds, threatening to swallow you whole — that's what always bothered me. When you're alone in the mountains you have none but yourself for company. There is no single distraction, only a grandeur that turns thought inward and makes you consider your own self and place. Never once did I find benefit in such a thing. I've always been the last person I wanted to know.

Nor did I have much interest in knowing myself that day, given what I had decided needed done. One way or another, I was going to find Earl Dullahan and hand him over to Clancy. And for one reason only: to save Micky. To get her away from Camden with me and preserve a future we were meant to share no matter who said otherwise, whether her or the Lord God Himself.

Saint Mary's was little more than a wide stream born among the mountaintops, a neglected cousin of the wide Maury that flowed through town. I followed the trail as best I could and told myself all would be well so long as I kept water in sight. The day was hot and muggy, the bugs fierce. I saw no wildlife larger than a wild turkey that scampered at my coming. The way was littered with the same smooth river stones Micky would leave as marks on our hilltop. A crow called from the trees. I had no way of knowing how long I would be in those woods and so occupied myself with the days and nights ahead rather than the day and night before me.

So much of my childhood was spent in such dreaming. The past was unchangeable, better forgotten, the present often boring toil. Yet my tomorrows shone like lights on some far hill, offering me guidance and direction. I walked a path that wound not through a forest patch but through days and weeks and months. Seeing myself at Youngstown State, coming back from class to an apartment that then existed only in my mind. Opening the door to a rank smell and Micky fanning smoke from the oven because she'd burnt our food, which I would eat anyway and ask for seconds. Scraping by because that's what college kids did, but only for a year. Two at the most. I'd get drafted, sign a big contract, a few hundred thousand at least and maybe even a million, guys signed for that much all the time. Camden no more than a memory, our last summer there lost among all the others come before. And at night we would lie in our nakedness, Micky's body pressed against mine.

My ears popped as the stream climbed higher. A roaring sound wormed its way through the thick trees ahead. I left the path and traveled down to the bank where the swift current swirled into deep pools of a blue so dark it looked like trapped night. Ahead of me lay a wall of white. Time had sheared away that part of the mountain, leaving a drop of what must have been fifty feet from which water captured near the peaks tumbled onto the mossy rocks below. I had reached the waterfall, and with it an end to my reverie.

The last bit I traveled was the longest, made harder by the June heat and the rough terrain. Maybe a mile I walked, could have been two or closer to three. I would have missed the cutoff completely were my head not hung so low. The trail pointed ahead clear and winding but branched off in little more than a worn place through the leaves toward my left. Far into the trees I spied a break where a stack of hewn logs formed something of a wall. *Cabin* was a loose term. All I saw of the place was a one-room windowless shack, its leaning wooden door cocked open to catch the sun.

It occurred to me Earl was likely armed. Not only must he suspect he was now wanted, but there was all the money he'd taken from the house as well. I backed away and spun in all directions, making sure I hadn't been spotted, then swept closer in a wide arc. I'd call out. Make up something that would get Micky away from there, then I'd call Clancy.

I kept low, just in case. "Hey to the cabin."

No answer came. I shouted again and set to counting, moving only when I'd reached twenty. The cabin was empty. A rough table sat in the center of the dirt floor. On it were two cans of beans and an empty Coke bottle. The radio beside them was on but low and tuned to static. For a moment I thought I had the wrong place, this was some squatter here or a moonshiner guarding a nearby still.

"He's gone," said a voice behind me.

She stood by the door looking harried and worn in a white dress soiled by dust. Lines were etched along Micky's forehead and the corners of her mouth, drawn tight into the first convulsions of weeping. It looked as though she'd lived a lifetime through the night.

"I can't find him, Owen. I been looking all day down along the river, but Earl's not come."

"The money?" I asked.

Micky shook her head, freeing a tear. It glimmered at her cheek before sliding down the side of her neck. "I think they got him."

"Didn't nobody get him. I was just to Clancy's. He's got everybody looking, Micky, but Earl ain't nowhere close. He's run off with that money."

The meaning of my statement slammed into Micky's chest with as much force as it did mine, though for differing reasons.

"Daddy wouldn't do that."

Wouldn't he? That had always been Earl Dullahan's way, trying to keep a step in front of whatever chased him. Always keeping close because he had no funds to flee. But that wasn't true now, was it? Now Earl had thousands.

"That's money for the people," Micky said. "It ain't his to do with. What's going on in the Pines? Is folk scared?"

"Earl don't count for nothing right now, and neither does anybody else. I got a way out for us."

" 'Course it counts." Her head began swinging in some unending *No*, arms clasped at her breasts.

"It don't. Listen to me, Micky."

"Them people's hurting, Owen. They trusted me to care for them. That money's gone, won't nobody have a dime in Shantytown."

Her head turning *No* and *No*, Micky not even listening to what I had to say. The picture that flashed to me was the time Mom and Dad took me to the Natural Bridge Zoo and the bear they had, a big brown bear stuck in a cage no bigger than it, shaking its head *NoNoNo* against those metal bars as its mind and soul fell bit by bit to darkness, and how I cried all the way

372

home and so had Mom.

"Listen." I went to her. Micky held to me like she was sliding off an edge. "We'll find him, okay? Clancy said. He's got his guys looking for Earl everywhere, and Earl's all they want. Me and you can still leave out of here. All we got to do is wait out the summer, then we'll be off to Youngstown and everything new."

Micky's head stilled. "What?"

"What we always said. You and me together, no more hiding."

"You still want me to go away with you."

"Ain't nothing left for you here now. You know that. Those Shanties will be after your head once they find out Earl took their money."

"All those people are counting on me, Owen. I can't let them down now. I don't have much time left."

"You got all the time if you just play it smart."

"You don't understand."

I could feel the anger rising in me, all of it and not just over her. Over Mom's lies and Dad's endless needling, over the whole cursed summer. "I understand. You're choosing a bunch of poor people who always been that way, who always *will* be that way, over me. Over everything I've

373

always loved."

"Everything you always loved will be the thing that breaks you. Don't you see that? The treasure you hoard is going to ruin your heart someday, Owen. You love what can't love you *back*."

I picked up the table and heaved it against the wall, breaking off the wooden top held by a single nail. Micky screamed and shrank away as it crashed onto the cot and released a snowfall of dust into the sunlight by the door. I felt no better a man than her father.

"Always been there for you, Mick." I couldn't look at her. "Spent all the life I can remember climbing up a hill just to see your face. Because I love you like I love no other. And now here I stand wanting a simple answer you won't give me."

"Give me your answer first. Tell me what you seen at that train. Speak it true, then stand there and say you don't understand why I can't go with you. I got to stay for when Daddy comes back. And my church needs me. It's the first thing I ever had in life to give me purpose, and I won't leave it."

"I'm trying to save you. Why won't you let me?"

Her head turned, one side and the other forming a single *No*.

"That's the thing, Owen. You still think you speak to the girl I was 'stead a the girl I am. That girl's somebody you could save, but not this one. This one's been saved already." She came to me, held my hands. "Don't matter what I want now. I can't go with you. God don't want me to. He says I got to stay because my time's drawn near."

"God don't talk to you," I said.

Micky delivered her line with the smooth elegance of practice: "God speaks to everybody. It's just so few listen."

I pushed past her, wanting air. Wanting bright sun and wide skies and a forest that swallowed me whole.

Micky called after me, "Where you going?"

"Stay here. Too many people looking for you. Clancy's got your barn all taped off. Shanties can get along fine without you for a while. So you just sit here and wait on Earl" — mumbling the last, because I knew even then Earl Dullahan would never be seen around Camden again. "Meet me at the hill tonight."

"Why?"

"Do you love me?" I stopped midway back to the path along the river, forcing myself to face her. "Can you at least tell me that?"

She stood in the small doorway, straddling

375

an edge of light and dark. "Of course I love you, Owen. I always have."

I wished I could believe her. Part of me did. The other half — the heart inside me that had given so much to Michaela Dullahan and gained so little — was simply tired. Never in my life had I reason to doubt what Micky felt for me. Never once had I asked her to prove her love. I would have that day were I not so afraid of her answer. But I knew as I left that old cabin and met the path leading home I would have her answer soon, finally and for certain. Whether she loved me as I loved her, or if our love was but one more thing meant to be left in childhood.

Either way, I would know.

6

Jeter is up and what remains of the crowd is on their feet, the stands filled with calls and yells and screams for their captain, calling forth the ghosts. Mike goes once more to the dugout phone. He plugs an ear with his finger and looks at me, making me look away. In the vastness of Yankee Stadium's center field stands Country. He pounds a fist into his glove, seeming to will the next ball his way, as all the best ones do. Johnson settles down enough to get Jeter on a fly ball to right. Richard calls off Country for the ball and fires his throw in to Hairston, keeping Knoblauch at second.

It's two down but Mike has seen enough. He makes the long walk out to the mound and holds his left arm aloft, touching it with his right as he signals the bullpen. The infield gathers in a huddle. Fordyce slaps Johnson on the butt as the bullpen doors open. It's B. J. Ryan coming out — a good call, bringing in a lefty to face the left-handed David Justice coming up next. Though the game seems far out of the Yankees' reach, it does not feel such a way. It is certainly not far enough out of reach that Mike Singleton will chance sending a rookie catcher up to the plate in the top of the ninth out of nothing more than pity and a favor to a grizzled veteran.

I take Country's bat in my hands, hoping the feel of Betsy can calm my nerves. The polished black wood holds the nicks and scars of hits untold. I flex my hands around the handle. Wiggle the bat to marvel at its balance. Country is still out there and still pounding his glove. Only once does he pause to look out at the crowd before and behind him. It reminds me of the way I must have looked years ago standing inside Cleveland Stadium.

Mike hands the ball off to Ryan. He turns and makes his way to the dugout and he spots me holding Country's bat. I let the bat wave in my hands. When it stills, my eyes settle on a small imperfection at the very top of the barrel. I move the bat closer for a better look. Rub my thumb across the spot. Where the wood should be smooth I find a ridge instead, sanded but not enough, and notice the grain there does not match the wood around it. I rub the spot again. Country isn't watching.

I reach beside me for a bottle of water left by one of the players and open the top, putting my finger over the opening as I turn it over. With the water I make a swipe over the circle of Betsy's top. The dirt clears away, leaving a smaller circle with the diameter of a dime in the center.

Fordyce lets one of Ryan's pitches get by him. The ball reaches the backstop, getting Knoblauch to third. I don't care because I cannot peel my stare off what I'm holding in my hand, Betsy, and the knowledge I hold as well — Bobby Kitchen, Country, the man *SportsCenter* calls the Kentucky Krusher, is using a corked bat. He's bored a hole into this Betsy's cap (*And how many before? I wonder. How long has Country been doing this?*) and hollowed out the barrel. One inch, that's all it takes, one inch around and ten inches deep. Fill it with cork, glue a plug to the end. Sand it all down and add a bit of paint. Rough it up real good. No one will know. No one.

Bat like that can add twenty feet to a fly ball and two million to a contract. Turns outs into home runs.

Gets you off the beaten path and onto the bypass to Cooperstown.

I set the bat down beside me. Can't touch it. Can't think. Justice singles, sending Knoblauch home and narrowing our lead, yet I am too overcome by what I know to care about the game. I am not angry; there is no room in me for righteous indignation. Country will be judged should he be caught, but he will not be judged by me. Let the papers find out. Let the reporters squeal. Let the fans turn their backs to him. I know. A man will do most anything in this world if he thinks it will get him what he loves most.

He will do it every time.

7

Nothing of the entire summer stood so plain to me as when I left Micky begging my name from the shadowed doorway of Earl's cabin. I knew my choice. It arrived with the clearness of sight restored, the way a hard cry will wash your eyes and leave the world glassy and cloudless after. The cost demanded was great. The price meant nothing. Nor could I claim any longer the thing I decided to do would be done in love's name alone.

Could love kindle such rage? Provoke me toward such action? No — what I felt for Micky was not so flaccid a thing as love but something beyond, more alive, savage as a blade's edge.

I would make her see that a life with me offered far more than a life mired inside Shantytown. What purpose Micky may have carried into the world was woven with my own. Why had she forgotten that? How could she have misplaced what we had always known: that apart we were but half a person, but together we made a whole? Isn't that what we all long for at the end of things? To be whole?

By the time I reached home it was close to five in the evening, meaning I had to hurry and be gone before Mom and Dad were let out of work. The note I left was enough to let them know I wouldn't be back until late, no need waiting up. I changed into old clothes I could throw away, put an extra pair of jeans and a fresh T-shirt into a bag. The only things I needed I found in the junk drawer by the sink, the shed out back, and the garbage cans left at the edge of the house — four items, all of which were small enough to be jammed into the bag of clothes without much notice.

The air stood calm and a perfect sort of dry. Grass crunched like glass under my shoes. People talked for years about that summer of 1990, I suppose many still do, but when their tongues wag of that long-ago it is not of Michaela Dullahan alone they speak and shudder. The drought that year ruined crops from Virginia to Georgia and left every yard in Camden a brittle, thirsty brown. It had been weeks since Dad mowed. He'd never miss a thing.

I drove away from the neighborhood and left my truck hidden in some trees before backtracking with the bag and its contents all the way to the hill. There I sat and waited for the sun to fall beneath the ridges. I remember no breeze that late evening, not a single bird's call. Never once did I reconsider what I meant to do. Not a single time did I believe it would damn me.

Beneath the cover of twilight I set out down Micky's side of the slope and followed the trail toward the Dullahan home. My sole worry was she had not heeded my warning to keep from Shantytown; Micky would be waiting at the path's end or meet me someplace upon it, tell me God had warned her, ruining it all. Yet as darkness settled, turning the woods silken silver, even that disquiet fell away and left me free. Not once did that thick canopy turn my thoughts inward. The wilds held back their reaching grasp, handing me over to myself.

The path ended. I did not bother to swing wide of the windows; the house lay dark, Earl himself a long way gone. The sloshing in my backpack came like a river's roar. I walked straight down the center of the dirt road beyond Micky's house and veered away only when it was time. The wider path to the opposite side of the road carried me the rest of the way. In the dim moonlight I could make out the bright-yellow police tape hung in a square around the barn's front, crisscrossed at the door. A bit of it had worked itself free. I shrugged off my pack and left it on the ground. No light came at me from inside. The barn looked a dying thing. I would take what life of it remained. From the knapsack I took the three empty two-liter cola bottles I had snatched from our trash, each now filled with gas Dad kept for the mower. I unscrewed the cap on one and hooked the other two in the fingers of my left hand. My thumb went over the bottle's mouth. I began at the door and worked my way around the barn to the right, sending a thin stream of gas at the base of the dry wood. One bottle, two, three, until I had come around to the door again. The last of the gasoline came out in a line extending from the front of the barn to the end of the path. I tossed the last bottle into the trees and reached for the matches in my pocket.

Micky's voice rose up from inside me: *Don't matter what I want now.*

I plucked one match free and struck it. A thin curl of sulfured smoke rose, nothing more.

I can't go with you, Owen.

Another match. I held it tight against the strip and pushed downward.

God don't want me to.

The flame burst into an orange and yellow tip at the end of my finger.

My time's drawn near.

Never in my life had I felt imbued with such power as when that spark met the rest of the matches still in the book. I dropped it all into the dust. Blue fire wriggled like a serpent toward the barn. It met the door and blew to a soft *whoomp* from which conflagration burst. A wall of heat and light crashed into me, singeing my clothes and face, yet I did not shrink from it. My arms instead opened as if to embrace light born in darkness. From its glow, my cold heart warmed.

All those years I had clung to Micky as I would my better self, only to find in the end she ran from me toward some vision, some passing fancy, as though she could find more comfort in the arms of her imaginings than in my own. Yet there is where I stood for my claim, plunging my stake into the hard heart of all the world's cruelty. God would not have what was meant as mine. I would take Him from Micky's soul and Micky from this place of pine and ruin. I could save her more than He could. And if I should be judged for that — for the very love Michaela Dullahan preached — then I vowed to let it be so. I would greet my burning eternity and dip my finger into the cool waters of our togetherness. I would suffer with gladness.

The fire gorged itself on the tinder of dried and rotting boards. Yellow flame yielded to orange above the roof and rose in thick ochre, blackening the sky into a demon's face uttering howls for mercy. And then I realized the voice was no demon. Someone was banging on the wall. What spell had overtaken me snapped when I heard the screams coming from inside. I woke as confused as one who had gone walking in his sleep.

Micky. It was Micky in there.

I answered with a scream of my own. Part of the roof collapsed into a storm of falling embers. Smoke poured from the opening. I ran and rolled the door free. The fire raged dim enough that I could push through. I covered my face with my shirt. Smoke stung my eyes. Bales of straw lit from the hot air alone. A body lay curled near the back, not blond hair but a shock of red. I crawled on my belly and picked up Todd Foster in my arms as a bit of the roof fell around us, timbers and struts crashing down, blocking our way. Flames higher, consuming us. Todd grew heavy in my arms. I kept to the center of the barn and away from the worst of the flames. We reached the door as the east wall of the barn fell with a noise of all things ending.

8

I laid Todd Foster in the soft bosom of a pine among the many he called home and stared in horror at the thing I had done. Add my abandonment of him to the long list of sins I committed that day, placed somewhere below Micky's death but above the lies I told. Place it anywhere, I don't suppose it matters. By then I heard the shouts of distant voices and horns blaring as Shantytown came alive. I counted it at mere minutes before the first people burst down the path, carrying pails and blankets and what water they could manage. No one saw me. I sprinted as though the devil nipped at my heels, which was only some removed from the truth.

All about those woods hung a thick layer of black smoke that reached into my lungs, making me retch. The taste was black in my mouth.

I had the strawberry moon to guide my way and the few stars the moon let shine. Not far I came upon the road and hid as a group of men and women and children ran past. Kept to the trees until I reached the Dullahans'. From there I ran bent and heaving until I reached the clearing and my final judgment. A figure stood at the edge of the slope leading from the hill draped in a white dress. I knew her shape even in the dimness. The soft curl of hair set against the broken outline of the limbs, head tilted downward to the right. I was too late. Micky too early. Whichever it was counted as nothing, because there could be no hiding now.

Even then I knew it should be no other way.

Micky kept motionless in her spot. I lowered my head and trundled up the slope feeling no less than a prisoner come under death, making his final walk to the gallows. My clothes reeked of smoke, my arms were blackened. Far down in the Pines burned what remained of the only purpose Micky had found in her life, yet her eyes never wandered from my own. Shame flooded me, and the fear it bore lay so great upon my heart I could not even look away. At the top of the hill I turned rather than face her wrath. Where for years I had looked out upon that nightscape to behold the dark swelling wave of the Blue Ridge, a ball of glowing orange now lay in that muted sea. Silence reigned where I had once heard song.

Beside me came, "Owen. What have you become?"

Only that — not *What have you done?* but *What have you become?* Everything in me longed to reach for her, hold the mere tip of Micky's finger. I deserved no such comfort.

There beneath the strawberry moon, I buckled under my own tears.

"There's no reason to keep here no more. You're unchained, Micky, from everything. We can be together now."

387

"No one is unchained."

My heart (was it my heart? even now, I cannot say) leaped to stifle such a lie, wanting to tell Micky my words were true even if she would not believe them. I beheld her in spite of my fear. Yet in Micky's face I saw neither anger nor the pain of my betrayal, nor even the sadness of seeing all she had come to love aflame. In that moment, I had never seen one so free.

She said, "I waited for Earl. I sat there until the sun went and then visited some folk in the Pines. I went back one more time in case he was there, but Earl ain't never coming back, is he? Because nothing in him ever changed. The bad of him was too much. That's when God spoke to me."

"God don't speak to nobody."

"He did me. He tole me I done all I could. Everything asked. I fought it, because nothing seems done. But He give me a feeling, like how you get to the last page of a book and know there's only one way you want it to end. That's how it was. I come down to say good-bye to my momma and I hoped I'd see her soon."

"Don't talk like that," I said.

"I will and you'll hear it. There's no going on for me no more, Owen. My time's come." She smiled, and in the parting of

388

her lips I saw not the gladness of a thing completed but a sweetness of its recollection. It was the very expression I had seen on her face between two iron rails at the edge of Brutal Simpson's field. "I'm going to die on this hill," she said.

My hand held her at the wrist. "Nobody knows you're up here, and no one will blame you for this. Clancy said he'd clear things. It's Earl they want. He stole that money. I'll call Youngstown, talk to Coach. Tell him I got to bring you along. Mom. They'll help, I know they will. I'll keep you safe."

Her hand swung free. The space between us grew.

"But you'll never be able to keep us safe from yourself. You got no idea what you did down there. The hurt you've caused. It won't go away."

"You think I took pleasure in it?"

Her eyes, so full of sadness. "Yes. I expect you did, some."

"What I did down there was for you."

"I know that. I knew it when I left the cabin. Knew it as soon as I stood up from under this oak and saw that flame of fire. I knew it was you before you stepped out from those trees. And I knew why."

My foot kicked out at the soft ground

under us, meeting a root growing from the oak. Across the other side of the hill, somewhere in town, a siren called. If Micky registered the sound, it seemed of little importance. She stood as though waiting — like she was packed and ready to go, only not with me. Even after all I'd done, I felt I was about to lose her forever. I could not bear such thinking.

I said, "You went away from me. All I wanted was you back."

"What you feel for me is only a shadow to the place you hold in my life. Always has been. I love you like no other in the world, Owen Cross, and that is why I would move heaven to keep you well. Your love saved me once, but it's a greater love that will see us home. That's all life should be, really. All I ever wanted was to help people find their way back home. You most of all. We'd fail each other in the end. Don't you see that? Like baseball will fail you. What you seek from me or some game is something we can't give you."

My lips thinned to a smile of their own accord. I whispered to her, "Don't you go preaching to me, now."

"Then I'll state it plain." She came to me and raised my hand and laid my palm to her breast. My fingers closed around her soft flesh. My body felt made of wires. "This," Micky said, "means very little. This means much more."

She took my hand away and rose up on her toes, leaning forward. Our lips met in a kiss, tender and soft, plumbing a depth inside me far down to where paltry passion cannot reach. A kiss that served not as a prelude to more but that held all the more I had ever craved, and a sureness beyond faith that ours was a bond that stretched across not days but worlds. I cannot say what part of me Michaela Dullahan's lips touched, only that by it I knew my own ignorance. My years had been spent pining for scraps while a feast sat before me.

Her mouth left mine. "Do you see?"

I stumbled backward, the hilltop feeling made of water. A chuckle flew from Micky's lips. It died in my ears as the streak of orange and red in the distance drew her attention once more.

"I think it's time," she said.

"No. I don't know what you think is going to happen, Micky, but it isn't. Nobody's coming up here. I won't hurt you. I won't let anyone else."

"Nothing you can do, Owen."

"There is. There's one thing." My eyes shut. I felt my jaw tightening. "I saw something at that train. Something . . . I don't know. I can't explain what it was or what happened, but it was so big . . . like my head can't even hold the memory of it, and I didn't know what to do. How to act. What to think or feel or . . ." I looked away from the fire and back to Micky, then back to the fire. "I don't know what it was other than a little of what you saw, like how somebody jumps into the water beside you and you catch some of the splash. I couldn't handle it. I tried pushing it away and forgetting about it but I couldn't, and then when you started telling everybody what you saw, I tried pushing you away but I couldn't. Because I love you. But I couldn't go where you went, Micky. I couldn't accept any of it, and you know why? Because it was too great. If I believed what I saw, really believed it, then it could only mean one thing."

Behind me, she said, "Tell me what that one thing is, Owen."

"That everything I ever wanted for my life, baseball and you and all of it, wasn't anything when set next to that. Those things were sand I'd gather up into a pile that'd one day get blown away by some gust of wind. But what I saw . . ." I shook my head. There weren't words for what I saw. "I couldn't, though. Couldn't go as far as you.

Because you're right — I had more to lose. Everything I'd worked my whole life for. Dad too. Baseball fills me up. There was no room for anything else."

"And now?"

I kept my eyes to the dying glow against the mountains.

"You're going to go away, Owen. You have to. I understand that now. Away's where you think you'll find everything you need, but someday you'll come back right here and find what you know you've always wanted. It'll be a strawberry moon like the one right up there now, and you'll come here to remember and forget."

"I think right now all I want is to get as far away from Camden as I can."

"You'll come here," she said, "because it's a special place. It's the most special place there is, that's why I don't mind it. It's where I always felt so good and where so many good things happened. There's so few places in the world that give you such a feeling. They're holy, I think. They're like a gate that swings open and leads you on."

"Come away with me, Micky. Please."

"I will, but not like how you want. My time's come. I done all I could."

The sirens had reached Shantytown. I heard them — three or four. Red lights blinked among the pine trees like mutant lightning bugs.

"I love you, Owen Cross. I will always love you. There's nothing more can be given me than what you have. You remember that, and don't you blame yourself. I want you to go on for as long as you're meant, knowing you'll find your way even when you don't think you will. I want you to know you're being watched over even when you call yourself hunted. I want —"

And that's all. Those are the last words Michaela Dullahan ever spoke to me, a single unfinished wish I have spent all these years wanting to hear completed. Only that: *I want* —

I begged her to finish. No answer came from behind me. I dug my heels into the soft ground and spun, meaning to grovel and plead as a peasant would before his queen, but what greeted me was only the wide trunk of the oak. In the place where my love once stood there lay only a fine white dress, cast off as one would a rag.

Micky was gone.

9

Adding to Mike's misery is Bernie Williams getting plunked by Ryan's third pitch. Two men on, two out. I hear Country from all that way in center hollering, "One more, one more, bay-bee," and I know if Tino Martinez somehow gets those runs in, there's no way Mike will let me pinch hit, no way at all. But the ghosts go quiet (*For now,* I tell myself. *Only for now, and you know that, don't you? Deep down? Those ghosts have been waiting years for you*) and Martinez sends a slow grounder to Bordick at short, which is gobbled and tossed to Hairston at second.

The dugout erupts. Ryan has worked his way out of trouble with only two runs in. He holds the Yanks down for three more outs, the game is ours. We'll pack up and head back to the hotel. Grab some food. Enjoy the New York City nightlife. Country will start at DH tomorrow and he'll take a loaded Betsy to the plate beneath a strawberry moon as big as the sun, looking to inch a little closer to his four hundred dingers. And I hope he gets there.

I do.

Top 9

1

Country's beside me long enough to slap his glove down and pull on his batting gloves. He eyes Betsy beside me.

"You watch over my bat?"

"Didn't nothing happen to her. Did hold her a bit, though."

He has one glove on and is fastening the other, but now Country stops, eyeing me. "Said you held her?"

"Couldn't help it. Guy's got the chance to hold one a Country Kitchen's black Betsies, he's gotta take it. Right?"

"She's lighter than she looks, ain't she?"

"Noticed that."

Country takes Betsy from beside me and hefts it with an arm that looks as big around as both of mine. Out on the field, Knight's already halfway through his warm-ups and Segui, our leadoff, is walking toward the plate. Country walks off, says, "I'm on deck," and turns when I call his name.

"You take care that bat. Wouldn't want it to splinter. You catch that ball square."

He winks at me. "Always do."

At the end of the dugout he takes the helmet Ethan hands him and then climbs the steps, pausing to say something to Mike. Country nods my way. Mike doesn't look. Segui steps into the box as Country centers himself in the on-deck circle. He uses Betsy to loosen himself up. Eyes cast toward the pitcher on the mound. Gauging Knight's delivery and speed, the tightness of his curve. Maybe even drawing a box around the point where the ball leaves the hand, just as my father once taught me.

2

I searched hours upon a hill that took only minutes to circle, peering into the full dark of night for a flitting shadow or a last, whispered call of my name. Scouring the slopes and the oaks for a trace of Micky beyond the clothing she left behind. Down one side and up the next, down and up again, forming a W in the tall grass. I stumbled what part I did not run. The remaining I crawled hands and knees like a beggar, tracing my hands over the uneven ground in the vain hope Micky had lost her balance fleeing and knocked her head against a stone or root. I beat upon the earth with balled fists and screamed her name toward a strawberry moon. Ripped at the grass as I would my own hair. And when I could search no more, I held Micky's dress against my face and felt cotton like her skin, soft and born of the earth. I breathed deep the aroma of her sweat.

The glow from Shantytown was now a snuffed candle. Inky tendrils reached heavenward — all that was left of the barn.

I left near to dawn. Before going I gathered a handful of dandelions and tied them in a knot at the stems. Those would be my final marker, forever unclaimed. I lit out for home after changing into the clothes I'd hidden and buried the ones caked in soot with Micky's dress in a grave dug by my own hands. They remain on the hilltop now is my guess, though I cannot remember where.

No one could pinpoint who called for help in battling the fire tearing through an old tumbledown barn in the heart of the Pines, though reporters from the *Record* exhausted every possibility. They had better luck ascertaining the call was received by a 911 screener and relayed without pause to the Camden Fire Department. Given the lateness of the hour and that the Camden FD has always been manned by a strictly volunteer force, no one was at the station. Men rose from beds and shook the sleep from their eyes, pulled on what clothes lay nearby. It took nearly forty-five minutes for the first trucks to reach the Pines. By then, the Fellowship of the Lost was naught but cinder and ash.

None from Camden much mourned the outcome other than my mother. No blame was assigned. You couldn't get a fire truck off that dirt road and down the path through the trees to where the barn sat. A bucket line of fire department personnel and Shanties was formed, though by then the only goal was to keep the blaze from lighting up the surrounding woods.

Whispers grew in the weeks and months after — mostly coming out of the Pines, but in some corners of town as well — that quite a lot more could have been done really, if the fire department had reached Shantytown earlier. Those mutterings stated someone else managed to catch wind of the fire in Shantytown (Mayor Henry's name was most mentioned, though Clancy's was a close second) and made a quick call to the firehouse, telling the boys to take their time, it was only some Shantie barn anyway.

The truth of those rumors eluded me. I wanted to believe our town leadership was made of stronger stock. But I remembered Clancy's face as I spoke with him in his office, looking so tired and undone, like all he craved was the whole mess being over. As did I, as did my father. In the end we were each granted our wish, which is a rare thing in this world. And in the end we found our reward somehow made our lives feel less, which is a thing exceedingly common.

The barn's loss was relegated to an afterthought compared to the disappearances. Word spread of Earl's running away with bags full of ill-gotten money. Tips poured in of his location, ranging from Mattingly to Kentucky and all the way to the Mississippi and beyond. Each day's newspaper became devoted to the search, every conversation its topic. It was as if all the rage and hurt felt by so many settled upon the shoulders of a single man. I remember standing in line at the Ace a few days before leaving for college, hearing an old-timer among old-timers go on about a blight that struck every farm in town when his daddy's daddy was a boy, and how it was somehow determined through prayer and divining the plague's cause was an old sow named Eloise, which was then branded with the mark of the evil eye and cast off into the woods. Such backward tales told by backward people were always at the root of my desire to leave Camden. It made me feel none better to know it had happened again, only this time the sow went by the name of Earl Dullahan.

Yet not even the furor with which Earl's name was discussed could shine a light to the conjectures surrounding Michaela's disappearance. Even her most fervent followers came to the belief they had run off together. Some — Louise Townsend among them, which drove Clancy to near hysterics — held to the likelihood that Micky had gone with her daddy by force. My mother held to this notion most of all. For Greta Cross, it was the only explanation for why Micky would leave all the beauty she had worked so hard and endured so much to create. No one entertained the possibility she was dead. In those early days afterward, I believe not even Clancy suspected something so macabre.

So unnatural.

Yet on the other side of that summer began a time of healing. Reverend Sebolt and the other preachers in town took up two Sundays' worth of offerings to replace what money Earl had stolen. Stephanie and

Jeffrey delivered the proceeds to the Pines. They went door to door together, giving what was needed.

By the end of that summer, little of Micky's preaching remained. Her talk of love drifted like the black smoke of her burning church, away and away. Only Todd sought something of a revival. For weeks he went all about Shantytown and Camden, telling everyone who would listen of the death that came for him on the night of the strawberry moon and the angel who saved him from it.

The hard shell around my father never did break, though it softened some toward Mom. I still wonder if it would have, were Micky not proven in the town's eyes the charlatan he had always suspected. Our home became solemn but peaceful, much as it always had been. I kept to myself. Washed Bubba's cars and cashed his checks and knew not what to do with the money. No one suspected what I had done. I was always such a good boy, the ballplayer who went off to college to chase a dream he could not help but love most of all.

I could hide my shame from Dad, from Jeffrey and Travis and Clancy, but I never could hide it from my mother. She knew in that mystical way mothers do — never anything so concrete she could come out and ask, but more impressions left in the soft parts of her heart. I could never tell her what I had done, never break her heart so. My secret became a wall she picked at until her death, chipping away layer upon layer faster than I could add to its thickness. We grew more distant in the years following than I ever imagined possible. I hated myself for it. Micky's going padded my father's pride and ruined my mother's faith, and though the truth of it would have brought him low and lofted her, I confessed not a word.

Don't blame yourself, Micky had said. But I did. My love had saved nothing. To me the burning of that barn was what caused Micky's disappearance, all to take what was never mine to have.

3

David Segui singles to right to start the top of the ninth. A smattering of cheers rolls down onto the field as Bob Sheppard announces the next batter ("Number twenty-three, Bobby Kitchen, number twenty-three") and jeers as well, the jeers bringing another smile to Country's face, him knowing they don't boo nobodies in the Bronx. He holds Betsy close to his chest as he steps in. Digs his back foot into the faint white line marking the back of the box. Looks over his shoulder to say something to Oliver crouched behind the plate and to the umpire.

Mike looks over to me as Country works the count 2–1. Segui leads off first. Takes an extra step. He's ready to run. Fastball count, gotta be a strike, Knight won't want to go three balls on Country. Not a hitter like him, past his prime but still a power threat, that bat he's got still has life.

Country knows it, knows this pitch is his. He cocks Betsy over his shoulder and rocks back as Knight falls into his windup, takes a small step and unleashes the bat.

The ball takes off like a rocket, the crack deafening. Those still in their seats stand as Country tears out of the box, already watching the flight of his hit as it arcs out toward the deepest part of center field, and I can nearly hear his thoughts — *Thirty-nine now, that's all I got.* But Bernie Williams is slowing his pursuit. He stops at the very end of the warning track where it abuts the center field wall and reaches up to snag Country's hit, then fires it back to the infield, chasing Segui back to first.

Cheers now from the stands. Country touches first and lowers his head as he veers off into foul territory, making his way to the dugout. Ten years ago, that ball would've been in the monuments. Now it's only a warning track shot, even with a hollowed-out Betsy to swing.

4

It was late February, a little more than four months ago, when Mom called me in Bowie to say the doctors had found a spot on her brain. I flew down while she started chemo. It was a hard time but filled with the sweetness hard times can bring. The gulf left between us for those seven years began to shrink. I'm not sure how many times in those weeks Mom sat with me and cried. Probably as many times as I put my arms around her and nearly told her everything about Micky.

Nearly.

She asked me outright two days before I was due back in Bowie. We were in her tiny living room watching *Jeopardy,* me sitting in Dad's old chair. Mom posed the question the way a contestant would who'd risked too much on a Daily Double and wasn't sure of the answer.

"I always thought you knew," she said. "And I always guessed you thought the truth would hurt me too much."

Her eyes never left the TV.

"You can tell me," she said. "Doesn't matter what it is. I need to know is all. It's haunted me these years. I need to know if I believed true or false."

I told her I didn't know, that for all I knew Michaela was down in Mexico with Earl and it didn't matter anyway, that was so long back. Then I got a beer from the fridge. Mom watched Alex Trebek and said she preferred him with a mustache. It was the last she ever asked me about Micky.

I stayed with her as long as I could and left only at her blessing. Spring training had already started. Skip was asking for me. Mom all but kicked me out of the apartment in an overeager way that convinced me she was afraid of my going. I hated myself for leaving and hated baseball for making me go. It was the first time I began to think hard on all the game had cost me, the much I had given it and the little it had given back.

"I'll be fine," she said. "And even if I ain't, don't you fret. Truth is I miss your father. I'm tired, and I'm ready for what comes."

I didn't fly to Florida but drove instead. I don't know why I did that. Maybe it was my way of trying to extend the illusion that nothing had changed, that the world was turning on as it always had and my life was still moving in something of a straight line. Change comes hard to us all. It takes a lot of hurting before we can be anything but what we've always been.

I called her every morning from the first of March, including the morning she died. She'd felt good that day. Said she had some errands to run. I told her to be careful and call me later. The Charlottesville police department did instead, five hours later. Mom was pulling out from a stoplight when a teenager more intent on updating his social media status than watching the road slammed into her. She was pronounced dead at the scene.

In all my mourning I believed my mother had been snatched from the world as well, no less than Micky. And just as it had been with Micky, it was a mercy.

5

Jay Gibbons strikes out. Two down, and Fordyce is up. Our catcher has gone oh-for-four tonight, has struck out three times and let a passed ball get by him behind the plate, but Mike leaves him in. He'd give Fordyce one more bat rather than give that bat to me, knowing I'm bound back to Double-A in the morning. Even Country won't sit with me. He's joking with Caldwell and some others. There is a wide space between me and the nearest player. It's like I'm dead now, a ghost myself. Just another busher on his way back to the minors.

6

You never know what to do when a parent dies. Doesn't matter how old you are, you feel four years old again and lost inside some huge department store where bright lights shine in your eyes and everywhere are strangers that look like they're one bad choice away from grabbing you. I never felt that way with Dad because Mom was still there, but her passing left me feeling utterly alone in the world. There were arrangements to be made and things to clean out and more papers to sign than I could imagine. Family night (a misnomer if I'd ever heard one, given it was only me standing by her casket) passed in a fog. I shook hands and spoke with faceless people, nodded my thanks to strangers. It was Mom's wish to leave the coffin shut. *You don't got to be showing people my bones, Owen. That ain't me there. What's me is gone to glory, the rest is old rags I won't have need of no more.*

Greta Cross saw to me even in death. Though in heaven, she was yet Momma.

408

I buried her beside Dad overlooking the Rivanna. Reverend Sebolt officiated. With him came dozens from Camden and Shantytown to pay their respects. I threw a fistful of dirt atop her casket after it was lowered and left a rose, then lingered as the crowd drifted back to their quiet lives on the other side of the mountain. Away in the distance, three men stood around a rusting yellow backhoe and smoked.

I did not mean to keep them long. It was just some old rags lying under there, right? A pile of bones and wasting flesh. And yet I could not turn away until I spoke what should have been spoken long before.

"Sorry," I whispered. I did not know where to direct that apology, sky or earth, and so settled for a place in the middle. "You were right, Momma. About everything."

Even then I struggled in my telling. No doubt I should have admitted the lies I'd told and the things I'd done, burning a church that had brought my mother such peace and helping to erase the girl who had brought her purpose and direction. I do not listen to those who say there is no world beyond ours, only a black quiet that goes on and on forever. I know better. Have seen better. The only question still left to me is whether those who have gone on before us keep an interest in the ones they've left behind, or whether all those things they died not knowing fall away once in the presence of a love that beckons us all in life. I wanted to think the former true. I still want it.

7

It has taken me this long to understand it, but I believe now that my return to Bowie three months back served as the beginning of an end. My hope was that after I laid Mom to rest, baseball would serve as my escape once more, this time from grief rather than guilt. But I went hitless my first three games back, ten times at the plate and ten walks back to the dugout. Skip said nothing beyond, "Don't press, your swing'll come." It never did. Every throw I made to nab a base stealer sailed into the outfield. A snap throw to first to catch a sleeping runner ended up along the stands. Players began to ignore me, the unspoken belief being I had contracted something that could catch and spread until it infected everyone.

By May, my average had dipped below .200. In desperation I called everyone I could, Frank Solis at Youngstown and even Coach Stevens back in Camden. I took extra batting practice and watched more tape than I could've imagined. Nothing helped. No one's advice worked. I suffered under the weight of all those empty words, knowing I no longer had a direct line to the only person who could pull me through.

Then came yesterday. Skip found me in the cage and watched my swings, grunted a few times. I couldn't tell if those noises were of encouragement or exasperation.

"Need you in my office when you're done," he said.

I bet I went through another hundred swings before I finally acknowledged the knot in my gut and made the long walk back through the clubhouse. I knocked at the door, which garnered me a "Yeah, come on in." A pep talk, that's what I told myself this was. Skip telling me to keep on what I'm doing, everybody goes through a dry spell and all you can do is fight your way through it.

I stepped inside. Skip had poured himself into a chair behind a chipped wooden desk. I couldn't read the look on his face.

"Go on and shut that door," he said.

Shut the door. My throat closed. Sweat broke out behind my neck. Couldn't breathe. I wondered if this was what Dad would have felt if he'd been awake just before he died.

411

My hand lingered at the knob. I pushed it shut.

"Won't be playing you tonight, Owen."

"Listen, Skip, I know I been in a funk —"

"Son, you ain't got no funk, you got a problem. Have a seat."

He motioned to the crumbling chair in front of his desk, a sad old castoff of scraped armrests and a stained seat that had taken on the imprint of the thousand guys who had sat there before, told they were being sent down or let go, and as I sat all feeling left my legs and Skip's face became a blotchy white smudge against the wall and, God oh God, please don't let this happen, please, Micky, tell God not to let this happen I don't want to die.

"Skip, I swear I'm trying hard as I can."

His voice was soft and grandfatherly and full of gravel. "Know you are, Owen. Why you're here." He reached into a drawer and pulled out an envelope. Slid it across the desk. "That's for you."

"What is it?"

"Plane ticket."

I looked at that envelope like it was a poisoned thing. My heart felt to jump through my chest, clouding my vision. It was as though Skip's face stood outside a rainy window. "Don't send me home," I said. "Please, Skip. I ain't got nothing else."

"Ain't sending you home, son." He tapped the envelope. "Ticket here says LaGuardia."

I blinked. Breathed. "What's in LaGuardia?"

He grinned. "The big team. O's are in the Bronx for a four-game set. Their backup catcher had to go home for a sick momma. Or daddy, I don't know. Need a body there tomorrow case Fordyce gets hurt or the game gets long. I put in a word."

I didn't want to say it fast, fearing I'd say it wrong: "A word for. Me?"

"You the one sitting here. Slumps don't mean nothing, Owen. They're just a valley with a peak on each side. You probably won't get one at-bat and you'll be told to pack your bags once the game's over. They'll send you back down to make room for some pitcher to see them down the stretch. But it's a day in the majors, and it just might be what you need to get your head straight." He winked at me. "Enjoy it, son. See it as a taste of what might come once you remember how to hit again."

My body felt like I'd gotten off one of those carnival rides put up for a week each spring in Camden. Krazy Kups or Monster Gulch, the kind that scare you not with loops and speed but with the rotting wood

413

and rusting nails that hold them all together. I'd gone into Skip's office thinking I was done, only to leave needing to pack my bag for the majors. I was so out of sorts I left the plane ticket on the desk and had to go back for it.

Skip chuckled and shook his head. "You act like you don't even want to go."

And that was the thing. I see that now, here and tonight.

God help me, Skip was more right than he knew.

8

I've always had the habit of making sure I leave no trace of myself behind when a ball game is over. Most guys will walk back to the clubhouse with bottles lying everywhere (energy drinks and water and even coffee — you'd be surprised how much coffee is gone through during a night game), half-eaten bags of sunflower seeds and wads of chewing gum, they don't care. Someone, Roy Campanella I think, once said you got to be a man to play baseball, but you got to have a lot of little boy in you too. Take a look inside a baseball dugout once a game is over, you'll know how true that statement rings.

So with two out in the top of the ninth

and even Country abandoning me, I start tidying up my spot on the bench. There isn't much: one catcher's mitt; one shiny rock, which goes back into my pocket; a mostly empty bottle of water I think is Caldwell's and not mine. I do all of this because I think the game is over. Little more to be played, nothing much to change the final outcome. You play baseball for so long it's easy to fool yourself into believing the game can no longer surprise you. Every facet of it is analyzed and set to numbers and trends and charts, the goal being to eliminate any surprise, but of course you can't. The heart of baseball — its very magic — rests in the undeniable fact that anything can happen at any time. And something happens now.

It begins with Brook Fordyce, our catcher with the oh-for-the-night slump who steps up in his last time at the plate and laces a clean single to right. Hairston follows with a single of his own, scoring Segui and moving Fordyce to second. Now Brady Anderson with his own base hit pulled through the right side of the infield. Fordyce scores, and now we have runners at the corners. All of this with two out in the inning and Knight looking in command on the mound. The score is ten to three, a deficit even the ghosts of Yankee Stadium would struggle to overcome.

And with Bordick coming up to bat and my mitt and a bottle of water in my hand, Mike turns my way and says, "Cross, bat for Richard. You're on deck."

My mind scrambles to decipher those words any other way. Country leans into the dugout path. His jaw is set, but he looks ready to burst. Mike waits.

"C'mon, Cross. I said you're on deck."

I toss the water bottle to the bench and reach into my other back pocket for my batting gloves. My head hurts. Bordick is already stepping in and I'm not even out there yet, not warm. Ethan hands me a helmet. He's beaming like it's him going out there and not me and I hear him ask, "What bat you want?" and I don't know, all my lumber is back in Bowie.

"You pick me one."

He slides a smooth and rounded stick of ash from the pile and promises it's good for a hit. I take it and climb the dugout steps as Bordick takes strike one. In the circle I find the pine tar and a weighted donut I slip over the barrel. Wide circles with the bat, letting it tug at the muscles in my arms and side. Keep loose.

Bordick lets a curveball go by for a ball — one and one.

Looking out onto the field. No longer overcome by all that beauty and history. The game shrinks. Runners at the corners. Two down. Infield shaded to the right, outfield a hair the other way, but they'll likely play me straight away because they don't know who I am, where I hit. That's good. Play me straight away, that means the alley in right center will be wide open. That's my power spot, where I'll take the pitch. Hit it on a line. Let the moon carry it, let it fly.

Another ball. Two-and-one, hitter's count. By now the Yankee dugout has seen me, surely Oliver has behind the plate. Bordick has had two hits in five trips tonight, and I think they might put him on. Walk him. It'll load the bases, but that might not matter to Knight on the mound because Bordick is a pro and I'm on my last sips of a single cup of coffee. The next pitch is a cutter that doesn't break but keeps to the outside corner for ball three. One more and I'll have my shot. One more ball or a little dribbler down the line, a ground ball with eyes, and the voice I hear will be the voice of God coming over the speakers announcing, *Now batting, number nineteen, Owen Cross, number nineteen,* and I will get my first at-bat in the majors inside Yankee Stadium. I can hit this guy. I've seen Knight throw four pitches.

417

I've watched his fastball and his off speed, and I can hit this guy.

Bordick steps out, takes a practice swing. My body feels loose. I tap the butt end of the bat into the grass to free the donut. Look over the crowd. There are maybe twenty thousand left, small for a big league game but more than twice the population of Camden, Virginia. Faces of strangers, tired women and drunk men and kids who can barely hold their eyes open. I smile, not being able to help myself, then feel my lips grow cold at the girl sitting alone four rows behind home plate. Hatless, one bare leg curled over the top of the seat in front of her, a deep line where the cutoff denim shorts bite into her thigh. Her T-shirt is black. It might say AC/DC on front, or Poison or Guns N' Roses. Might even say Def Leppard, like the shirt she wore for a state championship game long ago against the town of Mattingly. Corn-silk hair spilling down over her shoulders. Smiling. Smiling at me.

Over the distance between us, Micky waves.

I hear the slap of Oliver's mitt and the umpire calling strike. The count is full. Bordick steps out. Knight removes his glove to wipe down the ball in his hands. Time slows.

418

The lights of Yankee Stadium are above me and the moon shining down, crowd buzzing, voices from our dugout telling Bordick to hang tough and wait for his pitch, the smell of dirt and grease and grass. Michaela Dullahan in the seats, cheering for me. It is all just as I had once imagined it to her on a hilltop set along the Appalachian Blue Ridge so long ago. A boy's dream now real. Now true, or as true as anything can be had in this life.

Knight gets the sign. Anderson takes off from first. I see the pitch coming in to Bordick high and the breath catches in my throat — it's ball four flying in, and I'll have my at-bat. I take one step, two, leaving the edges of the on-deck circle, ready to hit. And at the last moment I see Bordick shifting his weight and his bat coming through the zone. His swing leaves a one-inch gap between the ball and the blur of his bat. Oliver squeezes his glove as the umpire turns and makes a pulling motion with his right arm, calling strike three.

Around me are bodies moving, Hairston and Anderson coming in along with the third base coach, our guys, Country included, running out to the field in order to claim the last three outs of the game. I stand alone with a bat not my own, watching.

Micky smiles from her seat as though telling me it's okay. Every single thing is okay.

Mike greets me at the dugout steps and extends a hand. He says, "Sorry 'bout that, kid. Took longer'n I thought to make sure game's outta reach of those guys. Wish you woulda gotten a bat, but I can't stand losing to the Yankees."

I hand Ethan the bat and shake Mike's hand. My words are maybe the truest I've spoken this night:

"S'all right, Mike. Turns out I didn't need it."

BOTTOM 9

It is a quiet three outs to end the night: O'Neill leads off and grounds out to Hairston at second. From my spot on the bench I see Micky stand and make her way down the aisle and the three rows between her and the netting that surrounds the area behind home plate. She stands there as Brosius gathers himself in the box. Still staring at me with that smile. Ryan works the count to two strikes and is winding to deliver the third when Micky reaches a hand to take hold of the netting. Her fingers pass through instead, followed by the rest of her body. She is out on the field and walking past Brosius as he swings for the third strike, and for a moment I believe I can see a quizzical look pass over his face, as though an unexpected puff of wind unfocused him for only a moment, long enough to upset his timing. He walks back to the Yankee dugout shaking his head. Micky strolls past the mound and past Hairston at second. It is as though she is tromping up the slope to our hill, so comfortable does she look. So in place. As though she has never left this world.

Oliver is the Yankees' last hope. Ryan nods at Fordyce's sign and delivers a pitch wide. Micky is now in the center field grass. She turns and looks at me again in a knowing way and moves within mere feet of Country, who does not even know the miracle that has just moved past him. Micky smiling, reaching out her hand. Curling her wrist toward herself, motioning me to come on, come on. At the center field wall she points upward to the moon over a darkened New York night, and now she is gone.

Ryan gains a strike on Oliver. The fans are filing out. In the field I see players in various stages of unconcern. Country is leaning forward, hands on his knees and head down. At shortstop, Bordick kicks at the dirt. Conine watches the waning crowd. Even Mike, calmed now for the first time tonight with a seven-run lead and only one out to get, seems to tire. It is like this for them all. The Yankee players are quiet on their bench, ready to go back to what homes they have, try again tomorrow. There is no joy here. Certainly none that I felt in the bright sunshine of this June afternoon. What comes now is a weariness I know too well, one that would follow me through my days as it must follow us all, for that is the way of this life. We're all trying to get from one end of it to the other the best way we know. In the end, we're all just trying to find our way back home.

Joe Oliver sends a two-one pitch on a fly to right. Country barely takes a step. Richard, still in the game since I never made it to the plate to pinch hit for him, squeezes the ball to seal things.

It is done.

In the clubhouse afterward there are congratulations and no small measure of ribbing directed toward those who managed not to contribute to the ten runs against Mussina and the Yankee bullpen. Reporters gather in front of Johnson's locker and inside Mike's office. Country huddles with a dozen microphones around him and Betsy on his knee, saying he got almost all of that pitch by Knight but it don't matter, those next forty homers are coming, you better believe it.

No reporters work their way to the end of the clubhouse where I sit. A few players, Country and Caldwell among them, stop by to wish me the best back in Bowie. *You'll be back,* they say. *Always a need for a good catcher.* Their tone of voice sounds the same as those who once made up the long lines of mourners waiting to greet me at Dad's funeral and Mom's.

I turn my uniform in to Scooter. Rick Mills finds me to say he's got my room at the team hotel all lined up and hands me a hundred and fifty dollars he calls meal money. I shake my head looking at it. In the Bigs you get as much to eat on in a night as my daddy did in a week of scrubbing floors at the high school.

My flight leaves tomorrow morning. I'll be back in Bowie in time for batting practice and the night game. Gotta hold this new kid's hand, turn him into something the big team would like. Gotta help prop wide that door so he can walk through. That's my life now. And it hasn't been a bad one, in spite of it all. For seven years I have come to a ballpark and been paid to do a job I'd do for free. And really, isn't that all I've ever wanted?

Isn't it?

POSTGAME

June 6, 2001

My flight from LaGuardia left at 10:35 a.m.
— a little more than twelve hours ago. I suppose by now they'll be looking for me. Skip
for sure and everyone in Bowie. Maybe even
Country, assuming word has gotten all the
way back to the guys in New York. Won't
take them long. These days about anybody
can be found. It's hard to stay hid for long.

The truth is I couldn't, Micky. Couldn't
go back. I'd reached my gate and had my
things and was sitting in a chair reading the
closed captioning of some CNN story on
one of the TVs. Weather guy on there talking about the moon tonight. He called it a
"harvest moon" but I whispered it another
way. I left my stuff (they're going to find my
mitt at that gate, Mick, or they already have)
and bought another ticket. Paid cash for it
but still had to show my ID. LaGuardia to
Charlotte to Charlottesville. At some point

I looked out my window and believed myself passing high somewhere over Maryland. Thought maybe that was Bowie down there, my old life. And you know what? I didn't miss any of it, not a single thing.

Rented me a car when I landed. Stopped by Mom's and Dad's graves to tell them how sorry I was and all about the game last night. How it was everything I'd always thought it would be but a whole lot less and more too. I stood there and wondered if there would be enough space between them for me. But maybe that won't matter, will it? I'm thinking it won't. If this is all what I think it's going to be, I just might go down as one of baseball's greatest mysteries, right up there with whether Shoeless Joe Jackson really did help the White Sox throw the Series in '19 and if the Babe really did call his home run shot in game three of the '32 World Series against the Cubs. Wouldn't it be funny if that's how I leave my own mark in the end? Not how I played the game, but how I left it?

From the cemetery I drove over the mountain and left the car downtown where the old Rivera's restaurant used to be. I left a note under the windshield wiper saying who I was and to call the rental place so somebody could come get it. Maybe it's Clancy who'll find it. I bet he'll understand, having spent all these years listening to his Louise go on and on about how you were a girl touched by the Lord and given secrets no human has business knowing. I walked around town most of the evening. Over to the Auto World and the IGA, the library. Spent a good bit of time walking the outfield grass at the high school. Didn't nobody notice who I was. I guess they all have their own lives now. Everything that went on during that summer so long back is mere memory to them, faded and gone like so many things.

When it got to evening I pointed myself westward past our old house and kept going, skirting the tall pines in the backyard and easing through the meadow on the other side and now I'm here.

I'm right here, Micky, just like you wanted me to be. Waiting to see what happens.

We risk nothing greater than when we love what cannot love us back. That is all I mean to say. Upon the rest I would hold my silence rather than violate a place that is as holy to me as any church. But as I wait beneath this clouded June sky in fear and wonder and hope, I know my quiet as sin. To say no more of love would be a selfish thing, and my days of miserly living are done. It is a change that has come as hard to me as the rest. It takes a lot of hurting before you can be anything but what you've always been.

I can feel the memories here, all those days and evenings we spent in this place piecing together a future we had no business dreaming of. All the way from New York I knew the past would be waiting, though I hadn't accounted for how that past has grown in my absence. My yesterdays stretch taller than this oak I sit beneath. They come not in broken and sharp-edged images but in words, hushed tones of voices not my own hidden in the folds of the breeze. They ride upon the perfume of the far woods below me toward Shantytown and the blue mountains rising beyond. They sprout like the dandelions on the slope, which have been left free to grow in the seasons since you and I wore this spot bare in our meeting.

But I will no longer run from what once was. I cannot, nor will I allow another hour to pass holding truth as secret. Time has a way of slipping like water through your fingers the more you try to lay hold of it. Sometime last night — maybe it was when I knew I would never get a bat in the majors, maybe as you strolled through the outfield and turned to look at me before pointing to that moon — I realized there were but a few drops left in my own hand.

It is time now, isn't it? I've done all I can do. That's why I'm here.

The one thing I always believed I possessed was choice. Maybe that was true at one time. But now I think the last choice I ever really made was climbing up onto those tracks to save you from that train, and ever since my days have been laid out for me in advance. Or maybe they always were. Either way, the illusion that my life was my own took years to be proved false, first when a future I once believed writ in stone became an unknowable present, then when Dad passed. Then Mom. Her dying was what settled things. In all the time since that summer, I had been chasing nothing and only running away. You saw that, didn't you? You were the one who stood where I stand now and said I would come back to our hilltop someday. You stood beneath this tree as the world crashed down upon us and said I would go off in search of all I believed I needed, only to return here to find all I ever wanted. And I stood in this very place and answered that all I needed and wanted lay as far from Camden as I could get.

God laughs at our plans.

Prophets do too.

I know what I want, Micky, now and finally. I know what I love most. It isn't a game. Isn't you. It's what you found and what you carried in your heart those precious last weeks of your life. It's the gift you tried giving to everyone.

Mom was right, the mob will always crucify Christ. We praise Him for His holiness and wisdom but cannot bow to His message. He stoops low for us, yet all we see is how the gods we fashion for ourselves stand taller. We would rather remain slaves to ourselves. That was why you were taken from us. You fled no less than Earl, though your going was an escape of a different sort. Your daddy ran not from Camden but from a damnation that will pursue him until justice is meted. Yet the same hand with which I pray Earl Dullahan will be struck down is the very one that reached down in mercy and love to snatch his daughter from a world unworthy of the woman you became.

And though you bid me not blame myself, though your last words were of love for me, it was never enough that I go on to live what small life remained. You knew my own gods were taller than your words. You knew I was not yet free.

Say what you will of your going. Tell me it was the last bits of sand running from a glass turned over by the hand of grace or that it was a postponement of your end so that you might crawl back into the dark hole that is this world and tell everyone what magic lies beyond its lip. It does not dull the truth of what I did that night. I burned your church not to save you but to make you a sacrifice to the god of my own selfish needs, and your loss became my judgment.

You told me neither of us was long for this world. I never believed you until now. We were so young, and what is life to the young but a road stretching ever on toward a moving horizon? It is the curse of life that we spend so much of it in slumber, waking to find our parents old and our dreams for nothing and all its gifts traded for what wilts and dies. What could I do then but what I did?

But as I wait upon this hill I am left with a faith that the vision granted you saw to a far greater distance than my own, and that you knew the end of my story. I pray such, here so near the end. I pray that was how you could look upon me with love even as I burned that church.

There are clouds here and no moon, but

I've heard the moon is coming. I will wait for it and drink in the silence of this place and its secret beauties. This night has come to me as a gift. It makes me glad for the life I've lived.

I think of Dad and whether he is looking down, if he's still proud of his boy. I think of Mom and what she said on the second story of the Camden library the day you left. It is true that baseball was ours alone — Paul and Owen Cross, to the bitter end. Mom had no place but to sit in the stands and cheer. What I could never find the words to say to her is that she had no place in my dreams for one reason alone: I knew Momma loved me as I loved her. There was no need to work out our love. But my father was different, wasn't he? You knew that.

I grew up with the knowledge that the only way to secure his love was to play a game even better than he'd once played it, and claim for myself a future stolen from him. And so I played it, Micky. I made baseball my life and never turned away, not even when you bade me for the sake of my own soul, and it was only last night I finally understood why. Never before had I seen brighter lights. They shone upon me only to expose my own emptiness. I always loved baseball for my own reasons, but I played it these many years to earn a father's love.

That is why I hung on as long as I could, crouched behind a plate until my knees felt made of brittle bone and sandpaper. The game I loved never loved me back, and yet I loved it still for him. Sitting on that bench last night, hearing the crunch of wood against rawhide as I held Country's bat, I knew even the having of all I ever wanted would only lead to more wanting. It came to me like the thunderstorms that used to roll through when we were kids, quick and sudden and with a noise you could feel deep in your bones. What can a man do when he comes to know all he has striven for in life is dust? What choice is left him when he realizes the race he has chosen to run has no end but keeps on and on with no finish, leaving him to die from weariness upon the very road he once believed would carry him to his dream?

At that moment the box I'd kept inside me marked *Do Not Open* sprung, and from it flew every falsehood I ever told myself and every wonder I ever denied. It was never what the game felt like that made me love it, or what I had always believed it promised me. It was what baseball meant. What it pointed to. There are nights I dream of baseball. I jerk myself awake by the moving of my hips as I settle into a swing. I have loved it so, and now I know why. Is it because baseball holds a promise of eternity with no clock and no time running out, and where played to perfection a single game can stretch on to always? How the plate must be seventeen inches whether you stand in Yankee Stadium or an old field in an old town in old Virginia, and the mound must be sixty feet, six inches away and the bases ninety feet apart but other than that there are no dimensions set, not one, Micky, meaning a field can cover one end of the universe to the other?

No, it is the impossibility of baseball I have always loved, nothing more. It is the art of hitting ninety-five-mile-an-hour gas and knowing the ball is fifteen feet before your brain can find it and another fifteen before you choose to swing, and how when the ball is upon you, your brain and eyes cannot work fast enough, so that the pitch itself turns invisible to your mind, and in that narrowest window of time, that bubble of eternity, you have seven milliseconds to meet a round ball three inches wide within one-eighth of an inch dead center on a round bat. And it all, every bit of it, happens faster than it takes the eye to blink.

That is the game to me, why I loved it.

Because to play should be impossible for mere mortals, and yet the impossible is done time and again. I played those many years for no other reason than to behold a small succession of miracles. Now I stand beneath this strawberry moon, asking for one more.

The moon, Micky. I see the moon. God, how beautiful it looks. Just like that night. Just the very same.

I am not afraid. Strange as it sounds, I have never felt more peace. Faith can do that to you, and love. I have come to know that these years. And I have come to know those are two words for the same thing.

No one is free. That is what you said on this hill when I proclaimed my liberty even as chains formed about me. It was freedom you offered by way of a love none of us understood because it seemed so great and ourselves so unworthy. Now here I stand to say you're right. Our souls are so large that not even the having of all our desires can fill them. Yet we try, oh how we try, only to find ourselves lost in all the darkness we create, our only hope to walk one another home. Is that not what you preached for a single summer in this town? And is that not why I have come back to this place you called special, where we would sit and bask in the magic of eternity? I have searched my life for all I wanted, only to come here for all I need. I love you, Michaela Dullahan. I have always loved you. There is nothing more can be given me than the greater love you said was mine for the having, and the last prayer upon my lips is for the grace of that gift offered once more. I want my journey to end with my way found. I want to know I have been watched over even as I called myself hunted. I want a love everlasting. I want —

ACKNOWLEDGMENTS

I would like to thank Ron Kitchen for his help in the crafting of this book, and for those long phone calls between Virginia and South Carolina that helped me remember what it was like to be seventeen. I played second base; he pitched. Back in 1990, Ron's nickname was "Heat." That was for a reason. Don't tell him I said it, but he remains the only pitcher I was ever afraid to face.

My thanks as well to LB Norton, and to my editor, Amanda Bostic, who wanted a baseball book. Daisy Hutton, Kristen Golden, Jodi Hughes, and Allison Carter: I'm so grateful to have gone on this journey with you.

Claudia Cross can talk the Yankees as well as anyone, but she is an even better agent.

And to Kathy Richards, who has suffered all these years as an Astros fan. Here's hop-

ing they have the pennant when you read
this.

DISCUSSION QUESTIONS

1. Early on, Owen tells Micky that everyone has a crutch, one thing they turn to when everything goes bad. Do you agree? What is your crutch, and how well does it serve you?
2. What do you think really happened when Owen and Micky were nearly killed by the train?
3. Why did Owen and Micky react to their near death in such different ways?
4. How does the way Micky views herself before the incident at the train impact her behavior afterward?
5. Both Owen and Micky suffer throughout the story from a lingering fear that their lives will count for nothing in the end. How common is this fear? How best is that fear diminished?
6. Micky's message is centered upon love, namely where our love is placed. Why is that so important, and how does where

we place our love influence the quality of our lives?
7. What change in Owen allowed him to be taken in the same way Micky was?
8. What role, if any, does pain and sadness play in the spiritual life?

ABOUT THE AUTHOR

Billy Coffey's critically acclaimed books combine rural Southern charm with a vision far beyond the ordinary. He is a regular contributor to several publications, where he writes about faith and life. Billy lives with his wife and two children in Virginia's Blue Ridge Mountains.

www.billycoffey.com
Facebook: billycoffeywriter
Twitter: @billycoffey

The employees of Thorndike Press hope you have enjoyed this Large Print book. All our Thorndike, Wheeler, and Kennebec Large Print titles are designed for easy reading, and all our books are made to last. Other Thorndike Press Large Print books are available at your library, through selected bookstores, or directly from us.

For information about titles, please call:
(800) 223-1244

or visit our website at:
gale.com/thorndike

To share your comments, please write:
Publisher
Thorndike Press
10 Water St., Suite 310
Waterville, ME 04901

443